Nobody Knows His Name

A Sheriff Jerry Valdez Novel

By
Gene Wright

PublishAmerica
Baltimore

First printing

ISBN: 1-4137-0247-3
PUBLISHED BY PUBLISHAMERICA, LLLP
www.publishamerica.com
Baltimore

Printed in the United States of America

DEDICATION

To Nora B. and J. D.
Golden friends both

And, as always, to LWW.

ACKNOWLEDGMENTS

No one writes a book alone. For this one, I owe a great deal to my friend and colleague, Dr. Don Smith, who guided me through the intricacies of botany and answered my many questions with great patience. And many thanks to the fine botanists at the Botanical Research Institute of Texas, Bob O'Kennon and Guy L. Nesom for their help. They generously spent time with me to find the particular hawthorn plant important to this story, although they could not understand why (since I was writing fiction) I did not just "make it all up." For help in matters legal, I thank my brilliant attorney (and my son) Patrick Wright, esq. for his great interest in my stories and his expert help in matters of the law. Thanks also to my friend Dr. G. Roland Vela, a microbiologist by trade and a humanist by disposition, for keeping my Spanish close to the idiom.

I appreciate the great interest shown in my work and the good advice given by my "front-line readers," Don Smith, Roland Vela, and Patrick Wright. And to my best and most gentle critic, LWW.

Chapter 1

Nine o'clock in the morning and already getting hot. The man sat uncomfortable and bored in the small plywood structure that served as a deer blind. He had been sitting on a short wooden bench since four thirty and had seen no deer—or maybe he had. Something had moved just before first light in the brush near the arroyo, some three hundred yards in front of the blind, but he had not been able to make out what it was. Last night's moon had been almost full this second week of November, and the temperature during the day rose to the lower eighties. The hunter supposed that the deer were likely feeding at night and snoozing during the day. What he *knew* was that they were not anywhere near him.

Douglas Leitch wanted to climb down out of the playhouse-like structure and walk back to the hunting cabin for breakfast. Forcing himself out of the sack at four in the morning to get to the blind by four-thirty left no time for breakfast. Not even coffee. But the agreement among the hunters was that no one left his blind before ten o'clock; it was just too dangerous to be walking around when hunters with high-powered rifles were just itching to shoot something. So Douglas Leitch squirmed uncomfortably and visualized coffee and eggs, potatoes and coffee and toast and jelly. And coffee.

The blind he sat in had been the landowner's child's playhouse before the youngster had outgrown it, and it was one of ten blinds on Harvey Phelan's 820-acre ranch in the Texas hill country. It stood near a windmill, supplying a large metal stock tank, and overlooked a rock-strewn pasture, with the arroyo three hundred yards away. The idea was that deer would climb up out of the arroyo in the morning to feed in the pasture and the hunter in the playhouse could take his pick and shoot the trophy buck. Or, in the evening, the deer would cross the pasture to enter the arroyo to bed down for the night. But Douglas Leitch could testify under oath that the plan was not working on this hunt. He had sat in the playhouse for four hours last evening and for over four hours this morning, and he had not seen anything he could positively identify as a deer.

Cows, now there had been plenty of Mr. Phelan's Hereford cows in the area, coming up the path from the pasture, their heads swinging side to side, to drink from the water tank, to scratch their backs on the playhouse supports that held the blind some ten feet off the ground. For the past hour, the hunter had been amusing himself by snorting at several cows grazing near the base of the deer blind. One was a fat cow that was rubbing her nose on the wooden 4 x 4 stanchions. The heifer was frightened by the snorting sound and took two quick steps backward, looking around for the source of the unfamiliar noise. Seeing nothing, she walked forward again to nose the brace; and the hunter snorted again more loudly. This time the terrified beast backed up so quickly that her hind legs tripped over a large rock in the path, and she fell unceremoniously on her bovine butt and sat there looking around for the danger. When the man snorted again, even louder, the creature bleated in fear, heaved herself to her feet, and loped away from the haunted area.

The amusement with the stupid cow was sporting enough to allay Leitch's boredom for a few minutes. When he looked at his watch again, he saw that the time was now almost ten o'clock.

Abruptly he heard a noise coming from the arroyo in front of him, and he picked up his loaded rifle, clicking the safety to the off position. His son, young Doug, had told his dad that if he had not seen deer by about nine-thirty, he might leave his blind overlooking an oat patch about a thousand yards south of the playhouse blind and walk through the arroyo, hoping to flush some deer out of their nests so that his dad could get a shot.

The elder Leitch knew the paths deer took coming out of and going into the arroyo, and he aimed his rifle in the general direction of the most-traveled path, waiting excitedly. When he heard the thrashing around in the brush grow louder and saw the top of a thin juniper move, he put his scope just were he had in past years seen deer move out into the open pasture and tightened his finger on the trigger.

"Dad!" he heard shouted loudly. Then three more times, "Dad! Dad! Dad!" When he saw his son emerge from the arroyo, waving his arms wildly, Douglas the elder jerked the muzzle of his rifle up and cursed softly. Ejecting the shell from the chamber of the rifle, he carefully leaned the weapon in the corner of the blind and climbed shakily to the ground to give his son as much hell as he could muster for doing something so dumb.

Douglas Leitch had hunted with his son, now in his teens, for over ten years, had taught him how to handle firearms, how to respect the land, and most important, how to practice safety. Now this damned-fool kid had just been running around a hunting site during a hunt and had almost gotten himself shot. The father was still shaking, partly from anger but mostly from the terror of having almost shot his son, when Doug the younger ran up to him.

"Dad, you better come see what I found!" The boy was wild-eyed and trembling as he pleaded with his father. He turned to run back the way he had come.

"Doug, damn it," the father said angrily. "What in the name of all that's holy were you thinking?"

The boy stopped and looked back at his father. "No, Dad, come on! Now! There's somebody dead down in the gully!" And he ran back across the pasture, looking back to make sure his father was following.

Chapter 2

Sheriff Jerry Valdez had just driven to his home to have lunch with his wife when Deputy Angela Wahlert called him on his home phone to tell him that a body had been found by two hunters out on Harvey Phelan's ranch, west of Boerne but still in Kendall County. The news distressed him, but it didn't much surprise him. The hill country of Texas was prime deer-hunting territory, and hardly ever did hunting season pass without some hunter or another being bitten by a rattlesnake, perfumed by a skunk, nibbled by an armadillo, skinned up or knocked unconscious by a fall, gored by a bull, pierced by a porcupine, or wounded or killed by a fellow hunter. What he'd probably find when he got out to Harvey's ranch was a drunk or hung-over insurance salesman, weeping his eyes out because he had accidentally mistaken his brother-in-law for a white-tailed deer and shot him through the gut.

He had taken his gun belt off and placed it on top of the china hutch. He wore his usual work clothes: his uniform for work, every day, was blue jeans and a sport shirt that buttoned down the front. His badge was the one issued to him by the county eight years ago: stainless steel, with "Kendall County" forged across the top and "Sheriff" across the bottom. It had the number "1" stamped in the middle. His pistol was the Colt .45 automatic he had qualified with in the Army. He had "lost" the pistol when he mustered out of the Army and had to pay for it, but he could not bring himself to part with the weapon he was certain had saved his life on more than one occasion.

Sighing as he eyed the two chalupas Anna Maria Velasquez Valdez had prepared for him, he put the phone on the hook and said, "Well, hell, you delightful female, I've got to go do some sheriff kind of stuff. Harvey Phelan just called the office to report that a couple of his hunters found a body. Miriam sent Willie Ward out to protect the crime scene, but Willie'll screw it up six ways from Sunday. I'd rather stay here and eat those wonderful-looking chalupas with my beautiful wife. But I'd better pick Archie up and get out to Harvey's place."

Anna Maria Velasquez Valdez, at age 41 two years younger than Jerry, had been his wife for sixteen years. They had been in college in Austin together and married as soon as Jerry had graduated from law school. To Jerry's mind, Anna Maria had only become more beautiful each year that he knew her. Her round face was framed by short dark hair as she looked up, smiling, at her taller husband. Her cotton shift with a print of small flowers did nothing to emphasize her firm, appealing figure; but her shape needed no help.

Jerry embraced his wife, with his hands placed firmly on her shapely derrière, and pulled her close to him, gathering the flowers on her clothing into his grasp and pressing her breasts against his chest. "Nice ass," he said.

She said, smiling up at her husband, "If you've got time for this, you have time for the chalupas."

"Time for what?" he asked innocently.

"Time for holding me in a most sexual manner, is time for what," she replied.

"Why, you beautiful creature, I'm just telling you good-bye."

"Seems it's more like hello," she said, averting her eyes and fluttering her lashes seductively.

"Nope," he said releasing his wife and taking one bite out of a chalupa, "this is no world to play with mammets and to tilt with lips. God's me, my horse!"

"Jerry, there are times when I'm sure you're out of your mind. What does all that mean?"

"It means I've gotta go, dear Kate."

"Name's not Kate, sailor."

"Yeah, well, I gotta go anyway."

"On your horse?"

"Well, no, 'horse' was just a manner of speaking. Shakespeare's characters didn't have a beautiful new Chrysler 300 patrol car. I do."

"So, you're going to mount your patrol car and ride off into the sunset?"

"First, it's just a little before noon. The sun won't set for some time yet. Second, if I'm going to mount anything, it's going to be…"

"Good-bye, dear," she interrupted, rising to her tiptoes and brushing his lips with hers.

He hauled his gun belt down from the hutch, using both hands to keep the gun, ammunition, and radio receiver from clunking against the furniture. Looking once again at his wife, and then at the remaining chalupa, he walked resignedly out the door.

Chapter 3

Jerry drove back through town to pick up his chief deputy, Archie Crane, his friend since childhood. When Jerry and Archie had graduated from law school and passed the Texas bar nearly nine years ago, Jerry had run for and won the position of Sheriff of Kendall County.

Archie Bedford Crane was the smartest man Jerry Valdez had ever known; and with his athletic 6'2" body, reddish-blond hair, and green eyes, Archie had received several offers to join established law firms in several states. The newly elected sheriff was reluctant to ask Archie to postpone a profession that would reward him well, but he really needed someone he could trust to help him run the Sheriff's Office. When he asked Archie if he would consider being his chief deputy at a salary much less than he could earn as a lawyer, the man's green eyes twinkled as he raised his right hand and said, "Swear me in, Jer." Jerry was Archie's friend, and for him that fact outweighed any amount of salary and prestige a law firm could offer.

Because he spent much of his time supervising the deputies, Archie Crane usually wore a more conventional Sheriff's Department uniform: khaki shirt and trousers with a shoulder patch on the left arm identifying him as a member of the Kendall County Sheriff's Office. His badge was almost identical to Jerry's, a simple stainless-steel star, but with Chief Deputy stamped under the number 2. His weapon was a Browning 9 mm automatic he wore on his right hip.

When the two officers turned into the dirt drive leading into Phelan ranch, Archie jumped out to open the gate and to close it when Jerry had driven through.

At the Phelan family house they found Harvey and his son, Charlie, standing outside, waiting on them by one of the two hitching rails in front of the house. Jerry angled his patrol car into one of the hitching rails and thought about getting a rope from the trunk and tying up the Chrysler 300M. *Hell, it has a 253 horsepower engine*, he thought. *Ought to tie those horses up.* But since there was a corpse somewhere on the property, Jerry decided he'd better restrain his humor.

Harvey Phelan was a fourth-generation rancher in the county. He looked to be about fifty years of age, but to Jerry the man had looked to be about fifty ever since he had known him. His well-worn leather boots were splattered with mud and manure and scuffed by the ever-present rocks that littered the hill-country. His young son, Charlie, stood behind his father, grinning, happy to see so many people all at once in his usually isolated home. The boy was a gangly boy of about thirteen, tall for his age, and shy in the company of others, as country boys tended to be.

"What've we got, Harve?" the sheriff asked, as he walked over and shook hands with Phelan. He had a rancher's rough hands and firm shake. "Some of your hunters shooting at each other?"

"No, Jerry, I don't think so," the rancher replied. "Now, 'course one of 'em mighta shot him. But I went down in the arroyo to make sure the man was in fact dead, and he weren't shot with a rifle. And it looks like he's been dead awhile. My hunters just got here yesterday afternoon. And, besides, these guys are real responsible hunters. I've never had a moment's trouble with them in the couple of years they've hunted here—they never shoot my cows, never even leave a gate open. They leave the place in better shape than when they found it. I actually look forward to seeing them each year."

Well, hell, Jerry thought. *Couldn't be a simple incident, could it?*

"The body those guys found's down in that arroyo that runs over on the east side of my land, just off the highway," the rancher said, waving his right hand to indicate the direction. "I'll just ride over with you to show you where. Some of your people are over there with the hunters."

"Harvey," Archie said, "did you recognize the victim?"

"Nope, I don't guess I ever saw him. 'Course, he don't have much of a face left. Critters got at him some. He's a Mexican, though. Or he was. I don't guess he's much of anything now."

Both Archie and Jerry knew that "Mexican" in this part of Texas did not necessarily mean "resident of Mexico." Jerry himself was often called a Mexican, although he had been born in Kendall County, Texas, and had never lived in Mexico. "Mexican" usually just referred to someone of Hispanic descent.

As the men walked to the patrol car, Jerry glanced over to the three long hen houses that stood a hundred yards from Phelan's residence. Four Hispanic men stood looking at the patrol car from the shadow of the first structure. *These men*, Jerry thought, *were almost certainly Mexicans and more nearly certainly living in Kendall County illegally.*

The rancher's main source of income was from the twice-annual sale of beef cattle, white-faced Herefords that he raised on his acreage. Most of the arable land, that which had most of the ubiquitous rocks removed so that it could be plowed, was sewn with either oats or rye during the winter for cattle feed. But like most ranchers in Kendall County, Phelan had to make all parts of the land produce if he intended to pay his taxes and provide for his family. He had less than an acre of land near his house he used for a vegetable garden and a number of native pecan trees down in the creek bottom. He made a bit of money from both the vegetables and the pecans. The only activities that came close to earning as much income as beef were hunting leases on the property and egg production. Like almost all the ranchers in the area, Phelan hired illegals to help him around the place; but mostly, Jerry knew, Phelan used them to take care of the chickens, feed them, gather and grade the eggs and load them in cartons, clean the hen houses, and similar tasks. Jerry's family regularly bought eggs produced on Harvey Phelan's property.

Just behind the hen houses was the old family residence, a rock and timber house Phelan's grandparents had lived in. His father had built the modern house to appease his wife, Harvey's mother, who had grown up in the city, with indoor plumbing, electricity, and other modern conveniences. Harvey's wife, Hazel, was delighted to inherit the new house. Harvey allowed the illegal Mexican help to live in the old house, and his wife was quick to agree that they were welcome to it. Jerry could not see the old house from where he stood, but he knew that some members of the men's families would be there.

When the Hispanics saw the sheriff looking in their direction, they melted back behind the henhouse. Jerry knew that their illegal status would keep them away from him. Not that he would have arrested them—or taken any unprovoked notice of them. As long as they conducted themselves civilly, he was happy to have them in the county. Without the illegals, who were willing to do work legal residents would not do and for wages far less than others, ranchers like Harvey Phelan would go bankrupt. But the foreigners did not trust the police, and Jerry tried not to intrude upon their privacy.

Phelan and Archie were waiting by the patrol car, watching Jerry stare at the hen houses. Archie said, a quizzical expression on his face, "What are you so interested in, Jer?"

Jerry was a bit discomfited at his own distraction. "Oh, nothing," he said. "Just wool-gathering."

Harvey Phelan stood looking at the sheriff. His face was brown and weathered by the elements, his hands rough, almost as though he had been crafted by the land he worked—as in many respects he had been. Land ecology in the hill country was a fragile problem and had to be managed the way a rider handled a good quarter horse, with care, pleasure, and affection. Phelan was an honest, productive man, protective of the land, its water, game and trees. He never thought of it as "his land," even though he worked it, protected it, and paid taxes on it. He had inherited the responsibility for the eight-hundred or so acres from his parents, they from their parents, and Phelan hoped to turn responsibility over to his son. Death was a natural part of life on the land but, to Harvey Phelan, murder was not

The rancher rode in the car with Jerry, directing him through two cattle gates over to the east side of his property, where they saw two other patrol cars parked near the windmill, two deputies talking with four men, all standing in the shade of a large oak tree.

As Jerry, Archie, and the rancher got out of the car, Deputy Willie Ward, the senior deputy in the department, walked over to them. Ward had been with the Sheriff's Department when Jerry was elected sheriff, and Jerry had seen no reason not to keep him on. Although he had seniority over everyone in the department, Ward was not the brightest star in that particular firmament. But he meant well. He was 42 years old and would likely be around for a while. A confirmed bachelor, Ward was a 5' 6" high-school dropout, who was as country as the cow manure on his boots.

"Hey, Sheriff, hey, Archie," the deputy said. Consulting the small notebook he held, he said, "That man over there," waving toward one of the hunters, "is Douglas Leitch and the kid standing near him is his son, also named Doug. That old fellow is Edward Ward and the fourth man is Eugene Wagoner. The kid found the body down in that gully," nodding in that direction, "and he took his daddy down to look at it. These other two guys never went down there." He flipped a page back in his notebook and continued, "Now, me and Deputy Patton got here right at eleven o'clock, and Hilton and Darrell, they got here a few minutes later. Mr. Phelan showed us the way to get over here. Me and Patricia, uh, Deputy Patton went down to look at the deceased and then came back up here to interview the gentlemen who found the deceased. I sent Hil..., uh, Deputy O'Brian and Deputy Schmidt down to the body site to, uh, protect the crime scene." Finished with his report, Willie Ward looked up with pride at his performance.

"Now, that's real good, Willie," Jerry replied. And in fact he was both surprised and pleased that his deputy had done so well. Ward was the senior deputy because of length of service, not by merit. He was usually able to put his foot in a pie as well as any Epaninambus. And Jerry was still apprehensive about what he'd find at what the deputy called the "body site."

"Willie," Jerry said, "did you remind Hilton and Darrell to protect the scene?"

"'Course I did, Sheriff," the deputy responded, offended that anyone would think he'd overlook so basic a detail.

"Good man, Willie," Jerry said, smiling, patting his deputy on the shoulder. "Did you ask Angie or Miriam to notify the medical examiner?"

"No, Sir, Sheriff, I never done that," the deputy said, fixing Jerry with his gaze. "That ain't for me to do. My job's to call you or Archie. I wouldn't have no way of knowing if you wanted the medical examiner or when."

Jerry could not think of a reason he would not want the medical examiner at the scene of a suspicious death, unless he intended to cover up something and did not want the doctor to find out. Willie Ward had not intended to make any such slur against the sheriff's honesty. He *had* insulted the sheriff, but he had not intended to.

"Well, please call in now, and ask Miriam to invite the examiner to come on out. I'd like for you to show him the way when he gets here so that he won't contaminate the scene. Or you can have Hilton or Darrell bring him over. Just tell them to be careful. Tell Miriam to ask the examiner to bring someone to take the body in when we're through with it. Did either you or Patricia recognize the victim?"

"No, Sir, Sheriff, I never seen him before. All's I know is he's a Mexican. And 'nother thing, Sheriff, he ain't got no hands, the body don't."

Jerry and Archie had started moving toward the hunters, but the deputy's last words caused them to turn back. Deputy Willie Ward often garlanded his reports with what seemed to him a natural kind of either hyperbole or understatement.

"No hands, Willie?" Archie asked.

"Right, Arch, no hands. Somebody done cut 'em off. He got feet and a head, but no hands. Feet but no shoes."

"Did you find the hands at the scene, Willie?" Jerry asked, knowing that the likely reason anyone would remove the hands from a body would be to complicate identification. Unless that someone had a hand fetish and collected them. But that notion was too weird for Jerry to deal with at the present. Either way, they weren't likely to find the hands near the scene. But it was possible that the removal of the hands was some kind of symbol that the victim had put his hands where they didn't belong. Anyway, the only thing Jerry disliked more than a body was an incomplete body.

"No, Sir, Sheriff, I didn't. 'Course, I didn't look around much past where the body was, 'cause I know you wouldn't want the crime scene all tromped around on."

"Okay, Willie, that's good, you did real good," Jerry said distractedly, patting his deputy on the back and turning to speak to the four hunters. "Gentlemen, I'm Sheriff Valdez of Kendall County. This is my chief deputy, Archie Crane. I need to ask you folks a few questions, and then I'll let you get back to your business."

He questioned intensively the young hunter who had found the body, less rigorously the father, and the other two only in a cursory manner—enough to assure himself that none of them either knew the victim nor had anything to do with his death other than by chance finding the body.

Archie pulled Deputy Ward aside to instruct him to make sure he had the full names, addresses, phone numbers, and accurate driver's license numbers of each of the men. He thought it necessary to remind the deputy to look at the men's drivers' licenses rather than just taking their words for the accuracy of the information.

"I looked at their hunting licenses, Arch," the deputy responded defensively.

"That's good, Willie," the chief deputy replied kindly, "but we're not game wardens. I'd appreciate it if you'd check their drivers' licenses. They've got pictures on them. I guess if hunting licenses have pictures on them, they'd probably be of deer or pigs or something."

"Nope, Arch, hunting licenses don't got pictures of anything on them," the deputy said, looking at Archie disapprovingly.

The chief deputy smiled and patted Ward on the shoulder and said, "Drivers' licenses does, though, Willie."

"They does?" said Jerry, smiling, as he finished questioning the four hunters and he and Archie walked away.

"Just trying to speak Willie's language, Jer."

"Godamercy," Jerry said, crossing himself.

"Methodists don't cross themselves, Jerry," Archie said, smiling.

"They do if they're around Archie Crane often."

Chapter 4

Jerry and Archie made their way down the steep sides of the arroyo in the direction pointed out by the young hunter who had found the body. The gorge was some two-hundred feet deep, with a somewhat flat floor, and covered with scrub oak, cedar, and stones both large and small. Along the length of the gulch meandered a wet-weather creek, now a few inches deep and two to four feet wide after recent rains.

Jerry and Archie struggled to keep from sliding and falling, holding on to limbs and roots of trees as they walked down the narrow path worn by deer.

When they reached the bottom, they saw Deputies Hilton O'Brian and Darrell Schmidt standing ten yards up the opposite bank of the arroyo and about thirty yards north. O'Brian (spelled with an "a" for some reason Jerry was unable to discover. Not "O'Brien" or "O'Bryan," but "O'Brian.") was a large black man, barely 22 years old. He had a round, friendly face and a pleasant manner. Darrell Schmidt stood four inches shorter than O'Brian's six-feet, four inches, and was a red-headed, quiet, muscular man. O'Brian, the more talkative of the two, shouted, "Hey, ya'll, up here."

As Jerry and Archie began walking up the hill toward the deputies, they were careful to step as close to trees as possible so that they would not contaminate any of the footprints in the area. When they reached the little flat area where the two deputies stood, they saw the body and saw that the two deputies were standing with their feet close to the bases of juniper trees.

"We were real careful coming up here, Sheriff," O'Brian said. "Willie told us not to step on any footprints or to leave any of our own."

"That's real good, Hilton," Jerry said, pleased that his repeated lectures on protecting the crime scene had sunk in. "But there are several sets of boot prints going down this hill and several more coming up."

"They ain't ours," the redheaded deputy said, looking hurt that his boss would think they could do such a thing.

Deputy O'Brian was briefly amazed at hearing his partner speak, since the man was unusually shy. But, recovering, he said, "Yes, Sir, Darrell and I saw them, too. There are footprints around the body, too. But they aren't ours. We were real careful where we stepped. Willie was too, he said. A couple of the hunters said they found the body, and then Mr. Phelan, he said he came down here with the hunters to look at the body. And Willie and Patricia came down here, too. But I don't think they left any prints. Willie and Pat didn't. The other might've."

Archie, looking around the area, said, "Jer, the body is maybe ten feet up this hill from the bottom of the arroyo. What do you suppose the kid was doing up here? I mean, he said he was just walking the bottom of the arroyo to scare deer up so his dad could get a shot. If he entered the gorge down near the south end, why wouldn't he have walked along the bottom, where it's flat? What was he doing ten feet up this side of the hill?"

Jerry looked down the hill to the bottom of the arroyo as he held on to the trunk of a small oak tree, and then up the hill. "Well, I'd guess that the kid was following a deer trail up on this side so that the deer he flushed would run up that west hill to get away from him. There's a deer trail just up there," he said, pointing with his free hand up the hill to the east. "But, of course, I don't know. We'll ask him."

Archie carefully made his way up the hill to the deer trail and, walking to the side of the path, looked carefully at the ground for nearly fifty yards. When he came back, he said, "Yeah, you're right, Jer, I guess. I see prints of a small boot coming this way along the trail."

"Maybe we better get a casting of the prints and compare them with an imprint of the kid's boots," Jerry said, as he pushed himself away from the tree and walked cautiously over toward the body. "Hilton," he said without facing the men, "you and Darrell go back up to where the others are and tell Willie that we'll need imprints of the boots of everyone who has been down here. There's a package of that sticky film stuff in the trunk of my car if you don't have any in your patrol car. Darrell, you bring back enough plaster and forms to get casts of the prints around here."

As the two deputies moved carefully down the hill and across the bottom of the arroyo, Archie joined his friend beside the body. The sun hovered overhead, a bit low in the southern sky, filtered through the yellowing and browning leaves still hanging on the trees, the growing-bare, ruined choirs, where late the sweet birds sang. The dancing shadows on the body of the man reclining calmly in the dirt gave the illusion of slight movement, the fluttering of the breast, the flickering of the eyes.

The man was a Hispanic male, 35 to 40 years of age. Decomposition had begun, but the full black head of hair remained youthful. The eyes were gone, the banquet of some bestial gourmand. The lips had been eaten away, leaving the blank face with an oversized grin framing a set of gleaming teeth. The nose, too, was gone, eaten away. *A delicacy*, Jerry thought, though he could not imagine why or to what. The corpse wore no shoes or socks. The toes on both feet were scratched and torn, almost certainly by feasting nocturnal creatures.

"Lots of insect activity," Jerry remarked, watching the worms crawl in and the worms crawl out.

"Insect activity," Archie responded archly. "That mean bugs are eating him?"

"Have and are," said Jerry. "As the bard says, we're food for worms. This guy sure is."

The corpse wore a wool suit, black with blue and brown threads woven into the fabric. Jerry drew a set of latex gloves from his rear pocket and put them on. Reaching down to the corpse, he pulled the jacket open to check the inside pockets for a wallet or some kind of identification. He found nothing, but he noticed that something, probably a label, had been cut from the left breast pocket, leaving a jagged hole. As he checked behind the head, he found that whatever label had been there was gone, cut away too. The other pockets, in both the jacket and the trousers, were empty as well.

And the body had no hands.

"I'll bet you a quarter," Jerry said to Archie, "that when we are able to examine the clothes fully, we'll find no identification anywhere. His hands were cut off so that we couldn't identify him by his prints. Look, here, Arch! Look how neatly the hands have been removed, like by a surgeon." He stood up and removed the gloves, placing them in his hip pocket.

"Or a butcher," Archie said, standing. "Who is he?"

"Dunno," answered the sheriff. "You know him?"

"Nope."

"Well, we got us a corpse. But we don't know who he is or who killed him," said Jerry. "I don't like deaths in my county, and I especially don't like unsolved deaths. I don't know whether this guy was good or bad. But somebody took it upon himself or herself or themselves to kill him and go on about their lives. Pretty easy, really, to kill someone. But it damned well shouldn't be easy to get away with it. So, I guess we'd better find out who killed him and bring whoever it is to justice."

Archie thought for a moment and then asked, "How?"

"Dunno," Jerry answered. After a few seconds, he said, "Did you kill him, Archie?"

Archie looked hard at his friend, dropped his head, and finally said, "No, I didn't." Then, lifting his head, he asked, "Did you kill him, Jerry?"

Jerry looked down at the corpse, then lifted his head to contemplate the clouds scudding high above the trees which climbed the sides of the arroyo. At length he turned his gaze to his friend and said, "No, Archie, I did not."

"Well, good, Jerry," Archie sighed. "See, we're making progress here. We've eliminated two suspects already."

The two men scanned the heavens, searching for the sylphs who they were certain were gathering to help them. They trusted their sylphs.

Chapter 5

No blood decorated the ground under or around the handless body, Jerry determined, although there was blood around two small holes in the back of the skull. Blood in the hair, but none on the ground. The head lay pointed west, the suit jacket and dress shirt pulled up high on the back of the neck. There was dirt, more than a cupful, inside the collar and down the back of both the shirt and the jacket, suggesting that the man had been shot at some other location and the body pulled along the ground from the north, which meant downhill into the arroyo from the county road running just a few feet from Mr. Phelan's northern fence. When Jerry and Archie began climbing the sides of the arroyo north, they immediately found the scuff marks in the soil. They followed the clear trail up to the top of the arroyo and over to the fence.

Harvey Phelan did not have deer fences, ten-foot high fences that white-tail deer cannot jump, around his property. Since his property lay in the heart of deer country and his neighbors never allowed their much larger properties to be over-hunted, he was just as happy to have his neighbor's deer jumping his fences for his hunters to harvest.

The fence on the north side of his property was, therefore, a standard five-foot high, four-strand, cow-tight, barbed-wire fence. The scuff marks clearly ran from the fence, under the fence, from the other side of the fence. There was a piece of black cloth smaller than a dime caught on the bottom-wire barb. Jerry pulled a small envelope from his shirt pocket and with a ballpoint pen pestered the piece of cloth off the barb and into the envelope. Since the wires were strung tight, with no room for an adult to get between the strands, Jerry and Archie agreed that the body-puller must either have climbed over or scooted under, as the corpse had evidently been scooted under. If they assumed that it was the corpse that had been pulled under the fence at the point of the track and the snagged cloth—a reasonable assumption, since the track was continuous from the body to the fence—they had to assume that the puller of the body had gone over the fence, because there were no more scuff marks on the ground. On the other hand, there were also no more snags of clothing on the upper-wire barbs to indicate that someone had gone over. But he must have. Or she must have. Or they. Jerry and Archie, stepping carefully on the fence wires where they were clipped to the posts, climbed over the fence. They left no part of their clothing or themselves on any of the barbs.

Beside the county road, they could see where a car or light truck had pulled off the road onto the shoulder near the fence. The road itself was gravel and oil, but the shoulder had just enough dirt mixed in with the limestone rock to show a tire print. The scuff marks made by someone's dragging the body started at that point.

Jerry pulled a white handkerchief from his right rear pocket and tied it around the top wire of the fence. He pulled his radio from his belt and called his office.

"Miriam, this is Sheriff Valdez. Will you please ask Smiley Wilson to bring a form and some plaster out to Harvey Phelan's ranch to make a casting of some car or truck tires? Tell him to take County Road…hey Arch, what is this road called?"

"I don't know, Jerry. I'm not sure it has a number posted."

"Okay—Miriam, tell Smiley to look at a county map and to find this county road that runs on the north side of the Phelan Ranch. Up near the northwest corner of the property, I've tied a white handkerchief to the fence on the south side of the highway—that's where Harvey's property is. Just outside the fence by where the handkerchief is tied are the tire tracks I want Smiley to cast."

"Sheriff, this is base. Okay, I've got that."

"And, Miriam, tell Smiley to keep his patrol car off this area. Tell him to park across the road—that is, on the north side of the county road—so that he won't contaminate the area."

"Sheriff, this is base, okay, 4-10. I'll tell him, but, Sheriff, Smiley doesn't always understand what he understands."

"Yeah, I know Miriam," the sheriff said. Then to Archie, "Hey, Arch, do you mind waiting here for Smiley to bring the stuff out to make sure it gets done right? You can just ride on back in with him when he's finished."

"Be happy to, Jer."

"Miriam, the chief deputy will meet Smiley at this location. Send him on out."

"4-10, Sheriff, understand G-E-M will meet Happy Face at that 20."

"That's it, Miriam," the sheriff responded. "Except, Miriam, a 410 is a shotgun."

"You want Happy Face to bring a shotgun out, Sheriff?"

"No, Miriam. One more thing. Have a couple of patrol units, whoever is available, to patrol along this road. Tell them to check all the houses or ranches in both directions for—oh, say five miles, to see if anyone remembers seeing a car or truck stopped out here by the Phelan ranch in the last couple of weeks. Ask them to stop folks driving up or down the road to ask them the same question. Tell them to stay at it the rest of the day. I'm out."

As Jerry hooked his radio back on his belt, his friend asked, "What the hell is all that 'Happy Face' and 'G-E-M' business?"

"Oh, Miriam thought that since the Secret Service has code names for all the White House staff, we should have code names in the department. Happy Face is, somehow this one makes sense, Smiley Wilson. G-E-M is short for "Green-eyed Monster." That's you. You've got pretty noticeable green eyes. At least Miriam notices them."

"Monster?"

"Yep."

"I mean, green-eyed I can understand. But 'Monster'? Who made these names up?"

"Miriam did, I guess. I didn't say they made sense. Anna Maria is 'Mama Bear,' Maria is 'Baby Bear,' Alex is 'Boyfoot Bear,' and so on. She even gave Jesse a code name: 'Guardian Angel.'"

Jesse Mueller was the young deputy who six months earlier had been killed by a drug dealer after a routine traffic stop. The members of the Sheriff's Department still mourned the likeable young man.

"'Green-eyed Monster'—that's envy, isn't it?" Archie asked, not reconciled to his code name.

"See, Arch, you're trying to make sense of it. I told you, Miriam made these names up, which means that consistency is not going to run far. Miriam is as consistent as a monkey on a typing test. And as politically correct as a commie in the Klan. She gave Johnson Washington the code name 'Sambo'

26

and she calls Hilton 'Kinky.' Johnson and Hilton thought it was funny, but I had to insist that she change those. She means well. G-E-M."

"Okay, my wise-ass friend," the chief deputy grinned, "what's your code name?"

The sheriff never broke a smile. "Don't ask!"

Jerry left Archie and walked back to the body and found the medical examiner and his staff were taking pictures and examining the body.

"Hey, doc," said Jerry to Able Martin, M. D., medical examiner for the county. "Can you guess at the time of death?"

"My dear Sheriff," he responded slowly without looking up, as he kneeled taking the temperature of the body. "I am a member of the medical profession, the scientific community. Scientists don't 'guess'; we examine and then arrive at conclusions." As he pulled the thermometer out of the corpse's rectum, he turned to face the sheriff and held the thermometer like a torch. "No, Sheriff, I'll see before I guess; when I guess, prove; and on the proof, there is no more but this; away at once with guessing!"

Jerry looked thoughtfully at the doctor for a moment before he repeated, "Time of death?" Then he added, "Doctor Othello."

The doctor smiled and answered, "An estimation, Jerry, nothing more at this point—I'd put it at about forty-eight hours. And not here. Cause of death is likely to be these two holes in the back of his head—probably .22 caliber. He clearly was not shot on this spot. I'd say that he was shot somewhere around forty-eight hours ago and dragged here almost immediately. Rigidity had not set in until he was placed here. As you can see, the body is straight as a board. Anyway, I'll have more to tell you after I've had a chance to examine him in the lab. And, oh yes, Jerry, I performed a cursory examination of his clothes and found that all labels had been removed. And, of course, you may have noticed that he doesn't have any hands."

"Yeah, Archie and I examined the area around here and saw no sign of them. My guess is that they are, as we law-enforcement types say, elsewhere. But I'll have some deputies scour the area to make sure."

"Almost certainly they are not around here," the doctor said, placing his instruments in his case and preparing to leave, "since the reason for removing the hands in the first place was probably to hinder identification. Well, Sheriff, I'll leave you to your detecting while I go practice science on this poor unfortunate."

"Okay, doc. Please ask your people to be very careful with his clothes when they take them off and bag them. I want to go over them carefully to see if there is something that will help us identify him."

"Will do, Jerry," the old man said, as he motioned to his crew to put the corpse in a body bag and to remove it to his lab.

"And, doc, be sure to get his fingerprints to me real soon, will you?" Jerry said seriously.

The doctor said nothing for a few moments, as he walked carefully down the hill, holding on to trees to keep from sliding. When he reached the flat bottom of the arroyo, he said, without turning his head, "And when you come by to get them, you young smart ass, remind me to give you an ice-water enema."

"Ouch," said Jerry, looking around the area to make sure he had not forgotten anything.

When he returned to the area of the deer blind, he found that the four hunters had gone back to the cabin and were preparing to leave for home, their lust for hunting having been slaked for the day. He made sure that his deputies had gotten casts of their boots and copied all the relevant information about the hunters. Harvey Phelan rode with him back to the residence, opening cattle gates for him as he left one pasture and entered another.

As they drove on the dirt trail in the middle pasture, Jerry saw two Mexican hired hands at a turnout on the side of the trail throwing large plastic garbage sacks into a hole in the ground. He pulled over near to where the men had parked an old Chevy pickup truck. The two men completely ignored the sheriff, never looking in the direction of the patrol car as they threw the last of the bags into the hole, climbed into the old pickup, and rattled off.

Phelan looked questioningly at Jerry as the sheriff thought for a moment, both hands still on the steering wheel. Then he turned his head to look at the truck disappearing over a slight rise to the west.

"Harve," he began, "once when you had a party out here, I helped you clean up all the garbage left over. We put it in boxes and plastic bags and hauled it all up here in your pickup truck, didn't we?"

"Yeah, that was the little-league football banquet or some damned thing. We had lots of venison sausage, burgers, and stuff. What of it?"

"You told me, if I remember right, that the garbage hole opens into a cave underground."

"It does. We put all our trash down that hole, and we never fill it up— deer guts, dead critters, everything. I have no idea how big the cave is, but it's big. About twice a year, when I think about it, I'll bring a five-gallon can of diesel fuel up here and pour her into the cave and throw a torch down into it to disinfect it some. Probably cooks 'bout a million rattlesnakes, too."

"Everybody on your property know about the trash dump, Harve?"

"Sure."

"Everybody have access to it?"

"Sure, Jerry. You need a place to bring your trash? Bring it on out. You're more'n welcome to use it."

"Good place to put trash, Harve," the sheriff said, starting the car and driving toward the Phelan residence.

Chapter 6

In his office, Jerry had given copies of the photos of the victim to his young deputy Angela Wahlert and put her to work at a table in the conference room so that she could sketch the face on a letter-size sheet of card stock, drawing in eyes, nose, and lips to replace those eaten away by varmints. The petite young deputy had wrinkled her nose in disgust at the sickening sight, but Jerry reminded her that as a deputy sheriff, she had not the leisure to be sick when her help was needed.

Angie was a natural copy artist, could draw anything she saw, and she had some imagination in her skills, enough to add hair, fatten or thin faces, make pictures of individuals look older or younger, and add or remove tattoos from her sketches. She was no good at trying to draw likenesses from descriptions by witnesses, although she had tried on several occasions to do so. She listened as closely as she could to the descriptions, erased and redrew at the directions of the witnesses; but no matter how hard she tried, the witnesses always shook their heads and said, "No, that doesn't look like him."

In most cases, Jerry or one of the more perceptive deputies would use a professional identification system to sketch out facial images from witnesses. A computer program designed to allow a trained operator to construct a "likeness" built from descriptions of witnesses had been created by a British firm some few years earlier and was used widely by Scotland Yard, the FBI, ATF, and hundreds of police units in many countries. The program, E-Fit it is called, allows an operator, after an initial interview with witnesses, to present complete faces. Even if witnesses can immediately remember only the general pattern of a face and not specific details, the program can insert a default nose on a draft sketch of a face with correct eyes. Often, then, the witness may be able to remember the nose of the perpetrator in relation to the eyes. It is a good and useful system. Angie was, however, not good at building up sketches from descriptions given by witnesses.

But give her something to copy and she was practically an Andy Warhol. Nobody ever asked her to draw a soup can; but if they had, she would have done a great job at it. And all that the picture of the dead guy needed was eyes, nose, and mouth—and a little of the left earlobe that had suffered from a gunshot and had been nibbled on a bit. Heck, all she had to do was to give her copy black eyes, a standard forty-year-old Hispanic nose, and some lips that fit around the mouth that was already there. Easy as pie.

Jerry walked back into the conference room just as Angie was adding one last touch to her work. She smiled proudly as she handed the sketch to him, "There ya go, Sheriff! There's your corpuscle!"

"There's my what?"

"Corpuscle. It means a corpse with the missing 'uscle' drawn back in."

"Angie, I love you dearly," the sheriff said, smiling at the beautiful young woman, "but I do believe you've got about a half-stick of butter missing from your noodles."

She grinned sweetly at Jerry and turned to walk away, her short uniform skirt swinging as she girl-walked toward the door of the conference room. When she got to the door, she turned, pulling her head into her left shoulder, and said, "Sheriff, my noodles have plenty of butter to get me through this world just fine." She dipped into a graceful curtsy, smiled, and minced out the door.

"They do at that," Jerry muttered under his breath, thanking his lucky stars that such female pulchritude graced his world.

"Angie!" he shouted as a thought struck him. When the young deputy pivoted in mid-step to face him, he said, "Angie, will you please fax a copy of this drawing and the height and weight estimates to the local and state guys and ask them to check their missing-persons files? Put your name on the request, please, and let me know when you hear back from them. I'll leave the drawing with Miriam soon."

"'K, Sheriff," she said smiling. Spinning again on the ball of her right foot, she continued on her way.

As he walked out of the conference room studying the drawing, a woman standing by the front desk spoke to him. "Sheriff Valdez, I'd like to see you for a minute."

Jerry looked up at the young woman. She was dressed in blue jeans, no socks, canvas shoes, and a tee shirt with writing on it. He recognized the woman as one of his deputies, and when he got closer he could read what was written on her shirt: "I'M OUT OF ESTROGEN AND I HAVE A GUN." A couple of weeks earlier Jerry had seen her in a shirt that announced WARNING: I HAVE AN ATTITUDE AND I KNOW HOW TO USE IT." Dorie LaDeaux had been a deputy in the department for three years. Her last two efficiency reports had been unsatisfactory, and Jerry and Archie had counseled her after each one. Her attitude had not promised improvement. Her tendency was to browbeat all whom she encountered, whether they be criminals, citizens, or other deputies. Soon, Jerry was going to have to fire her.

Jerry sighed, then said, "Deputy LaDeaux, I'm right in the middle of a murder investigation. So, if it can wait...."

"It can't wait, Sheriff!" Her words were not loud, but they were spoken slowly and with emphasis. Her face was somber, lines of a frown etched in her forehead. A somewhat plain woman of some twenty-five years of age, straight black hair cut little longer than a man's, a well proportioned and muscular body, she stood five feet, seven inches. She had the habit of hunching forward to cover the nicely shaped breasts which would have, had her shoulders been carried erect, attracted attention. The pronouncements on the shirts she favored called attention to her chest, while her stooped posture tended to hide. She seemed to be proud of the sayings, ashamed of her breasts.

Jerry took a brief glance at the drawing in his hand, then said resignedly, "Okay, Deputy, come in for a minute." He preceded her to his office at the back of building and asked her to shut the door and sit down. When he was settled in his chair behind his desk, he put the drawing face down on his desk and said, "Okay, Deputy, what is it?"

"Sheriff," she said gravely, "I want to file a case of sexual harassment."

Jerry was immediately alert. He had no patience with men who used whatever power they might have to intimidate or exploit women and children.

"Tell me about it, Deputy," he said, moving forward in his chair and placing his arms on the desk.

"It's Deputy Carroll, Sheriff, Avon Carroll. He called me a bitch in front of two other deputies. You can call them for witnesses. I have their names here." She pushed a scrap of paper across the desk. "I want to file a formal complaint against him!"

Jerry did not move for a moment, but then he exhaled perceptibly, sat back in his chair, and reached for his phone. "Angie," he said to his office manager, "is Deputy Carroll out there?"

"Yes, Sir," the deputy said in her musical voice, "He and Billy Joe are in having coffee."

"Ask him to come to my office right away, please Angie," he said and put the phone down and looked at the young female across his desk. He said nothing.

Less than a minute later, Avon Carroll knocked on the door of the office, opened it, and said, "You want to see me, Sheriff?"

"Yeah, Deputy Carroll, I do. Come in, close the door, and stand in front of the door." When the deputy had done so, Jerry said, "Deputy Carroll, did you call Deputy LaDeaux a bitch in front of two other deputies?"

Carroll glanced briefly at the woman sitting to his left and then looked back at the sheriff. "Yeah, I did, Sheriff."

"Why did you do such a thing, Avon?" the sheriff asked.

"Well, Sheriff, that was about a week ago, and I don't rightly remember exactly why I called her a bitch. But it was because she was being a bitch about something. She's pretty much a pain in the butt about some things."

"Deputy Carroll, I want you to listen very closely to what I have to say to you. It is uncivil behavior to call a female, any female, a bitch. I don't ever want you to call Deputy LaDeaux—or any of our deputies, for that matter—a bitch. Do you understand me?"

"What if she's acting like a bitch, Sheriff?" Carroll asked in all seriousness.

"Avon, a bitch is a female canine of some kind. It is uncivil to refer to a female human as a bitch."

"Well, Sheriff," the deputy said, "I didn't mean that she's literally a bitch. It's just that she's ill-tempered most of the time, and on some subjects she's really a bi…, ah, well it's like calling her a shrew, like I don't…."

"Don't call her a shrew, either, Avon."

"…mean she's *literally* a nasty little rodent that'll take your hand off if you try to pet it. I just mean that sometimes she's really bad tempered and malicious for no good reason."

Jerry put his head in his hands, rubbing his temples with his thumbs. Sighing, he said, "Deputy, let me say once again, it is uncivil behavior to call a female, any female, a bitch. I don't ever want you to call Deputy LaDeaux—or any other female—a bitch. Or a shrew. Do you understand me?"

"Okay, Sheriff, sure," the young man said. Then looking at the female deputy, he said, "Sorry, Dorie."

"You may go back to work, Avon," the sheriff said.

When the young man left, Deputy LaDeaux's eyes grew wide and she asked, "Is that all you're going to do, Sheriff?"

"Yeah," Jerry responded. "What did you want me to do?"

The woman stood up, her hands fluttering as though she did not know what to do with them. She seemed to want to lean over the desk to face the sheriff in a dominant manner, but she clearly also did not want to confront him. After a moment, she controlled her hands by moving her right arm across her body and grasping it above the elbow with her left hand. "I want," she said then, with some vigor, "I want you to fire him!"

"Now, Deputy LaDeaux, I'm not going to do that. I'm sorry he embarrassed you, and I have told him never to do it again. It's over. If he ever uses such language about you again, let me know and I'll sandpaper his ass. But I don't think he will. Avon is a good kid."

The deputy stood trembling with anger as she sought to control her emotions. "Sheriff," she said evenly, "I'm going to file a lawsuit against this department and you and everybody concerned, charging sexual harassment."

"Deputy LaDeaux," the sheriff said quietly, "sit down for a moment." She remained standing. The sheriff continued, "You don't have a case for sexual harassment. The guidelines we use are the same guidelines that the courts in this state and in the country have used for several years. They have been well adjudicated. I know you are angry, and I can understand that up to a point. Sometimes people—including, of course, Deputy Carroll—are not the essence of kindness in the way they treat others. He has apologized, and I have told him to control his language. That's got to be the end of it—for now, at least. I'd like for you to look upon this as the actions of a rather ignorant country boy who needs to be educated in what to say and when to say it. I'll certainly insist that he be educated. But, Deputy, there is simply no substance in this situation to take further action. Read the departmental guidelines carefully and you'll see that you do not have a case for sexual harassment—unless there is something you haven't told me. Is there?"

"No, there is nothing else. There doesn't have to be. I have been sexually harassed, and I am filing a lawsuit!"

Jerry sighed and said, "Okay, Miz LaDeaux, that is certainly your prerogative. Give me your gun, your badge, and your identification card. I am placing you on indefinite unpaid leave." He held his hand out.

The young woman was immobile with shock. At length she sputtered, "You can't do that! I'm exercising my constitutional rights, and you are punishing me for standing up to you! You can't fire me for filing a sexual-harassment suit! First one man insults me sexually, and now you think you can fire me! Well, Buster, you've assaulted the wrong woman! I won't give you my badge, and if you try to take it from me, I'll sue you for every cent this county is worth! You lay one hand on my body, and I'll make sure the world knows what kind of pervert you are!"

By now tears were in her eyes, mucus dribbled from her nose, and saliva flew from her mouth as she spoke. Jerry picked up his phone and called his office manager. "Angie, come back her for a moment, please."

When Deputy Wahlert knocked and entered, the sheriff said, "Angie, I have asked Miz LaDeaux to give me her gun, badge, and identification. She has refused to do so. Please take those items from Miz LaDeaux and put them on my desk.

Angie Wahlert smiled sweetly and said, "Yes, Sir, Sheriff." Then in one motion, she grabbed the taller woman's right arm at the wrist, pivoted 360 degrees under the arm pulling the arm behind LaDeaux's back, clamped her left arm around the woman's neck, and immobilized LaDeaux's right arm with her body. With her right arm free, Angie lifted the service revolver from the holster in the small of LaDeaux's back and placed it on the desk. She reached around the woman's body to pull the badge from LaDeaux's left-front shirt pocket and tossed it on the desk. From her right hip pocket, Angie pulled a wallet and flipped it open to make sure the identification card was in it. Discovering that it was, she released her hold on the woman, removed the card and tossed it on the desk, and gave the wallet back to LaDeaux. "Anything else, Sheriff?" she asked sweetly.

"Hang around a minute, please Angie," he said. Turning to the other woman, he said, "Miz LaDeaux, as I said, I am relieving you of your duties. If you leave now, I will not have you arrested. If you do not leave now, I'll have Deputy Wahlert arrest you for criminal trespass and take you to jail."

Dorie LaDeaux had no more fight left in her. She looked at the wallet in her hands and slowly placed it back in her pocket. Without looking at either the sheriff or Deputy Wahlert, she lethargically turned and left the office.

"Just follow her, Angie," the sheriff said, "to make sure she gets out of the building."

"Okay, Sheriff," the deputy said. "You okay?"

"Not really, Angie. That's not my favorite thing. Thank you for your help."

"It's not my favorite thing either, Sheriff," she said, quietly walking from the office, closing the door to the office.

Chapter 7

Jerry had just picked up the drawing of the victim when he heard a gentle knock on the door. He did not really want to talk with anyone right then, but when he heard Archie Crane's voice call his name softly, he said, "Oh, come in, Arch."

Archie stuck his head in the door, smiling at his friend. "Is today still Friday?" he asked. "Seems like I've been up and at 'em for a week at least."

"Yeah," Jerry answered, waving his friend into a leather chair in a small area to the right of his desk. He picked up the drawing from his desk, reminding himself that he needed to copy it and leave the original for Angie; and as he walked over to sit on a couch facing Archie, he said, "As if a murder in the county isn't enough to occupy us, I've got Avon Carroll calling Dorie LaDeaux a bitch, and Miz LaDeaux more than a little upset."

"I guess that's all the yelling I heard?"

"Yep," Jerry answered with a sigh, heaving his feet up on a small table in front of the couch. "Miz Dorie insists that she's going to file a sexual harassment suit, just to start things off, and then she's going to sue me and the county and everyone else she can think of because I put her on unpaid leave. Actually, I fired her skinny ass, but I didn't say so in those words. You know we've talked about firing her after her last two efficiency reports. She's so damned concerned with the minutia of her own life, she can't pay attention to more significant things going on around her. Anyhoo, Arch, unless she hires a lawyer that will give her good legal advice, she'll probably sue. I'd like for you to serve as my lawyer."

"Sure, Jer, be happy to," the chief deputy answered. "Did you tell her she has no case on the sexual harassment allegation?"

"Yeah, I did. But she's sure that I'm another chauvinist out to dominate women. She's not going to listen to me."

"Okay, we have no problem on the original charge," Archie said, taking a mechanical pencil and a small notebook from his shirt pocket. "I've got a pretty clear picture of the parts of Title VII of the Civil Rights Act of 1964, and Deputy LaDeaux's case doesn't come close. But on firing her because she's a pain in the butt, there the timing may be bad. There's this case in the U. S. District Court in Illinois, some female plaintiff versus the Chicago Housing Authority. The plaintiff was fired after she filed a sexual harassment case, and the court found in her favor. I'd guess that there was some pretty heavy wampum changed hands there."

"Yeah, I've read that case. It's in the sexual harassment folder in the file. But I remember thinking at the time I read it that the defendant retaliation against plaintiff was a dumb move. I don't remember all the details of the case—it was a motion for summary judgment filed by the employer I read. But our case is different. I just don't remember exactly how right now. And, Arch, there's another case summary in that file, a Writ of Certiorari to some circuit court of appeals on a retaliation suit. The U. S. Supreme Court reversed the lower court's ruling that a woman's protected activities were violated when she was fired after filing a sexual harassment case against her employer. I don't remember all the details, but review the law and let me know what you think."

"Okay, Jerry," Archie said. "Let me handle it. I know you want to work on that other petty little problem, the murder. I'll take care of this LaDeaux problem and make it go away."

"Thanks, Arch," Jerry replied, ready to put the concern out of his mind.

"Just one more thing, though, Jer," Archie said, smiling.

"We don't need any more things, Arch."

"*Exactamente, mi amigo estimado!* But we got Miz Gladys M. Hump, don't we now."

Jerry looked at Archie for a moment, a look of dismay on his face. He said, "Angels and ministers of grace defend us! What's Glad Ass Hump to do with us or we with her?"

"Well, Glad Ass ain't too glad, I'm afraid," Archie responded. "Miz Hump called while Deputy Dorie was savaging you. Since she couldn't get through to yell at you, she lit in on me. Seems she's upset by 'rampant prostitution' up in her neck of the woods."

"Glad Ass is always distraught at anything that doesn't meet her standards of moral conduct. She averages a call a month to me complaining about some moral degradation or other up near Solace."

Gladys Hump, she insisted upon being referred to as Mrs. J. Maurice Hump, was the wife of a rancher in northwest county. Maurice owned several thousand acres on which he ran Hereford cattle and an interesting variety of white-tail and exotic deer. Maurice was the best of the good old boys, common as dirt, but friendly to a fault. He might well put his boot directly into the middle of a cow patty and then walk across an exquisite white rug in someone's elegant house, treading the manure into the material. Indeed he had, to his wife's distress, done so on a somewhat regular basis at his own home. But he would never think of doing such a thing on purpose, for revenge or because of general malevolence. And he was moderately wealthy. He had gone to high school in Solace with Gladys Finch, whose family had moved to Solace, Texas, from Pennsylvania when Mr. Phinnias Finch purchased the local newspaper, *The Solace Sun*.

Young Miss Finch was not amused by her new surroundings. A not unattractive, short, dark-haired girl with a stuffed shirt, both literally and figuratively, she caught the attention of young Maurice Hump, whom she thought to be the epitome of crudity. He was rather a lumbering hulk of a man who loved to work the land, to load the plenteous rocks onto trucks to free the land for the plow, to feed and tag and tend the cattle. Gladys had never seen him wear anything but blue jeans or overalls and cotton tee shirt. He always seemed to her to have just walked in out of the pasture, manure still on his boots. When she could not ignore his presence, she scowled at him. He, on the other hand, saw her as angelic, beautiful, the most flawless creature God had ever created. She thought he was the perfect oaf.

When high school was over, and when her father could not afford to send her back east to school—or anywhere to school—Miss Gladys Finch took a train to New York to make a new life in the Big City. Nearly three years later a Greyhound bus brought the young woman back to Solace a sadder, but wiser, person. Maurice was overjoyed at the return of his sacred and sweet Gladys, brought her flowers daily, and looked down at her like a large puppy that wants his ears scratched. But Gladys, whose expectations of life had declined considerably during her time away from Solace, still could not imagine a life with Maurice. But when she grew bored to tears working as a clerk in the First State Bank of Solace, young Maurice began to change in her sight. His family had money for big houses, new cars, fine clothes, flamboyant furnishings, whatever they wanted.

Although Maurice wore overalls and was oafish, the alternatives for young Gladys in Kendall County were worse. And she saw no acceptable way out of Kendall County. She married Maurice Hump and set out to refine him.

Failing to make a silk purse when all she had to work with was homespun, she turned her attention to improving the morals of those around her. And she especially seemed to loathe those women who brazenly displayed their bodies in public and sold their favors. Her main goal in life became to rid, if not the world, then her own county from such lascivious women. She formed and was the president of Ladies Shakespeare Society, an organization devoted to flower arranging, bridge playing, and improving the morals of all and sundry. They once asked Jerry to speak to them at their monthly luncheon. When Jerry had asked them which of Shakespeare's plays they were reading, the program chairwoman, Ms Wilhelmina Frost, widow of a former mayor of Solace, had looked embarrassed and replied that they were not "at present" reading of any of Shakespeare's plays. "His sonnets, then?" Jerry had asked. No, not his sonnets either. "His longer poems?" Jerry asked, surprised, because few people were aware that Shakespeare even wrote these early poems. As it turned out, the Ladies Shakespeare Society of Solace had nothing to do with Shakespeare. They wanted Jerry to talk to them on "The Enforcement of Moral Law." Jerry continually found himself too busy to talk with the ladies.

Miz J. Maurice Hump's husband was aware that if the young men in the county sought to have their ashes hauled for a modest fee, they would find a hauler without much trouble. But he did not think prostitution an epidemic in the county. He certainly did not argue the point with his wife, however. She was too bad-tempered on the subject of sex without his aggravating the situation further. If she wanted to chase all the whores out of Kendall County, he was not going to stand in her way. He also knew that the only way to rid the county, any county, of prostitutes was to castrate all the young men. He did not figure that was going to happen. He hoped not.

"Well, Arch, what's Glad Ass's complaint this time?" Jerry asked, not really interested.

"More than just normal complaining this time, Jer. She says that whores are coming out to cars and trucks parked at rest stops and service stations on I-10 soliciting."

Jerry raised his eyebrows. "That doesn't sound right. The only prostitution I know about in the county is controlled by our friend over in Kerr County. I know one of his commercial ventures supplies female company to business men who come to the area to hunt or attend meetings. But these are high-dollar commodities. They don't frequent truck stops."

"Well, Jer, she insists that such things are really going on. You know Glad Ass; she's likely been out patrolling the area to keep dirty sex out of our clean truck stops. And also, Jer, we had a report from Charlie Lewis this past week that he'd heard the same thing, that women, he said 'girls,' were soliciting sex for pay at points along I-10."

Since Lewis was the deputy assigned to the Solace area and made his home there, Jerry assumed that he was a good source for the information. "Has Charlie witnessed any of these women actually soliciting truckers or tourists?"

"No," Archie replied. "He says all he knows are the rumors, truckers talking about it on their CB radios and tourists mentioning it when they stopped for gas in Solace. Charlie told me he checked out the rest stop and three of the truck stops and he didn't see any sign of solicitation."

"Probably wouldn't have," Jerry said. "Even if the women are there, when they saw the patrol car drive up, they'd disappear."

"Want me to handle it, Jer?"

Jerry stroked his chin for a moment and said, "Arch, I'd really like to spend time trying to understand something about this corpse we have over at the morgue. Can you put off this Dorie LaDeaux thing for a while—we're not being pushed on it right now—and look into this spate of sluts that seems to be invading our fair county? If you could meet with our big buddy sometime on Monday, I'll try to set it up."

"Be happy to, Jer."

"Good. Thanks. I'll call him—and then I want to take Angie's drawing out to Harv's place to see if he or any of his workers know who the dead guy is."

Archie pushed himself out of the comfortable leather chair. "Okay, Jer. Let me know. Until I hear from you, I'll look over our files on sexual harassment and be ready if and when young Deputy LaDeaux brings action."

"Miz LaDeaux," Jerry corrected.

"What?" asked Archie, stopping on his way to the door to look back at his friend.

"She is no longer a deputy. She's Miz LaDeaux. Let's not honor her with the title of deputy."

Archie smiled. "Right, Jerry. Miz LaDeaux."

Jerry was walking back to his desk when Archie Crane left the office. He opened the large drawer on the lower right of his desk and pulled out a steel lock box. He found the right key on his ring and opened the box. Taped to the top of the box was a phone number, which Jerry dialed. As the phone rang, he closed the lid of the box, locking it, and returned the box to the drawer. The phone was answered with a growled, "Yeah?"

Jerry said, "This is Sheriff Jerry Valdez. I need to speak to him."

"Not available," came the gruff response.

"Give him a message, please," Jerry replied. "Inform him that we need to discuss a problem. Ask him if he can meet with my chief deputy at the usual place at noon on Monday next. If a meeting is not possible at that time, I'd appreciate a call so that we can reschedule."

There was silence for a moment, then a click, breaking the connection. Jerry looked at the receiver for a moment with some irritation, and then hung it up.

He wrote a short note to Archie: "Arch—I've asked our friend for a meeting on Monday at noon at the Wilderness Area Turkey House. His amanuenses did not say yea or nay, so I'm only assuming that MB will be there. At worst, you'll get a good smoked turkey dinner. Jerry." He put the note in a small envelope, sealed it, and wrote Archie's name on it. He'd ask one of the deputies in the outer office to see that Archie got it this afternoon. Then he made several photocopies of the drawing Angie had made.

Chapter 8

The phone rang five times before it was picked up. When the soft, feminine voice answered, Jerry said, "Hi, babe. It's now…" as he looked at his watch "…five o'clock and I'm not finished yet. I'd hoped to get home in time to cook dinner, but it ain't gonna happen. Have you planned anything?"

"Yes," she replied. "Since I didn't hear from you, I assumed that the call you got turned out to be complicated. So I got some frozen chicken breasts out to cook. I've got them marinating in a ginger-soy sauce. I'll boil some rice and heat a can of green beans and make a salad. The kids and I'll eat about six. Can you be here by then?"

"No, sweetheart, I've got to drive back out to Harvey Phelan's place tonight to ask a few more questions. Keep a plate of food hot for me and I'll eat when I get in. Should be no later than eight."

"Okay, Jerry. Be careful."

Jerry had telephoned Harvey Phelan before driving out, and Phelan was waiting for him as he drove up to the house at a few minutes before six o'clock in the evening.

"Evening, Harv," Jerry said, getting out of the car and shaking hands with the rancher. "Sorry to bother you so late in the day, but I'd like to do as much as I can as soon as I can on this incident."

"You mean murder, don't you Jerry?" Phelan asked, looking the sheriff straight in the eye.

"Well, yeah, almost certainly, Harv. But since the doc hasn't finished the autopsy yet, I can't officially rule it a murder. That's what it is, of course,

42

unless the victim accidentally shot himself in the back of the head twice, threw the pistol away, cut off his hands and disposed of them, walked out here to your ravine, had a heart attack, and died. I guess that might have happened. But I'm betting it's a murder. I just can't call it that yet. Anyway, Harv, I've had Angie Wahlert sketch what the victim might have looked like before the critters spoiled his good looks." Jerry opened a blue folder and held a copy of Angie's sketch for Phelan to see. "Do you know this guy, Harv? Has he ever been out here before he walked onto your land and had his heart attack? Ever see him anywhere before?"

Phelan looked at the picture, took it from Jerry and held it where the last remaining light of the setting sun would hit it, and looked at it closely. Closing the folder and giving it back, he said, "No, Jerry, I don't know who he is. As far as I know, I never saw the feller. Jerry, you don't figure anyone around here killed him do you? I've lived in this area all my life, know most of the families. I don't know nobody'd murder nobody. It ain't natural."

But Jerry knew that many in the county had no such bond with the nature of things. Land to some was there to exploit or merely to live on. Such people cared little for the sanctity of life, probably never thought about it. Others were to them things, like the land, to be used for personal profit. Harvey Phelan, Jerry knew, cared more for the land, for his family, and for his neighbors than for himself. But for every Able, a Cain or two grew parasitically and would thrive until the host was dead. Kill someone? Sure, why not?

Jerry slapped the folder against his leg and looked around at the setting sun. The sky was growing burnt orange, the glow stretching behind the narrow clouds across the horizon. He felt a passionate desire to sit and consider the beauty of the evening, to sit with his wife and children near him, to sit quietly on the large porch of his father-in-law's home overlooking a small lake, with miles of woods stretching as far as one could see west of the pond. But his mind summoned his thoughts back to where he was, where he was required to be by promises he had made, to the problem, to the murder. Slapping his leg one last time reluctantly to send the happy image away, he said, "Well, okay, thanks Harv. Uh, I need to talk with your workers for just a few minutes. How many you have now?"

"Well, I've got four boys, and two of 'em got their wives with them— them girls came up from Mexico just recently. The boys all been here longer. Juan and Eduardo have been with me for four years, and Miguel and Victor— they're the younger boys—they been here less than a year." The rancher thought for a moment. "Them younger boys came together last spring—in

March, I think. Them younger ones have the wives here. Sorry, I don't guess I know the girls' names. Hazel tries to keep them girls busy by giving them light chores to do, but mostly they stay out of sight. 'Course, they're in a strange place and scared and naturally shy. Before the girls came, the boys would now 'n again take their meals with us and play around with Charlie in the evenings. But since the girls came, they mostly keep to themselves. They're staying in the old place just behind the hen houses."

"Okay, thanks Harv," Jerry said, glancing over his shoulder to see the last glow of orange, now diminished to a small blush on the western horizon. Slapping his leg with the folder once more and forcing his attention back to the matter at hand, he walked a few steps over until he could catch a glimpse of the old rock and timber house that Phelan's grandparents had built. He asked, "You mind coming with me to let them know I'm not out to deport them or anything?"

The rancher grinned knowingly as he began walking over to the old house. "Shore, Jerry. You're Mexican and all, like them, but they're scared to death of anybody in authority. It took me several months to get them comfortable with me. They figured I wouldn't pay 'em or cheat 'em somehow, just because I own the ranch. They trust me now, but you're likely to scare the hell out of them."

When the two men arrived at the old house, the rancher stopped about ten feet away from the lighted porch and shouted, "Hey, Eduardo, Juan, *Salgan todos aquí por un momento, por favor?*"

After a moment, the two men Eduardo and Juan cracked the door and peeked out. The rancher smiled and waved them on out. The two men glanced briefly at the sheriff and then dropped their eyes and came out the door.

"*Necesitamos ver a Miguel y a Victor, también,*" the rancher said.

The two men looked at each other for a moment. Jerry thought they were going to question the request, but the older of the two shrugged, pushed the door open, and said, "Miguel, Victor!"

The two younger men edged slowly out of the door, their eyes down, never looking at either the rancher or the sheriff. Jerry noticed that each man had a silver cross suspended from a chain around his neck.

Jerry spoke to the men in Spanish. "Please forgive me for interrupting your evening meal, men. I know it is late, and I do not mean to intrude."

All four men looked up at the smiling sheriff, who spoke their language in their own idiom, with their own inflections.

Harvey Phelan said, in language that was to Spanish what the Rio Grande

River is to filtered water, "Boys, this here's Sheriff Jerry Valdez. Now, he's a good Mexican and a long-time friend of mine—best sheriff we ever had in this county. He needs to ask you boys some questions, and I want you to give him all the help you can. Now, he's not out here to send you back to Mexico or nothing like that. He just needs for you to answer some questions for him, okay?"

The four men nodded at the rancher, but they did not shift their gazes to Jerry until he spoke to them. "Gentlemen," he said in the most formal Spanish he thought they would be comfortable with, "you are aware that we found a corpse down in the arroyo this morning, are you not?" He waved his left hand, indicating the direction of the arroyo.

The men glanced at each other, shrugged, and Eduardo gave a sort of shrug with his mouth and nodded.

"Okay, gentlemen," Jerry continued, opening the folder and extracting the drawing. "Do any of you know this man?"

The Mexicans glanced furtively at the drawing, as though they were fearful of involving themselves with anything having to do with death or crime, even a drawing. But as they glanced at the drawing, then looked longer, they seemed to relax and move closer. Jerry, seeing their willingness to look at the drawing, handed the copy to the oldest of the men. Eduardo accepted the drawing and looked at it carefully, his brow furrowed. He passed it to the other men, each looking at it in his turn. After the last man, Victor, had looked at the drawing thoroughly, he began shaking his head and looked up at the others, passing the drawing back along the path it had taken to him. They all shook their heads.

When Eduardo received the drawing back, he gave it to Jerry and said, "I am sorry Sheriff. We don' know who this is. Wha' is his name, please, señor?"

Jerry sighed as he received the drawing and looked at it. "Nobody knows his name. Any of you ever see anyone around here who looks like this?" He held the drawing up again for them to see.

Again, the four men looked attentively at the drawing and shook their heads.

"You ever see anyone anywhere who looked like this?" Jerry asked.

The men looked surprised to be asked what seemed to them the same question. Eduardo pulled himself to a more formal stance and said, "Señor, I have never seen this man. I believe my frien's when they say they have never seen this man."

Jerry saw that he had insulted the men by seeming to call their honesty into question. "I am very sorry, señors," he said, with a very slight bow of his head. "I did not mean to question your honesty. I am investigating a murder, and I am trying to be thorough. Please forgive me for seeming to disrespect you."

The four men appeared shocked to be spoken to with such deference by so high an authority as the sheriff, and Eduardo was mortified at having spoken so bluntly to so powerful a man. "Señor," he said, "of course, we understan', and we are only shamed that we canna' be of service to you in this matter."

Jerry once again bowed his head slightly and briefly and said, "Señors, thank you. I have taken too much of your time. Go with God."

As Jerry and Harvey Phelan walked back to Jerry's car, the rancher asked, "You don't think those boys had anything to do with the murder, do you Jerry?"

"No I don't, Harv."

"Well, I don't either. 'Course, you can't always tell what a man might do. But these boys, it seems to me, don't have any meanness in them at all. I don't see that they could kill somebody. And even if they could, they wouldn't cut his hands off. I know you can't tell no book by its title, but I don't think these boys have anything to do with murder."

"Cover," said Jerry, almost lost in thought.

"What?" asked the rancher, looking puzzled.

"You can't tell a book by its cover."

"Well, sure, I just said that. But I still don't think they done it."

Jerry smiled, "Me neither, Harv."

It had been a long day.

Chapter 9

The front page of the *Boerne Bugle* carried the story of the murder above
the fold in the Saturday edition, the headline MURDER MOST FOUL! in
what looked to Jerry like 48-point font. The report, accurate enough, Jerry
thought, was written by Nina Thornton, a competent reporter. The paper did
not run a copy of Angie's drawing, but there was a physical description of
the victim, described as "an Hispanic male in his early forties." Near the end
of the article, Jerry was annoyed to find a quotation:

*A highly placed source in the Sheriff's Department reported confidently,
"We'll have this homicide solved within the week. The perpetrator or multiple
perpetrators will be in our jail, count on it. We have several Mexican males
we can place in the vicinity at the time of the crime, and we'll be bringing
these individuals in for questioning."*

Willie Ward, thought Jerry angrily, making a mental note to scorch the
deputy's ass for presuming to speak for the department.

He looked up a number in the phone book and punched in a number.
"Nina," he said when a woman answered, "Jerry Valdez here. When the hell
did Willie Ward become 'a highly placed source in the Sheriff's Department'?"

The woman laughed. "Well, hello, Jerry. Nice to hear your voice. When I
can't get you or Archie to give me a comment, Jerry, that's when I have to
look elsewhere for a highly placed source. I thought it was nice that whoever
it was who gave me that inside information promised you'd have it solved in
a week."

"Whoever it was, my Aunt Fannie," Jerry snorted. "Only Willie Ward talks like a bad television deputy. I wish you wouldn't ask him to speak for the department, Nina. He can hardly speak for himself."

"I know, Jerry. I felt kinda bad about that part of the story. But my source, whoever it was, was convenient, and I couldn't get either you or Archie on the phone. Since it's really not important and it looked kinda good, I put it in. But I apologize."

"You owe me, dear heart," Jerry said. "Next time you can't get Archie or me on the phone, call Angie Wahlert."

"Not jolly likely, Jerry," Nina said. "She protects that office like it was her own prize kitten. All I ever get out of Angie is, 'You'll have to take that up with the sheriff.'"

Jerry laughed. "Good girl, Angie. I wish I could get Willie to learn from her."

"You're a bastard, Jerry Valdez. With sources like Angie Wahlert, newspapers would have nothing to print. Other than the quotation, how'd you like the story?"

"Accurate, well written, as I would expect from you. You write the headline?"

"God, no!" she said, the embarrassment evident in her tone. "Wasn't that horrible? Mr. Lane believes that an owner of a newspaper should participate in getting the paper out—and sometimes he chooses to write what seem to him appropriate headlines. I wish I had negotiated in my contract the right to compose my own headlines. Thanks a lot for bringing that up, Jerry."

"Okay, Nina, I accept your apology and I am a bastard. But don't call Willie 'a highly placed source.' He's not even a lowly placed source."

"I did not say who my source was, Sheriff. For all you know, it might have been Archie Crane or Angie Wahlert."

"Right, Nina. 'Bye."

After he hung up the phone, he kissed Anna Maria goodbye and drove downtown.

Jerry hated working seven days a week, but during hunting season twenty-four/seven emerged as his cosmic numerical authorities. That he found the county medical examiner, Dr. Able Martin, also at work in the morgue on Saturday did not make him feel any better. Being county medical examiner was not a full-time job during most of the year, and usually even during hunting season there was little forensic science to be practiced. But German by family, heritage, and disposition, the good doctor hated a mystery. He did not care who had killed his patient; that was not his business. But he hated having a patient he did not know. Jerry found him standing over the undraped cadaver staring attentively.

"Watcha think, Doc," Jerry said, as he pushed open the door and walked into the examining room, holding out his right hand to greet the examiner.

Dr. Martin looked up as Jerry approached, but did not put his gloved hand out to shake hands. Jerry saw that the latex gloves were flecked with blood and tissue, and he quickly lowered his hand.

"Jerry, goddamn it, tell me who is this man."

"Well, hell, Doc, I was hoping you could tell me. I can't get any fingerprints since the fellow did not have either the manners or the foresight to keep his hands attached to his body. So, if he's going to tell us who he is, I guess it'll have to be someway other than by fingerprints. Anything else you can think of, Doc?"

The ME looked at the sheriff distastefully. "Sure, my most illustrious sheriff. I can give you a retina scan—well, no, I guess I can't, since your corpus evidence here did not choose to present me with eyes. But I can give you his blood type. He is five feet, eight inches tall and weighed about a hundred eighty pounds at time of death. I can give you his DNA structure. I can give you an imprint and analysis of his dentures. I can tell you that he has no tattoos, no evidence of surgery, no evidence of disfiguring disease. I can tell you that he was probably murdered sometime Wednesday evening. The cause of death is gunshot wound behind the right ear. I can tell you that he was shot twice, but I cannot tell you which of the two shots killed him because the second shot probably followed hard upon the first. Either one would have killed him. I can tell you what he had for dinner about an hour before he died. I can tell you that he had a rather serious case of acne as a teenager. I can tell you what kind of grease he put on his hair, what kind of deodorant he put under his arms, and what kind of aftershave he put on his face. I can tell you that he was not injecting himself with drugs nor inhaling. I can tell you that his penis is on the small side of average, measuring in the flaccid state two inches and firm likely five to five and a half inches. I can tell you he has been on this earth just under forty years, that he has an ingrown toenail on his right great toe and the beginnings of calluses on the heals of both feet. Now, if I tell you all this, can you tell me who he is?"

Jerry looked at the medical examiner for a moment before he said, "Probably not, Doc. Not right now. We don't have enough of a data base on retina prints, even if you had them, or hair oil choices or penis size. But I'd like a list of all that other stuff, when you get around to it. Anything useful on his clothes?"

"I don't autopsy clothes," the pathologist said, unfolding a sheet and pulling it over the body. "They're in that plastic tub over on the shelf by the door. You got anybody out looking for the hands?"

Jerry had glanced over at the shelf, but turned back and said, "We looked a reasonable radius around where we found the body. Didn't find anything. I wouldn't know where else to look. Would you?"

"Nope," the doctor replied, pushing the gurney over near the refrigerated room where the corpse would be stored until final disposition. "I can tell you what he is, but not who he is. I guess we'll just call him 'Nobody,' as Quasimodo called Ulysses."

Jerry thought for a moment before he said, "Not Quasimodo." It was that Cyclops guy—what's his name?"

"Quasimodo. I told you."

"Naw, Quasimodo is the hunchback of Notre Dame," Jerry responded. "Homer's guy is somebody else."

"You're really having difficulty with names nowadays, my good Sheriff. First you can't name Nobody and now you can't remember the name of a one-eyed giant."

"Polyphemos. That's the guy's name," Jerry remembered.

Doctor Martin mused for a moment before he responded. "Well, you're right, Jerry. Polyphemos, son of Poseidon, god of the sea. Now you're on a roll, Sheriff. Who is this guy?" he said, gesturing toward the corpse.

"I wish I knew."

"He's Nobody, Sheriff."

Jerry said, "Well, nobody knows his name, that's for sure. I don't suppose you found anything under the fingernails that might help? Like flesh scraped off in a fight or drugs or soil or anything?"

The doctor did not pause in his ministrations. "You remember that ice-water enema I promised you? Best not upset the good doctor, lest when you least expect it your colon is visited by an unpleasant guest," the doctor said, pulling his gloves and lab covers off and tossing all into a lidded bin. Winking and smiling at the sheriff, he opened the door and left the room.

Jerry found a box of thin rubber gloves and pulled one on each hand, wiggling his fingers into the talcum interior and snapping the wristbands in place. He walked over to the shelf to remove the plastic container from the shelf and set it on a workbench.

The shorts and undershirt were on top of the neatly folded pile of clothes.

Jerry examined each of the undergarments thoroughly but found them to be no help. The undershirt had no tag to identify brand or size, and no visible laundry mark. Jerry put it aside to check with ultraviolet light for possible hidden marks. The underpants were common cotton jockey shorts. The remnants of a label were extant on the elastic band, but worn so that neither brand nor size was discernable. Again, no marks.

The shirt was a white cotton dress shirt with a small collar. The brand tag usually found sewn just below the collar band in the rear of the shirt had been slashed out, probably with a knife, since the cuts had left a jagged hole in the shirt. There were remnants of another tag sewn up and to the left, also hacked out. *Probably*, Jerry thought, turning the collar over in his hand, *a tag giving washing instructions*. No other marks were in the collar. Probably the collar and sleeve length had been on one or the other of the excised labels. Jerry then checked the single pocket on the shirt and found nothing, not even lint. No ink spots to indicate that a pen had ever been carried in the pocket, no lead or pencil marks on, in, or around the pocket. He ran his fingers along all the seams to see if anything had been sewn in. Nothing. He checked for markings on the shirttail. Sometimes clothing manufacturers will print "care instructions" in that area. Not this manufacturer, not on this shirt. He laid it aside for the ultraviolet check.

The suit jacket was soft wool, like cashmere, black with blue and brown threads woven into the fabric. *Handsome*, Jerry thought, *and probably expensive*. The material was cut so that the vertical threads on the pocket flaps were aligned with the jacket. Dirt was imbedded in the material around the center vent on the back of the jacket, probably from being dragged down into the arroyo. Just to cover all bases, Jerry would have the dirt analyzed to find out if any soil was embedded that could not have been picked up on the trip into Mr. Phelan's arroyo. The three buttons were black leather. The lining of the jacket appeared to be blue silk to match the threads in the wool fabric. There were two spare leather buttons sewn inside the left side of the jacket, along with two smaller leather buttons—*probably*, Jerry thought, *spares for the jacket sleeves*. All the labels were gone, cut out seemingly by the same knife used on the shirt. No hint was left to indicate who constructed the jacket, who sold it, who bought it, or the name of the man who died in it. Jerry carefully searched each pocket, finding only a bit of lint in each of the inside pockets. He took several plastic bags out of his shirt pocket and placed the lint from each pocket in a separate bag and sealed it, marking each one with one of the lab's black markers. He was surprised to find nothing, not even lint, in the outside pockets. The body had been dragged along the ground for a considerable distance, but nothing in the pockets. Probably protected from the dirt and the lint elves by the pocket flaps. He laid the jacket in the ultraviolet pile.

The trousers were the last item, and he laid them on the counter top. They matched the jacket and were seemingly little worn. The pockets contained nothing, not even harvestable lint. Jerry held the pants up by the waistband to get a general look. He saw no worn places on the seat, no indication of stretch bulges where a wallet was carried. A small amount of dirt was embedded in the material, again, Jerry surmised, from being dragged into the arroyo. He'd get the lab to check. As he searched the pants from waist to rolled cuffs, he could find no identifying signs. He stretched them back on the counter top. The inside waistband was a heavy white material and clearly not much worn. No tags to indicate manufacturer or size were anywhere to be found. Jerry ran his fingers over all the seams, but found nothing obviously secreted there. He stepped two paces to his right to run his fingers over the rolled cuffs, thinking of J. Alfred Prufrock. But these were not white flannel trousers. There was some lint in the left cuff, and a bit of what appeared to be grass or leaves and some seeds in the bottom of the cuff. Nothing in the seams. He found a bit more of the same stuff in the right cuff. He scrapped as much from the cuffs as he could, put the bits and pieces in a bag, and labeled it. As he ran his fingers over the seams of the right cuff he felt something flat and hard, wedged between the stitch that secured the cuff to the pant leg and the bottom of the cuff. Worrying the disc out of its place, he spun it onto the counter top. It appeared to be made of copper or brass, a token of some sort. Jerry picked it up with a pair of forceps he found on an instrument tray.

On the obverse side of the quarter-sized disc "The Riviera" was stamped around the top and "Las Vegas" around the bottom. An image of a building, presumably "The Riviera," was stamped in the center. The reverse side was encircled with leaves of some sort and "25 Cents" stamped in the middle.

"Hello," said Jerry.

He placed the token in a plastic bag, the clothes back into the tub, all the evidence bags on top, and took them down the hall to the forensics lab. He was somewhat more optimistic than he had been an hour earlier.

Chapter 10

Jerry knew better than to expect anything in the forensics lab to be done on Sunday. And he was right. Nothing was done.

But early on Monday morning, he dragged himself unwillingly out of bed at the indecent hour of six in the a. m., had but a brief breakfast with his wife and two children, and drove to the lab, there to make himself as insufferable as possible until he got the results from the tests he had requested.

He did not like the results when he got them.

Disinclined to wait for the report to be written formally, he cornered Albert Berger, the chief lab technician, to try to get some answers. Berger was thorough, proficient—yet German and arrogant. He would not let God herself tell him how to run his lab, and he bridled at anyone's hurrying him. And Jerry was hurrying him. But Jerry had the prudence to approach Berger with a smile and *einer Apflekuchen* fresh from the magnificent *Deutcher Wunderbar Bäckerei* on Main Street.

Jerry had thought, *What the hell*, and got one for himself, too.

Even with the apple tart, Jerry had to drag the information out of Berger, who was more inclined to talk about how his tasks were made impossible by people who wanted him to draw on some sort of magic to do his work, how science required precise measures and patience and could not be forced into hasty conclusions.

Still, with the pastry and his smiles and his persistence, Jerry finally got the results of the tests.

There were no fingerprints on the token—well, there were some smudges, but nothing remotely usable. There were no hidden laundry marks on any of the clothes. The lint in the pockets was just lint—pieces of wool and cotton scuffed off of some unidentifiable material, probably even the article of clothing itself. The dirt imbedded in the jacket and trousers was consistent with the soil in and around the Phelan ranch, and with the soil for about a hundred miles in any direction. The stuff in the cuffs was vegetable—grass or flowers or weeds or seeds of some sort, but not marijuana or poppy or any drug; those Berger knew readily. Berger had no idea what it was. It was probably picked up, Burger assumed, while walking through some field or other. Could be anywhere.

Jerry thanked the technician with as much fervor as he could muster, but he felt no enthusiasm. The tests were almost dead ends. All he could do was to follow up on the Las Vegas token—probably a goose chase. And the grass stuff, whatever it was. Since it was not Mary Warner, he figured it was another dead end. Grass, a wise man once said, is grass. Alas.

Back home for lunch, Jerry tried to talk with Anna Maria with his mouth full of chili con carne, corn chips, cheese and onions. And catsup. "Waya whank out goin to Wegus?"

Anna Maria, having a small salad, slowly put her fork down, looked up at her husband, and said quietly, "Jerry, I can't understand you with that cigar in your mouth."

This was an old joke. In the evenings, while Jerry sat in his recliner reading his paper, he habitually chewed on a piece of a large-ring cigar. When he tried to discuss something he had just read in the paper with Anna Maria, the cigar seemed to inhibit communication. Only when he freed a hand from the newspaper and took the cigar from his mouth did she pay any attention to him.

Jerry smiled, chewed the mush in his mouth, swallowed, and said, "What, my dear, do you think about going to Las Vegas with me?"

"No!" she responded, as though he had asked her to fornicate with Satan himself. "Why are you going to Las Vegas?"

"Well, I'm not, unless you want to go. I've got to track down a lead—not much of a lead. But I can probably get in touch with the sheriff's office out there and get them to help out. I just thought you might like to fly out for a day or two."

"I've been to Las Vegas, Jerry, and I don't care if I ever go back. You might as well ask me to go to Sodom. All the lights and music and naked dancing girls, and for all I can tell nobody having any fun. I've sat for an hour at a time looking at people pulling those levers on slot machines looking bored and vacant. What's the fun in that? The naked dancing girls, you've said yourself, are only attractive for a while. And there are so many of them, you stop looking at them after awhile. I hate Las Vegas."

Jerry sat for a moment. "How about Gomorrah?"

"Neither Sodom nor Gomorrah, thank you."

Jerry knew his wife was no prude. She was reared in a strict Catholic environment and had to be weaned away from many of the strict teachings of her youth, but she had never been a prude. She knew the official attitude of the Church had been that sex was for procreation within the bounds of a holy, that is, Catholic, marriage. She knew that birth control was alien to that opinion. She knew that the Church argued that she should never look with sexual interest at a man not her husband, be he ever so fetching.

She also came to understand very early that most of these teachings were thoroughly unrealistic, irrational, and probably unnatural. Those who believed them might just as well be one of those religious sects whose concept of Truth was so unnatural and unreasonable as to deny God-given reason. The Catholic moral conventions were fashioned and sanctioned by a group of celibate men who, Anna Maria often thought, must be as frustrated as a starving man who could only look at, but never have, a standing prime rib of beef fresh from the oven. She had great admiration for those men and women who choose to serve others through the Church. But she could never have been celibate. She liked men too much, she loved Jerry too much, she liked sex too much. Early in her marriage to Jerry she had worried when she became uncontrollably passionate during sex, giving herself totally to the moment, to the feast of pleasure. She would feel guilty, confess her sins, repent, and do penance. Then a wise young priest who had heard her contrite confession, a scholar from Rome visiting her church for a summer, asked her a simple question: "Do you express your love in the sex act?"

When she had, wide-eyed and a bit indignant, said, "Of course I do, Father."

He had responded, "Remember that God is love. Bless you, my daughter, for being close to God in your love."

So she took the teachings of the Church with a reasonable and realistic measure of salt. But Las Vegas was something else. What she saw there was not sex, the way she understood and experienced and loved sex. What she saw there was dissoluteness, sadness, confusion, loneliness.

"I don't want to go to Las Vegas, dear," she said and picked up her fork again.

"Aw-wite," her husband replied, this time with half a jalapeno in the mix in his mouth of chili, corn chips, and cheese, as he glanced over to his large glass of iced tea, in which were submerged three wedges of lime, wondering how he could take a drink with his mouth already full of food.

Chapter 11

At ten minutes before noon Archie Crane parked his patrol car in the almost-full gravel lot of the Wilderness Area Turkey House, on the Interstate nearly twelve miles northwest of Boerne. The chief deputy chose to drive a marked patrol car, a new Ford Crown Victoria with all the decals and lights, rather than the unmarked car his rank permitted. His theory was that the more presence law enforcement could show in the county, the better.

The Turkey House was often crowded at noon this time of the year. Not only did travelers along the Interstate, having been alerted of the imminent presence of the Wilderness Area Turkey House by large signs placed strategically along the highway in both directions, and advised by even more smaller signs of the gastronomic delights of the food served there, stop by for lunch, but during hunting season the woods would empty of hunters who could depend upon the Turkey House cooks to provide the turkeys that their own hunting skills could not.

Archie often wondered why Mr. Biggs chose such a public place to meet. Maybe he liked the food. Probably he owned the place.

John Wesley Biggs was the most powerful gangster in four counties, one of them being Kendall County. He supervised all of the prostitution in those counties, ran the numbers games, brokered business and political schemes, controlled several oil leases, and generally lived like a king in quiet isolation somewhere no one seemed to know about. His "family" included mob bosses in all the major cities in the United States, and he had himself controlled a large part of the rackets in Chicago before he opted for a quieter life in the hill country of Texas.

He had called Jerry in the sheriff's first year in office to ask about the son of one of his "business associates," who had been arrested for transporting a truckload of liquor into a dry area of the county. When Jerry learned that the kid had been dispatched to San Antonio to buy the liquor for a party his mobster dad was throwing, Jerry had let him out of jail and dropped the charges against him. Biggs had called him soon after and asked him what he could do for him. When Jerry told him "nothing," that the boy had broken the letter of the law, but not the spirit, Biggs had said simply, "I owe you."

Through the years Jerry had called Biggs when the man's enterprises began to disrupt communities—like when one of his prostitutes turned out to be the fifteen-year-old daughter of a Dallas banker, or one of his enforcers mistook a country preacher's son for a man who had welched on a debt. In every case Biggs set his business right. Several times Biggs had called Jerry to comment on departmental activities that Biggs insisted were too stringent and were hurting his business. Jerry never warned Biggs, and Biggs never threatened the sheriff. But Jerry knew that a total confrontation between the sheriff and Biggs would be a dangerous war.

As Archie entered the Turkey House, he noticed two members of the mobster family sitting to the right of the door, their table placed so that they were partially obscured by the open door as one entered. Archie stood for a moment upon entering, looking around the room and spotting the two goons almost immediately. They were looking at him, but they gave no indication that they wanted to confront him.

Mr. Biggs's "family" members were always well dressed—not, however, in the style of a big-city mobster. Armani suits, Italian shoes, and silk ties would have attracted as much attention in the Texas hill country as *La Sauce Auscitaine* on chicken-fried steak. These guys, both large men, wore new chino trousers and silk shirts. The gravy on these chicken-fried steaks had a bit of caviar mixed in, but it was not French.

Two more similarly clad men sat at a table near the door to the small dining area off to the left of the main dining room. Archie noticed that neither group of outriders sat in a booth. *Probably too difficult to exit a booth in a hurry*, he thought.

As he walked to the door of the small room, the two men at the nearest table stood and moved in front of the door, blocking his entrance. Archie stopped and held his hands away from the Browning 9 mm automatic he wore on his right hip.

As one of the men fixed his gaze on the pistol, the other attached his eyes on Archie's face. Both men had dark hair and black eyes. The one staring at the pistol had a hint of a moustache, and the other had a scar on his right cheek. Other than those characteristics, Archie was not sure he could tell them apart in a lineup. "Who are you?" the one with a scar asked, without a hint of gentleness.

"My name is Archie Crane. I am Sheriff Valdez' chief deputy. I am here at the sheriff's instruction."

"I don't know you," the man said.

Archie shrugged. "I don't know you either."

As the mustached thug continued to stare at Archie's pistol, Scar Face grasped the chief deputy's right arm above the elbow with his left hand and opened the door with his right, ushering Archie into the small dining room.

Inside the room were two men sitting at a table for six. Archie was about to speak when Scar Face pulled his right hand up and Moustache unsnapped the restraining clasp and removed Archie's pistol from the holster. When he was disarmed, Scar Face patted him down to check for other weapons. Finding none, he handed the weapon to one of the men at the table, motioned to Moustache and both left the room.

Archie remained passive as he was disarmed and searched. When the two heavies left, he looked at the two sitting at the table, trying to determine which one was Mr. Biggs. One was clearly older than the other, although neither was young. The younger was likely in his forties, the other maybe mid-fifty. When the one who had received Archie's pistol glanced at the older man, Archie also turned to him. "Are you Mr. Biggs?" he asked.

There was an ill-humored smirk on the mouths of both men. The older man asked, "Who are you?"

No 'will you please join us? Please sit with us?' Archie was beginning to grow irritated with these two clowns, but he was here to gather information for his friend, not to smack some civility into a couple of social Neanderthals. Still, it would be enjoyable. "My name is Archie Crane. I am chief deputy sheriff of Kendall County. I am here at the instruction of Sheriff Valdez. Now, are you Mr. Biggs?"

Again the smirks. "What do you want?" asked the older man.

"Right now I want to know if you are Mr. Biggs," Archie responded.

"Don't use that name again," the younger man interjected threateningly, moving the slide on Archie's weapon slightly to see if there was a round in the chamber. There was not.

59

Archie thought for a moment. "Okay," he said, glancing from one to the other, "I was asked by Sheriff Valdez—is it all right for me to use that name?—to drive up here today to meet with someone whose name you seem not to want me to use. Is either one of you that man?" He was proud of himself.

The younger man smirked again while the older man said in a bored manner, "What is it you want?"

"We're not getting too far, are we, guys?" Archie said. "I really don't have time to play games with you people. The sheriff asked me to meet with Mr. Biggs to clarify a possible problem. Now, can I do that or not?"

The younger man stood and pulled the slide back on Archie's Browning, levering a cartridge into the chamber. He held the pistol in his right hand across his chest, the muzzle pointing at the ceiling. "I told you not to use that name!" he said with sand in his voice.

Archie's rein on his annoyance disappeared, rather like a shadow vanishes in a blaze of light. His left hand shot out to grab the right wrist of the younger man, and his right hand grabbed the pistol, twisting it up and counter-clockwise. When the pistol cleared the man's hand, Archie quickly eased the hammer into the safe position and returned the weapon to his holster. But he did not fasten the restraining belt. Then he said, "I tried to accommodate you insulting bastards, but now I'm not interested in what you want. From what Sheriff Valdez has told me, Mr. Biggs has better manners than you shitheads. I'll assume that neither one of you is Biggs." He looked at each man but got nothing but scowls in return. The younger man was still standing, but the older man had remained seated. "So, what's it to be, guys? I was sent to talk about a problem. You guys want to talk about it and give me some reasonable assurances?"

The younger man, turning red in the face, opened his mouth to say something, but restrained himself when the older man held up his hand.

"Sit down," the older man said to the other. After a moment, the still seething younger man sat stiffly in the chair. Then the older man turned to Archie, "You do not speak to us in such a manner. You do not treat us in such a manner."

Archie looked at the older man for a moment, then glanced at the younger man, and then back at the older man. "Am I to go back to the sheriff and tell him that you refused to discuss with me the situation he asked me to bring to you?"

"You can go to hell!" the younger man said, rising threateningly.

The older man again held up his hand to restrain the other. When the younger man sat down, the older one said, "You may tell the sheriff that you have insulted people you should not have insulted."

Archie once again looked into the eyes of the two men—men who were used to intimidating anyone they faced. He would like to take each of them apart right here in this room, to teach them a bit about the dangers of attempted intimidation. But Jerry was always concerned about his tenuous peace with so powerful an entity in the area. Archie was clearly not going to get any information from these guys, and he did not want to escalate the conflict naturally existing between organized crime and the law. At least not right now. So he left the room, left the Wilderness Area Turkey House, and drove back to the office.

Chapter 12

After some searching in his Sheriffs' Association directories, Jerry finally found a listing for the Clark County Sheriff's Office in Las Vegas, Nevada. The sheriff of Clark County was not in, and no one seemed to know when he would be back. Jerry talked to the chief deputy.

"Deputy Berry, Jerry Valdez here. I'm sheriff of Kendall County in Texas. I have a favor to ask of you good people."

"Sure, Sheriff," the deputy responded. "How can we help you?"

"I've got a murder vic here we need to identify. Reason I'm calling you guys out in Vegas is that he had a casino token on him when we found him. Token's from 'The Riviera' in Las Vegas. What I'm asking is that if I fax you out a copy of both sides of the token and a drawing of the corpse, if you could check out at the Riviera to see if they know who the vic is. And, of course, maybe check with others in your office and local police and state guys."

"Sure, Sheriff, shoot me the pics out and we'll check around for you. You got anything else that might place him in Vegas?"

"No, I don't, Deputy. Whoever killed him sanitized him pretty well. This token was pretty well hidden in his trouser cuff or I guess we wouldn't have that."

"Not much to go on, is it? Why not send me a photo of the vic instead of a drawing? It might be easier to recognize."

"Not in this case, Deputy. We found him in the woods, and I'm afraid the critters have been gnawing on him some. I don't think his mama would recognize a photo of him as he is."

"Yeah, well, I copy that. Send us what you have, and we'll run it as far as it'll go."

Jerry got the fax number and closed the connection. "Angie!" he yelled out the open door as he put a photocopy of the token together with a copy of the drawing of the victim.

A moment later, a smiling Deputy Angie Wahlert stood in the doorway, leaning against the molding, her right hand on her hip. "You bellowed, Sheriff, Sir?"

Jerry smiled at the young woman. "Sorry, Angie. I wanted you to hear me. Will you be so kind as to fax these two sheets to Las Vegas at that number I've written on the front. Put one of our standard cover sheets on and send all of it to the attention of Chief Deputy Berry."

"Okay, Sheriff," she said, pivoting to leave, but turning her head to smile winningly at her boss again. Her skirt flipped in the pivot, drawing Jerry's eyes to the back of her legs—as the presence of an angel would entice the adoration of a priest. The fact that Angie was no angel and Jerry no priest enhanced rather than diminished the allure.

As she walked away, she ran full into Archie Crane, who clutched her in his arms to keep her from falling.

"Oops, sorry Archie," the still smiling young woman said, leaning back in his arms to look at him.

"Anytime, Angie," Archie said, setting her free to dance back down the hall to the lobby.

Archie watched the young woman walk away, swaying and clapping her hands to some unheard melody and then turned to see Jerry watching him. Archie grinned. "Just wanted to make sure she wasn't hurt in the collision," he said, closing the door.

"Sure," Jerry responded. "You meet with our friend?"

"You don't use his name, either, do you?" Archie said, surprised that he had not noticed before. "Everyone I've met today has avoided using his name, and several of them have warned me to do the same."

"I try not to refer directly to him," Jerry responded. "He's kinda like a hornets' nest. I know he's there and dangerous. But I don't want to disturb the nest unless I'm willing to take it out. And that's one hornets' nest that would be damned hard to take out. Lots of folks would get stung. And even then we might not get rid of it. So, yeah, I'd rather not disturb it any more than I have to."

Archie nodded understanding. "'Our friend,' then, was not at the meeting today—at least I don't think he was."

Jerry stopped pushing things into his desk drawer and paid attention. "Who was there?"

"I dunno, Jer," Archie responded. "There were two youngish guys near the front door and two more outside the door to the small dining room. But I guess they were outsiders."

Jerry nodded. "They were," he said. "Biggs takes them whenever he's outside his own compound. They give you any trouble?"

Archie shook his head. "Nope. One of the guys guarding the door to the small room took my gun and patted me down when I got into the room, but..."

Jerry was angry. "Well, goddamn it, that won't do. I won't have them treating you like that. Who was in the room when that happened?"

"There were two guys already in the room. I thought one of them had to be Biggs, but you had told me that Biggs had some refinement to him. Neither of these guys did. I asked them several times if either one was Biggs, but all they said was not to use that name."

Jerry listened intently to his friend.

"When I decided that Biggs wasn't there, I asked them if we could discuss the problem, but they were too busy trying to impress me with the size and mass of their balls to discuss anything else. I made one last attempt and came away empty. Sorry, Jer, I didn't get the job done."

Jerry shook his head and said, "Not your fault, Arch. I don't know what got into Biggs. He doesn't want a war any more than we do. Did they give your gun back to you?"

"No, well, I kinda got angry and took it back. They must not have sent the first string to meet with me. It wasn't hard to take it back."

Jerry smiled at his friend's humility. "You break any of their bones?"

"No," Archie responded. "Only thing injured is their egos. But they are angry. I don't guess the king hornet was there, but some of his worker bees might be swarming."

Jerry thought for a moment, and then he opened the large drawer on the lower right of his desk and pulled out the steel lock box. He found the phone number taped to the top of the box and dialed it. As the phone rang, he closed the lid of the box, locked it, and returned the box to the drawer. The phone was answered with a growled, "Yeah?"

Jerry said, "This is Sheriff Jerry Valdez. I need to speak to him."

"Not available," came the gruff response.

"This is Valdez. Get him. Right damned now!"

The receiver on the other end clicked and the connection was broken.

Jerry sat immobile for an instant, thinking. He then flashed the receiver and dialed another number. When the phone was answered, Jerry said, "Artie, Jerry Valdez here. Do you have some guests in for a hunt this week?"

"I do Sheriff," Artie Commons responded. "A group—from Chicago, I think. Why?"

"Artie, I'm not going to ask you these questions and you're not going to answer them. Understand."

"I understand, Sheriff."

"How many 'hunters' do you have there tonight?"

"Eight."

"How many locally furnished hostesses?"

"Aw, Jerry!"

"How many?"

"Damn, Jerry." His voice got very soft. "Eight. But, Jerry, this is really high-class stuff. And you know who the provider is. Nobody's getting hurt here, Jerry."

"When's dinner over tonight?"

There was an audible sigh from Artie. "We have dinner at six; they're finished by seven-thirty. Then they have cigars and brandy and cards until eleven in the great hall. And then to their individual rooms. Just like always. Jerry...."

"Artie, not a single word to anyone about this conversation we did not have. Do you absolutely understand me, Artie?"

"Jerry...."

"Do you absolutely understand me, Artie?"

"What conversation, Sheriff?"

Jerry hung the phone up and buzzed Miriam. "Miriam, get Deputy Lewis on the radio and ask him to report to me ASAP. And get Deputies Carroll, O'Brian, Potts, Patton, and Schmidt and ask them to see me when Charlie Lewis gets here."

"Okay, Sheriff," the communications deputy responded.

"You gonna knock the nest down, Jerry?" Archie said, worried.

"No, not if I don't have to. But I'll be damned if I'll let the hornets just light on anything they want just because they're hornets."

"They got stingers, Jerry."

"Yep. And as long as they stay in their own orbit, we'll leave them alone as best we can. But when they get too aggressive, we'll have to pull their stingers out."

"If we can."

"If we can."

Chapter 13

At about five Monday evening, Jerry reached for the phone in his office and punched the quick-dial for his home phone. When Anna Maria's cheerful voice answered, he said, "'Afternoon, beautiful. How's my girl?"

"I'm fine, dear," she responded tentatively. "Does this call mean that you're going to be late again?"

Jerry sighed. "Yeah, babe, 'fraid so. I've got a bit of evening sheriffing to do. It'll probably be really late when I get home. You guys go ahead and have dinner. I'll get a sandwich or something around here and see you later. Give the kids a hug for me."

"Okay, sweetheart. Please be careful," she said.

"I will, babe," Jerry responded. "And give yourself a hug—oh, never mind. I'll take care of that when I get home."

As soon as he hung up, his intercom buzzed. It was Miriam. "Sheriff, I've got Solace, Christmas Carol, The Oboe, Shooter, Peppermint Patty, and Big Red here. I believe the Guardian Angel is with them."

Jerry thought for a moment. "Is that Deputies Lewis, Carroll, O'Brian, Potts, Patton, and Schmidt?"

"Yes, Sir."

"Oboe?"

"Yes, Sir, O'Brian."

Jerry sighed. "Oboe" was better than "Kinky." "Okay, Miriam. Ask those people with weird names to meet me in the squad room. Is the chief deputy in his office?"

"4-10, sheriff. The Green-eyed Monster is waiting in his office."

Jerry shook his head as he replaced the receiver. Walking down the hall to Archie's office, he smiled at his friend, nodded, and waited for Archie to accompany him to the squad room.

When Jerry and Archie walked into the room, Hilton O'Brian rose to his feet. The other deputies glanced at him for a moment and then turned their attention back to the sheriff and chief deputy. O'Brian waited until both had sat before he resumed his seat.

"Hey, guys," Jerry said. "How is everyone?"

The deputies all smiled and answered with a cacophony of responses: "Great, Sheriff." "Fine." "Good." "Real good, Sheriff." "Great, how're you?"

"Good. I need for you guys to go with me this evening to Artie Commons' commercial hunting lodge to arrest some women and charge them with prostitution. I want this done with a minimum of disruption at the scene. There will be eight women. When we get there, I expect them to be in individual rooms in the company of one man each. But we will not know that for sure until we get there, and maybe not until we get into the different rooms. So, we'll need to be flexible. Deputy Lewis, the ranch is in your district, but I want Deputy Patton to be directly in charge of this operation. I'll be along to help and to supervise, but you'll take your direction from Deputy Patton. Since we will be arresting eight women, I want Deputy Patton to make sure that the arrests are, without question, professionally done. I'm asking Deputies Wahlert and Smith to accompany us and to assist Deputy Patton. Any searches of the females will of course be done by one of the female deputies, and I'd prefer that any touching of the female suspects— such as handcuffing or forcible removal—to be done by one of the female deputies."

"All the female suspects are to be cuffed, Sheriff?" asked Patricia Patton.

"Yes," Jerry responded.

"Are the males with them to be cuffed as well?" Patton asked.

"No, keep an eye on the men and don't let them interfere with the arrests," Jerry said.

"I have some trouble with that, Sheriff," Patton said, fidgeting in her seat, looking uncomfortable. "Prostitution is illegal, and I have no qualms about arresting perpetrators. But if we are arresting women engaged in prostitution in the rooms of men, the men are at least as deserving of arrest and conviction. I'm sorry to be contentious, Sheriff. I hope you all know that I want to do the best job I can, and I love my job. But I don't believe I can participate in this raid with the rules you have given us."

Jerry sighed and said, "Yeah, Patricia, I understand. It's my fault for not explaining better, and I apologize. This little foray is not a usual raid. There is prostitution going on and it's illegal. But ridding Kendall County of all illegal sex is not high on my agenda right now. What's going on here is more complex. I'm arresting the women not because I want to prosecute them but because I need to send a message to the man they work for. If everything goes as planned, Patricia, I will release the women without ever charging them. Arresting the men would not do what I want done. It would only muddy the waters. I'm asking you to trust me on this one, Patricia."

"Of course, Sheriff," she answered. "I'm sorry to have questioned you."

Jerry shook his head. "Not at all, Patricia. You did exactly what you should have done. And I thank you for it. You were exactly right. It's just that this is an unusual situation. If I were arresting the women for prostitution for the purpose of prosecuting them, then I'd certainly arrest the men as well. They are, as you say, at least as culpable. But I don't mean to prosecute anyone. Of course, I may have to if things don't go the way I've planned. But I don't intend to. Are you okay with that?"

"Certainly, Sheriff," she said. "I understand, and you'll have my full cooperation."

"Thanks, Deputy," Jerry responded. "Charlie, I'll want you to drive the van. The rest of you double up in patrol cars. That will give us enough room to transport prisoners in case we have to arrest more than the eight women. We'll leave here at eleven sharp and travel in convoy out to Artie's ranch. We'll enter the lodge together and, assuming that all the 'hunters' and women are upstairs, as I expect them to be, each of you will go to an assigned room, enter that room, and arrest the woman in that room. Artie Commons will give each of you a passkey to take upstairs. When you enter the rooms, if you find the suspects unclothed—that means naked, Avon—as I expect they will be...."

Deputies Carroll and Schmidt glanced at each other and grinned. Patricia Patton gave them a withering look, and their smiles disappeared.

"...you are to hand the woman a sheet to cover herself with and call one of the female deputies to attend to getting them dressed and cuffed.

"How about the men?" Charlie Lewis asked.

Jerry responded, "Keep an eye on them to make sure they do not hinder the arrests. Otherwise, don't concern yourself with them."

"I mean," Lewis continued, "do we tell them to get dressed—assuming they're naked, uh, unclothed too?"

"No, Charlie," Jerry repeated. "Don't concern yourself with them. If they have no clothes on, they can't very well hide a weapon. We are not concerned with them unless they break some other law. Leave them be. Now, Artie's lodge house has twelve guest rooms upstairs." He stepped to the moveable chalkboard and sketched two rectangles. "Here's the front door—they're double doors—where we'll enter. This area here is the great hall." He shaded most of the area in the lower rectangle. Moving the chalk to the upper shape, he drew in a hall and twelve smaller rectangles, indicating rooms. "Up here are the guest rooms. There are twelve of them, but only eight should be occupied tonight. Artie will tell us which ones. Patricia, you will assign each deputy a room to see to. I want you to position yourself in the hall between rooms four and five. I want one female deputy on room three and one on room six. That will put the female deputies in the best position to take care of what they need to take care of. You men, I expect you to behave yourselves. The female suspects are not likely to be a threat to anyone's safety, and you are not to touch them unless absolutely necessary, and you are not to ogle them under any circumstances."

He looked at each of the men, all of whom nodded. "Okay, get something to eat. Be back here no later than ten thirty to assemble; we'll leave at eleven."

Jerry had begun to gather his notes and the deputies were shuffling out of their chairs when Avon Carroll raised his hand and said, "You suppose Shelby'll be there, Sheriff?"

Jerry looked up, shrugged, and said, "I don't know, Avon. Why?"

The deputy grinned. "Well, everybody just talks about how pretty she is. I thought I might volunteer to arrest her."

"Avon," Jerry said, with as much sternness as he could muster, "Deputy Patton will assign you to an area, and you follow her instructions without question. Do you understand, Deputy?"

"Yes, Sir. I just hope she's there, that's all."

Jerry could not much blame the young deputy. He had seen the young woman named Shelby on several occasions, a bright, athletic, vigorous, distractingly feminine, silken brunette, whose profession and vocabulary suggested an attractive earthiness, but whose appearance seemed to bespeak elegance. Jerry hoped she'd be there too.

Chapter 14

Jerry was late arriving at the office on Tuesday morning. The arrests at Artie Commons' ranch had gone off without a glitch the night before, but by the time the eight women were transported to the jail and housed in the rather comfortable quarters reserved for non-dangerous, female detainees, it was almost three in the morning when Jerry showered and crawled into bed. He was still sleepy the next morning as he walked into the outer office and was greeted by the smiling faces of Miriam Smith and Angie Wahlert.

"Both of you ladies are looking mighty cheerful after I kept you out almost all night," he said.

"We had a ball," Angie said. "I wish we could get out of the office more often to arrest bad guys."

"You didn't arrest any guys, Angie. Didn't you notice that all eight of the suspects we arrested were female?" They could hardly not have noticed. Each of the eight was thoroughly naked when the deputies entered the rooms, all of them caught in the act of some variety of vigorous sex. Two women and two men were in the same room doing whatever they were doing to whoever they were doing it to. When Morgan Potts was trying to explain what he had seen to the other deputies, he kept getting confused. Too many parts, he had finally said, going in too many different places. "Damnedest thing I ever seen!" he had concluded.

"Yeah, okay, Sheriff," she said with her usual smile. "We arrested ladies."

"Nope, Angie," Jerry corrected. "A lady is a female with the attributes of nobility, with the virtues of thorough civility. You arrested some females last night, but they are not ladies."

"They sure are purty, though," said Miriam, her stringy hair and skinny, freckled body barely identifiable as a woman's. "That Shelby woman's as pretty as everybody says she is."

"Pretty is as pretty does, my delightful Miriam," Jerry responded, with a bow toward her. "Yeah, those women are well coiffed, beautifully toned, properly manicured, trained to walk and sit elegantly, and expensively dressed—when they are dressed. But to me they do not even approach the beauty I see before me at this moment."

Miriam stood open mouthed. When Jerry finished, she gulped and said, "Oh, my, Sheriff. Where'd you learn to talk like that?"

"'Tis from my mother wit," Jerry responded, with another bow.

"A witty mother," Angie mumbled, "witless else her son."

Jerry grinned. "You been reading again, Angie?"

"You had a call from Las Vegas, Sheriff," she said, shifting the subject, having made the point she intended. "You going to Vegas, Sheriff? You need a really dependable deputy to go with you?"

"I hope I don't have to go to Vegas, Angie. But if I do, I'll certainly not take you. My wife would beat me soundly about the head and ears if I took off to Vegas with the likes of you."

Angie tried to look innocent. "Why, Sheriff. I'm sure I don't know what you mean. I look upon you as a kindly grandfather."

Jerry smiled as he took the call slip from her hand and opened the door leading to his office. "I'll get you for that, Angie."

"One other thing, Sheriff," Angie said. "I got calls from both the local and state missing-persons folks. They've got no files on anyone matching our victim. You want me to send the information over to the Fibies?"

"Yeah, Angie," Jerry sighed. "They won't have anything either, likely, but let's cover all the bases."

Chief Deputy Warren Berry of the Clark County Sheriff's Office was on the line in less than ten seconds. "Hey, Sheriff Valdez. How's it hanging?"

"'Preciate your call, Deputy Berry…"

"Call me Warren, Sheriff. We're kinda laid-back out here in the desert."

"Yeah, us too. Kendall County isn't exactly uptown. Call me Jerry. Whatcha got for me?"

"Not much, I'm afraid. No one in any of the agencies recognized the vic. If he was ever out here, he didn't stink the place up to the extent that anyone remembered him. I went over to the Riviera my own self. I know the folks over there real well. That was their token right enough, but no one recognized the drawing. I even had our sketch artist here add a moustache and made a copy and then a beard and made a copy. I showed all the copies around. Nobody knows who he is."

"Many thanks, Warren, for the really good and fast work on this," Jerry said.

"Well, Jerry, we weren't able to do much. Sorry we couldn't identify your vic."

"You were a great help by eliminating a road that went nowhere. Now I know we'll have to look elsewhere. Our thanks to you, and I hope you'll pass along my thanks and greetings to your sheriff. You guys ever need anything I can help you with, let me know."

"Will do, Jerry. Best of luck."

Well, damn, thought Jerry, as he hung up the phone. He turned the token in his hand, flipped it (it came up tails), and put it back into the plastic bag. He looked at the grass or leaves or seeds in the other bag, but they did not speak to him. After a moment's thought, he reached for the telephone. But at that instant, his phone rang, startling him. His calls regularly were routed through the front office, where they were screened. When Miriam or Angie or someone from the lobby wanted to reach him, they used the intercom, which had a distinctive buzz, not a ring. But his private line, the number known to very few, rang directly through to his office. Even Anna Maria called on the regular department line.

On the third ring, Jerry answered, "Jerry Valdez." A brusque voice said, "Don't think you can strike me with impunity. I will not tolerate it."

A cold chill ran down Jerry's spine. A few times in his life he had been distinctly afraid. Several times in Korea, when an attack was feared, as he lay in a shallow hole, sweating or freezing, waiting for hordes of screaming Chinese troops to attack, he felt the shiver in his spine. Once when his wonderful Anna Maria had been injured in a fall and he found her unconscious in a heap at the bottom of the stairs, the fear had almost incapacitated him. He had expected the reaction from the man, had arrested the women in order to get his attention. But still, he felt the fear now.

Collecting himself, Jerry said, "I have tried on three occasions in the last two days to communicate with you so that the action you refer to would not be necessary. I was rebuffed on all three occasions. Do not think you can ignore me with impunity." Then he hung up, his hand shaking. Rubbing his hands together to control the shaking, he sat staring at the phone. He did not know how he might have handled the situation differently. In three minutes, the private line rang again.

Jerry lifted the receiver and said, "This is Sheriff Valdez." The same gruff voice said, "I suggest we meet. Noon. Usual place."

"Yes," Jerry responded and, finding that he had been holding his breath, expelled a lungful of air as he hung up. He looked at his watch. He had twenty minutes to reach the Turkey House.

Chapter 15

The two heavies sat at a table to the right of the door as Jerry entered the restaurant, and the two guards sat on opposite sides of the door to the smaller dining room. Jerry ignored all four men and moved toward the room on the left, where Biggs would be. Where he hoped Biggs would be. As he approached the door, the two men at the table near the small room stood and blocked his path.

"Who are you?" one of the men, who had a scar on his face, asked.

"I am Sheriff Valdez, and I am going to go into that room. Either you get out of my way, or I'll get you out of my way."

Scar Face smirked and said, "I'll tell you what, Valdez, first we'll take that gun, then we'll search you, and then we'll tell you what you'll do."

As the other man, one with a moustache, reached for Jerry's gun, Jerry reached over with his left and grabbed the man's hand. Pulling his .45 Colt Army semi-automatic from his holster, he laid it with some vigor on the side of moustache's head. As the man fell, Jerry thumbed the hammer back on the weapon and pushed it up to the right eye of Scar Face. "When the Sheriff of Kendall County wants to enter a room in his own county, he will by God enter that room. Now if you want to continue that pitiful life of yours for another heartbeat, open that goddamned door and move your ass in. Do it now!" Scar Face did so.

When the two men pushed into the small dining room, Mr. Biggs was seated nearest the door. Two other men were in the room, and they jumped to their feet and reached for weapons as they saw Jerry's gun in the face of their companion.

Mr. Biggs held his right hand up to stop the two men to his right from drawing their weapons. When they continued standing, their hands under their jackets, he looked at them until they sat down. Then he said to Scar Face, "Antonio, get out of this room." Seeing for the first time the unconscious body of moustache lying outside the door, he continued, "And drag that idiot to the men's room. Then both of you sit in the car until I tell you otherwise."

Scar Face, or Antonio, listened to the orders without moving his face, Jerry's gun causing him to stretch taller, as though trying to escape the point of contact. Only his eyes had shifted in the direction of Mr. Biggs. When he had heard Biggs's order, his eyes shifted to look at Jerry. After a moment, Jerry pulled the barrel out of the man's face and holstered it. Antonio, or Scar Face, hustled out of the room, dragging the unconscious Moustache behind him.

Biggs turned to the other men in the room and motioned them outside.

"But boss!" the younger of the two began. His outburst earned him a withering look from Biggs. Both men scurried out the door. Jerry closed the door, sat down, and turned to face Biggs.

With a severe face, Biggs said, "You are interfering with my business."

Jerry, with as severe a face, answered, "If you mean that I arrested eight women on suspicion of soliciting last night, yes I did."

Biggs stared into Jerry's eyes for a few moments before he asked, "Do you intend to start a war with me?"

Jerry's response was brief: "Only if I must."

Again, Biggs thought a moment before he answered. "Why are you doing this? We have coexisted peacefully for some time. What has changed that you could not call me, discuss it with me?"

"I have already told you that I tried on three separate occasions in the past two days to talk with you. On one of these occasions, my chief deputy, who is my friend, came to this very room to discuss a matter with you face to face, after I had phoned and asked for a meeting. He was disarmed, searched, and insulted by your men. My friend's name is Archie Crane, my chief deputy. As he is received, I am received. The extreme disrespect with which he was treated was also disrespect to me and to my office. Your men are very lucky that I had asked my friend to keep your name and your presence low key. Otherwise he would have arrested the six men who met him here, and they would be in my jail instead of your eight women. They are also lucky that only one of them got hurt, and only slightly, rather than all of them landing in the hospital before they enjoyed the hospitality of my jail. In short, I needed to talk with you, tried three times, and was rebuffed. I cannot tolerate that treatment."

Biggs was silent for a moment before he spoke. Then a trace of a smile was suggested on his face. "I wondered how Victor received a swollen finger. But I did not ask." He was silent for a time before continuing. "Your deputy is your friend?"

"He is my friend."

"That is important to you?"

"It is of primary importance to me."

"He works for you?"

"He works with me."

"Words," Biggs shrugged, a slight smile on his lips.

"Sometimes words have solid meanings," Jerry responded, still looking seriously into the other man's eyes. "He is a friend. For me that is as real as life."

Biggs almost imperceptibly shook his head at such a notion. Then he said, "I have been out of state for over a week. I have not heard that you called me. That is a problem in communications that I shall have to deal with. Had I been aware that you called, I would have responded. The men I left in charge handled the situation badly. I shall see that they learn from their mistakes. Now about the people you have arrested...."

Jerry interrupted, "Before we get to that, I need to speak to you about the situation that led me to call you first."

Again, Biggs was silent for a moment. Then he said, "Yes, of course."

Jerry drew himself up, feeling more secure, feeling that the discussion was proceeding effectively. "We have had many citizens of the county, one especially, complaining that prostitutes are doing business in the truck stops and rest areas along the Interstate. I called to ask if you..." Jerry had to be careful of his language here, "...have any information about any such activity." Okay. He had not insulted the man by even hinting that he would be involved in such an activity—though it certainly would not be the immorality of the activity that would restrain the mobster.

Biggs fixed Jerry in his gaze. "I do not do business in truck stops and rest areas."

Jerry, with as intent a gaze, responded, "I did not believe that you did. I need to know whether you had any information about any such activity."

Again a pause. After a while, Biggs said, "I assume you are suggesting that some of my business associates might be engaging in free-lance business without my knowledge. I assume you suggest that because I seem not to have been able to control their actions regarding you and your chief deputy." For the first time since the conversation began, Biggs shifted his gaze from Jerry's eyes and looked vacantly at the ceiling. Jerry was glad for the respite. He needed to blink his eyes. This macho stuff is hard on a man's eyes. By the time Biggs dropped his eyes again to stare at the sheriff, Jerry had had time to lubricate his eyes by blinking several times. Now he could be macho again. Biggs continued, "I shall address the behavior of my men regarding you and your office. It was ignorance on their part that caused their behavior, and I am responsible for not educating them better. I shall educate them. Such conduct on their part will not recur. But it is impossible that they would have engaged in independent business activities. They are well schooled in that regard. They would not. It is quite as simple as that."

Holding his gaze for a moment, Jerry suddenly nodded, spread his hands from the serious clasped position in front of him to an expansive gesture, and said, "Well, that's it then. I had to know in order to determine how to proceed with the complaints."

Another hint of a smile visited the face of Biggs. "And now about the women you hold in your jail?"

Again an expansive gesture with his hands, Jerry said, "They will be released immediately."

"No charges?"

"No charges."

Biggs nodded his satisfaction.

"Shall I have them returned to the hunting lodge?" Jerry asked.

Biggs shook his head faintly "Is it convenient for a limousine to call for them this evening?"

Jerry thought. "A van," he answered. "At the back door might keep civilian attention to a minimum."

Biggs nodded.

"If you will call to tell me when the van will be at the back door, I shall have the young women ready."

"My representative tells me that they have been treated with dignity."

"They have been."

Biggs stood and nodded again. He did not offer his hand. They did not sit down for lunch. It was past lunch time, but Jerry was strangely not hungry.

Chapter 16

"Well, hell, Jer," Archie was saying as he paced the floor in front of the desk where Jerry had his feet firmly planted. "If there are any prostitutes plying their trade in our fair county, they are damned covert about it. Glad Ass says that throngs of whores are flashing their asses in every truck stop and rest area between here and the county line, that a decent citizen can't drive a mile without being propositioned. Yet Charlie, Patricia, and I have been looking under every man in the county and can't find even one whore."

"Yeah," Jerry said, relaxed after the dangerous confrontation with Biggs. "Whores are like cops: can't ever find one when you need one."

Archie grinned and sat down across from Jerry. "You believe Biggs when he says he has nothing to do with prostitutes at the truck stops?"

"Yeah, I do, Arch. That's not his style. I mean, he's certainly into prostitution, but his whores don't sell at truck-stop prices. By the way, Arch, did the young women get picked up from the jail last night?"

"Yeah, Steven called me when the van drove up to make sure it was still okay to let them go." Steven Abbot was the jailer.

"Good," said Jerry, nodding. "That's one less thing to deal with."

"Do you trust Biggs, Jer?"

Jerry pursed his lips for a moment as he thought. "No, not to any distance. I believe him when he says he's got nothing to do with the spate of whore sightings, but only because such a thing is not his style. And I trust him not to break the peace in the county intentionally, but only because it is not in his best interests to do so. He's a businessman, not a friend; and I can't treat him like a friend. He doesn't have the moral virtues that friendship requires, and he frankly doesn't even understand such a relationship. He uses me and I use him. But I don't have any quixotic notions of his undergoing a moral reformation." Jerry rubbed his hands together as he thought again for a moment. "Biggs is an ethical man. But he's not a moral man. There are certain rules of doing business he follows, as long as it is good business for him to do so. But I can't see that he recognizes any freestanding moral law. He and I generally understand each other, and I have a certain amount of respect for him."

Archie nodded. "Yeah, I can see that. So where did all the truck-stop whores go? You suppose the stories are just urban legends? People fantasize about sexually active women, and the stories become real in the minds of most who hear them? Like a big buck standing out near an oat field in the dark of the morning becomes a bush in full light?"

"Well, maybe," said Jerry. "But probably not. If it was just Glad Ass, I wouldn't pay any attention to it. But we've had too many reports from too many different sources."

"Yeah, you're right, Jer," Archie admitted. "But why can't we find them? We've used unmarked cars, trucks, motorcycles, even a horse. Charlie worked the rest areas and I worked every truck stop and service station, major and otherwise, between here and the county line. Patricia has talked to women all along the Interstate. Nothing. The employees of the truck stops who reported an epidemic now say they don't see or hear anything. Truck drivers who a couple of weeks ago were being harangued in this area on CB radios to stop and have sex now say they hear absolutely nothing. And believe me, they are looking. But not finding. What happened?"

Jerry shrugged. "I dunno. I guess they either quit or moved on. Let's don't spend any more time on this, Arch. If you'll call Glad Ass and tell her we've got it stopped, maybe she'll be placated for a while. I really need to spend time on this murder, and you're going to have Ms LaDeaux to deal with. You heard any more on that, by the way?"

"Nope," Archie responded. "'Course it's only been since last Friday she decided to sue your sheriffly ass. It'll take her a while to get a lawyer. And maybe lawyers have become so honest that any she approaches will tell her she has no case."

"Yeah," said Jerry, "and maybe pigs will fly."

The intercom buzzed. "Yeah, Miriam?" Jerry responded.

"Phone call for you, Sheriff. She says she's Miz Estelle Enright and she's a San Antonio lawyer."

"Pigs don't fly, do they Miriam?" Jerry said sadly.

"What, Sheriff?" the deputy said.

"Never mind, Miriam. Put her through, please." When the phone rang, he answered it. "This is Sheriff Valdez."

"Sheriff Valdez?" a high-pitched female voice asked.

Jerry closed his eyes and prayed for patience. He'd just told her who he was. He hated to talk on the phone for any reason, and he especially hated irrelevant conversation on the phone. Even the delightful Angie Wahlert would occasionally call him and say, "Hi, Sheriff, what are you doing," when she knew damned well what he was doing. People he did not know would call him and ask, "How are you?" when they did not give a dead rat's ass about the state of his health. Gave him a pain. But, "This is Sheriff Valdez."

"Sheriff Valdez, I am Miz Enright, an attorney, representing Deputy Dorie LaDeaux in a wrongful termination lawsuit...."

"It's Miz Dorie LaDeaux; she is not one of my deputies; and it is an *alleged* wrongful termination," Jerry corrected.

"Whatever," Ms Enright responded.

What the hell's that supposed to mean, Jerry thought irritably. "Whatever." In a lawsuit, "whatever" had no meaning, no relevance. It was just a sound, just air. "Miz Enright, please be good enough not to take my time or cloud my usually sparkling character with anything to do with Miz LaDeaux. Speak to my lawyer, only my lawyer, and nobody but my lawyer."

"Very well, Sheriff Valdez, if you will tell me how to contact your lawyer...."

Good god. "Contact." My lawyer's male pride would shrivel into insignificance were this irritating harpy to "contact" him. The only thing Jerry could think of worse would be for her to "impact" him. He handed the phone to a smiling Archie Crane.

Chapter 17

Miz Enright was calling to set up a conference prior to formal depositions in the LaDeaux matter. After speaking pleasantly with her for a while, Archie pushed the hold button on Jerry's phone and walked down to his office to check his calendar, waving to Jerry as he left.

Jerry picked up the bag of debris he had collected from the cuffs of Nobody and peered through the translucent plastic. Some dirt was in the bits and pieces of stuff, and some lint. But some of the stuff was vegetation of some species or other. Some pieces looked like bits of grass or leaves, others like seeds. Making sure the bag was tightly sealed, he slid it to the side of his desk and picked up the phone, dialed information, and asked to be connected to the main operator at the University of Texas in Austin.

Dr. Emil Brunner, who had taught Jerry biology at UT, had had a great influence on the young student. When Jerry's call reached the professor's lab, the lab assistant found the good professor out in the green house and transferred the call. Brunner remembered Jerry fondly and was happy to agree to meet with him at four that very afternoon.

Jerry was pleased at his good fortune when he hung up the phone. He immediately dialed another number.

When a pleasant female voice answered, he said, "Good morning, you beautiful creature. How are things over at the Valdez house?"

"Things are quiet, Jerry. You want to come home and make things exciting?"

"Well, now, that's a right friendly invitation, school marm. And I have a little something that you might find exciting. But, unfortunately, I still don't know who Nobody is, and I'd better stick to finding out."

Anna Maria was quiet for a moment. "You don't know who nobody is? Does that mean the same thing as you don't know who anybody is, or do your double negatives cancel out each other—so that you know who everybody is?"

"Now you've really got me confused, dear heart," Jerry said, leaning back in his chair, pleased to be talking to this woman and, as usual, charmed by her. "But Nobody is not nobody. He's really somebody. Nobody is somebody, not nobody."

"Who *is* on first, Jerry?"

"I think Who is on second, dear. But I really can never remember. Anyway, reason I called is to ask if you want to go up to Austing with me."

"Austing?"

"Yep, Austing. Up to the forty acres. To the land of the burnt orange and longhorns and Truth."

"Truth?"

"Yep, says right there on the tower, 'You shall know the Truth, and the Truth shall make you free.'"

"Okay, dear. What are you going up to Austin for, the burnt orange, the longhorns, or the Truth?"

"Truth, dear heart, Truth. We've got burnt orange and longhorns aplenty right here in Kendall County. But while I've got Nobody, I need Truth."

"You've got me, dear. Which is the truth."

"Well, I know I've got you, sweetheart. But I've got Nobody too."

"You're very confused today, dear—even more than usual."

"Right, sweetheart, now you understand. So do I have you with me up to Austing?"

"You have me, dear, but not up to Austin. Your two delightful offspring have school and appetites and dirty clothes and homework. And they need a mother. When will you be back?"

"Dunno, babe. I'm going up to see Dr. Brunner to see if he can give me any help on some botanical material I found on the body—on Nobody."

"Oh, Nobody is the body those hunters found out at Harvey Phelan's place! That's the game you've been playing."

"No game, dear. Nobody calls."

"Then, don't answer, dear."

"Gotta, babe. Dr. Brunner can meet with me this afternoon at four, and

I'll get back here as soon after that as I can. But if he has any idea what this stuff is he may have to check around at some botanical maps, if any such things exist. I just don't know. I'll call you as soon as I know anything, okay?"

"Okay, Jerry, be careful."

Chapter 18

The voice of Gladys Finch Hump began in the lobby of the Sheriff's Office, but it traveled at what everyone who heard it was persuaded was a speed faster than that of light and penetrated the offices down the hall and in the rear of the building, where Jerry and Archie had their offices. Hearing the clamor, Jerry gathered his things and began to steal, guilty-like, out of his office even before the phone rang on his desk. As he snuck out and down the hall, Archie stuck his head out of his door and said, "Chicken!"

"Damned straight," Jerry admitted, smiling and turning to face his friend. "I'm off to Austin, Arch. Um, would you mind dealing with whatever might be going on out in the lobby?"

"You know damned well enough what is going on out in the lobby," Archie said. "Hell, people in Siam can hear the melodious voice of Glad Ass. And that's your phone ringing, Sheriff. I can assure you that an irate citizen is asking to see her duly elected sheriff, and that's young Miriam or Angie calling back to inform you of that fact."

"Well, Chief Deputy, since the sheriff is not in, I suppose you'll just have to deal with it," Jerry said, putting a serious look on his face.

Archie Crane smiled and waved at his friend. "Be careful on your trip, Jer. Keep in touch. I'll try to placate Glad Ass."

As Jerry hurried out the back door to his car, feeling a bit craven—but not too much—Archie walked up the hall to smile at the fuming Gladys Hump and invite her back to his office for a nice chat.

He sat behind his desk and indicated a chair for Gladys. But she was too agitated to stand still, much less to sit.

"Archie Crane," she said with irritation, "where is Jerry Valdez?"

"He's gone to Austin, Gladys," Archie said quietly, trying to bring a new tone to the interview. "We've got a murder in the county, and Jerry is trying to get that all straightened out."

"Well, for his information, we've got whores in the county, too," she said, finally standing still, left hand on her hip and pointing at Archie with her right index finger. She pronounced "whores" like "who-ers." "And I am here to tell you and Jerry that the decent people of this county will absolutely not stand for such moral degradation around our families!" She had left her stationary pose and returned to pacing.

"Gladys," Archie began. But she turned on him and adopted her hip and point pose again.

"You will refer to me as Mrs. Hump, Deputy Sheriff. Too much familiarity has bred contempt, Deputy Sheriff. You and the sheriff don't seem to take me seriously. But you *will* take me seriously. I am not going to have whores parading their wares around decent people and our law enforcement officers doing nothing about it. Well, Mr. Crane, you big manly men may think it's all just a big joke, having them flaunting sex in front of devout Christians, but I will not have it!"

"Gladys," he began again.

"You will refer to me as Mrs. Hump, Mr. Crane," she shouted, her face fixed and as menacing as a short woman whose cheerleader body had begun running to chubbiness could be.

"No, Gladys," Archie said calmly. "I will not refer to you as 'Mrs. Hump.' I've known you since we were kids, and I'm damned if I'm going to call old friends Mrs. anything. You can call me what you like—although you've always attracted my attention by calling me Archie. And I'll call you Gladys. Because that's your name. Now, sit down and let's talk about what's got you disturbed."

Gladys Hump did sit down, but it took her a while to say anything—not so much because she was enraged, but because she had not formulated in her mind really what she wanted to say. Finally she said, "Archie, I don't want prostitutes flashing their…plying their trade along the highways in my county. I don't want whores practicing their business in my county. I want my county, even though it might be the last one in the whole world, to be a safe place for moral people to live morally. And I can't seem to get you and Jerry to understand how important this is." By the time she finished, she was no longer shouting. Her last words were barely audible, and she had tears in her eyes.

Archie listened without interruption and was moved by her obvious sentiment. Gladys was a pain in the ass, but she was not a bad woman. And she was certainly not actress enough to feign this emotion.

"Gladys," Archie said, "Jerry and I do take this matter very seriously."

"Have you arrested them all yet?" she asked, her anger and her vigor returning.

"No, Gladys, we...."

She was on her feet again. "How can you tell me that you take it seriously when you have taken no action at all?" she shouted. She had taken her hip and point stance again.

Archie looked up at her, waiting until she finally lowered her finger and dropped her hand from her hip. "Sit down, please, Gladys," he said. When she did so, he continued, "I certainly did not say that we have taken no action at all. In fact, we have spent a great many hours tracking down every lead we could come up with in this case—*every* lead, Gladys. The reports we got were that women were offering themselves for sale in truck stops and rest areas along the major highways."

"Well, that's exactly what they are doing," Gladys Hump interjected. "And if you and Jerry and a whole sh...passel of deputies can't find people who seem determined to thrust themselves in the faces of every traveler and law-abiding citizen in this county, then...."

"That's just it, Gladys," Archie said, holding up his hand to try to get a word in. "I have no doubt that some women were vigorously offering their bodies to the general populace along the highways, but they are not doing so now."

"You can't find them?" she asked, amazed.

"They aren't there, Gladys. Have you heard any reports of such activity in the last couple of days?"

Gladys Hump thought for a moment, then said, "I certainly heard plenty last week!"

"But, Gladys, by the time the incidents were reported to us and we began investigating, they were not there anymore. Believe me, we've looked everywhere. We've had no reports from anyone since last week. We've sent plainclothes men to the truck stops, to the rest areas, and we've even had them stop randomly along the highways to see if anyone would approach them. They just are not there now. Maybe they'll come back, but they're not there now. And if we can't find them, we can't arrest them." He spread his hands in frustration and looked at Gladys Hump.

"It's those who-ers from north county come down here to expand their territory," she said, like a teacher lecturing a backward child who could not grasp a simple equation.

"No, Gladys, it's not," he said, hoping that she did not know about the parties at hunting leases around the county. He didn't think she knew about those practices—and even if she did, she probably had only rumors.

"Now, how do you know, Mr. Smarty-pants?" she asked, again the teacher with the slow child.

"We've checked that all out thoroughly, Gladys. Both Jerry and I have conducted separate investigations. We're certain that the incidents that were reported had nothing to do with previous problems with prostitutes from northern county."

She was quiet for a moment. Then she looked up with tears in her eyes. She reached over to take Archie's hands in hers. "Archie, please don't let them do that—please don't let who-ers be in our county. This is our county."

Then she left.

Archie had never seen Gladys cry. He had seen her angry at almost everyone—him, Jerry, Maurice, her father, her mother, the weather, life. But he had never seen her cry. Don't let whores, what had she said? Not "don't let them work in our county." "Don't let them *be* in our county." Curious.

Chapter 19

Traffic around the University of Texas campus was still heavy at a quarter 'til four on Wednesday afternoon. Guadalupe Street, "The Drag," was bumper-to-bumper from MLK for a mile north of the campus. Jerry found a place at a parking meter south of 24th Street and parked the Chrysler. He pulled his brown leather jacket over the seat from the back and put it on. The wind had shifted northerly, and the temperature had dropped twenty degrees since he had left Kendall County. The upper fifties was not cold, but the north wind made the jacket feel comfortable.

Jerry looked at the parking meter and fished his change purse out of his pocket. Since he had exactly seventeen cents and the meter took only quarters, he pocketed the purse and walked away. His car had on the doors the decals of the sheriff's badge, with "Kendall County" lettered above and "Sheriff's Department" below and "To Protect and Serve" emblazoned across the trunk. He figured the local cops would not ticket his car. And his conscience did not trouble him. He was on official business.

A direct route from where he had parked to the Botanical Greenhouse, where he was to meet Professor Emil Brunner, would take him north along The Drag up to 24th Street and east to the Biology Building. The Greenhouse lay just south behind the Biology Building. But Jerry's ritual route anytime he was on campus was to walk up the Mall across the street from the Co-op, past the Union Building, the Undergraduate Library, then north between the library and Tower to the Biological Greenhouse. Memories of the campus, the exciting mixture of youthful exuberance and intellectual substance each time overwhelmed him as he walked across the familiar ground near the familiar buildings. This was the forty acres, the place where most of the community worked very hard to get things right. He loved the community when it encompassed his life, and he loved it no less while he was away. He could separate himself physically from the campus, but he was nevertheless a part of it and it was a part of him. The faces he saw, the clothes they wore, the spiked hair and pierced bodies were new, different in some respects. But he felt very much at home, as he walked past the statue of the torchbearers and glanced at the tower. Maybe like an older son come home again for a visit rather than a present resident. But home nevertheless.

Jerry felt the warm air engulf him as he entered the Biological Greenhouse through the glass door. Professor Brunner was sitting on a high stool in front of a zinc-topped worktable. In a tray before him were rows of small plants. The professor was lifting the leaves of the plants with a small metal probe and then writing notes on a form held by a clipboard. When he saw Jerry approach, he set the clipboard down and extended his hand.

"Jerry Valdez, how are you?" he asked, shaking Jerry's hand. "I knew you wouldn't be able to stay away. Came back to enroll in graduate school, did you?"

"No, Professor," Jerry smiled. "I'm sure I need to go back to school, given the state of my ignorance. But being sheriff seems not to give me time to do too much else."

"Well, what can I do for you, then, Jerry," the professor said, sitting back down on the high stool.

"I need some help, Professor Brunner," Jerry said, removing a plastic bag from the pocket of his jacket and handing it to Brunner. "I found these leaves and seeds on a corpse in Kendall County, and I was hoping you might be able to identify what they are. We don't know who the deceased is, and I'm grasping at straws—literally grasping at leaves, here—to see if they'll help me identify him."

The professor held the plastic bag up to peer at the contents, shook it a couple of times to rearrange the contents, and looked again. "His fingerprints didn't help you, Jerry?"

Jerry smiled. "No, Sir, whoever killed him was ill-mannered enough to remove his hands. So we have no prints. One of our artists drew a reconstruction of his face, but nobody knows his name. So, I'm down to grasping at these straws."

Brunner opened a drawer in the table and withdrew a small, rectangular, metal tray, about the size of an entrée serving dish used on airlines. He removed the plastic wrap from the tray, threw the plastic away, and emptied the botanic debris from the baggie into the tray. Using the metal probe, he separated the small pieces of rubble, turning some of them over so that he could peer at the reverse sides.

"Some of this is not botanical," he said, snagging a piece of what looked like lint on the end of the probe. "This stuff is probably wool or cotton fluff. You've also got some seeds and pieces of leaves here, Jerry. Truthfully, I don't recognize any of the botanical matter. The leaves look to me as though they are some sort of plant indigenous to the Southwest. But I wouldn't recognize what it is or where it might come from. As you know, I spend almost all my time on international economic plants, like soybeans and energy-producing plants. I'd have to send this stuff off to a specialist in plants of the Southwest to see if it might ring a bell. But you can do that as easily as I can." He opened the bag and poured the bits and pieces back inside and then resealed it.

"Yeah, Professor, if I knew where to send it," Jerry said, taking the plastic bag and looking at the contents again, as though some miraculous answer were going to glow out at him. It did not.

"Well, hell, Jerry, that part is easy," Brunner said, waving his hand as though to flap away any problems. "Get this stuff to Professor Wiley Haskell up at the University of North Texas. He's a botanist who's most likely to be able to identify this stuff. And if he can't, he can put you in touch with someone who can."

"Okay, doc," Jerry said. "Uh, doc, you think you could let him know I'm coming and maybe make an appointment for me to see him? I don't know him, and I imagine he's busy. I hate to just walk in cold. I guess he's one of your former students?"

Brunner smiled and pulled a telephone across the table and dialed his office. After a moment he said, "Marie, will you be so kind as to look on your rolodex for the number of Professor Wiley Haskell up at UNT and tell me what it is?" He jotted a number on the top of the form on his clipboard and said, "Thanks, Marie." Glancing at his watch, he continued, "Marie, it's after four, and I'm not going to get back over there this evening. You go on home, now. Give Ben my best, and hug your kids for me, will you?" Then he dialed the number he had jotted down and waited until he had an answer. "Wiley, you old sonofabitch, how are things up in the frozen north land?... Yeah, well, the wind has already turned to blow from the north down here, but we're still in the fifties here…. If it's still in the fifties in Denton, I guess it won't be what you Texans call a 'Blue Norther.'…Reason I called, Wiley, one of my former students is now a sheriff. He's got some botanical debris he found on a murder victim, and he needs to have the stuff identified to see if it can help him. I want to send him up there to see if you can look at it for him. Tomorrow around noon okay?" He glanced over at Jerry, who nodded. "Okay, good, Wiley. His name is Jerry Valdez. He says he can be there by noon tomorrow. He was one of my best, Wiley. Do what you can to help him, okay?…How's Rolando doing? …Well, that's typical of microbiologists. You ever think, Wiley, that micro-pukes are just lying to us. I mean, they can *say* they see anything, and who's to know? Unless you carry a microscope around with you. I believe those guys get away with a lot of fuzzy science just because nobody can see what they are doing. Anyway, tell old 'Londo hello for me …Thanks, Wiley. My best to Nelda."

When he hung up, he turned to Jerry. "No, Dr. Haskell wasn't one of my students. He went to school in one of those middle northern schools. But he sort of specializes in plants of the southwest. Wiley is one of the good guys in the academy. You'll get on with him immediately."

"Thanks, Professor," said Jerry. "I really appreciate your help." He looked at his watch, seeing that it was a few minutes before five. "I guess I'll stay in Austin tonight and drive up to Denton in the morning. The traffic north out of Austin will be heavy at this hour, won't it?"

"A bear," Brunner said, frowning. "Jerry, I'm going to have to work late tonight. These damned plants are just at the right stage of their growth for me to do some cutting and splicing. But how about dinner, say, right about now—if you don't mind eating this early? These plants need to sit under the grow light for a couple of hours before they'll be ready for me."

"Sure, doc. Kendall County can buy us both dinner. I sorta been dreaming about the Nighthawk. That okay with you?"

"Sure, Jerry. I loved eating at the Nighthawk. Main problem with that is it's not here anymore."

"Yeah, Anna Maria and I went by 19th and The Drag on our last trip up here and found the Nighthawk had disappeared. That's really too bad. 'Course it's not 19th Street now—it's MLK. But how about the Nighthawk on South Congress? Or the one out north on 35 at 290?"

"Gone and gone," said Brunner sadly.

"Well, damn," said Jerry, suddenly very sad. "What possible reason can there be for the demise of the Nighthawk? They had the best beef around."

"I agree," replied Brunner. "I guess they were just not chic enough for the new Austin crowd."

"Chic?" Jerry asked.

"Yeah, many of the new arrivals have up-scaled Austin to chic," Brunner replied.

"Well, damn, doc, I leave Austin for a few years, and you let it all go to hell," Jerry said. "Have they also up-scaled Tex-Mex food here, too?"

"Like you wouldn't believe, Jerry," the professor replied. "A text-book agent took me to dinner last week at a place called La Casa Hermosa de la Virgen. Wasn't an enchilada or a chalupa on the menu. They served things like Blue Corn Soup and sautéed breast of game hen."

Jerry shook his head in sadness. "Any good Tex-Mex places left here?"

Brunner grinned. "Hell, Jerry, this is still Austin. The tight pants can put the frou-frou places in all they want, but East 6th Street is still Austin. You got a car? I'm afoot today."

"Yes, Sir," Jerry responded. "I'm parked out on The Drag."

"Hell, boy," Brunner snorted. "You'll get towed out there faster than fast!"

Jerry smiled. "I don't think so."

Chapter 20

Archie Crane followed Miz Estelle Enright into the conference room just off the lobby of the Kendall County Sheriff's Office and took a seat across the large oak table from her.

"Mr. Crane," she said primly, after she had taken a sheaf of papers out of her leather briefcase and placed them on the table in front of her. "As you know, I represent Deputy Dorie LaDeaux in both the wrongful termination and sexual harassment cases she intends to file against the Sheriff."

"It's Miz LaDeaux, counselor," Archie replied, with a faint smile as he looked at the lawyer intently. "She is not a deputy sheriff, at least not in the Kendall County Sheriff's Office."

"Whatever," the attorney responded, waving her hand as though to clear some fog from her face. "Am I to assume that you are the attorney of record in this case?"

"I am dealing with this unpleasant incident for Sheriff Valdez, Miz Enright," Archie said. "There is no 'attorney of record in this case' since, as far as I know, your client has not filed suit. If your client is misguided enough to file suit, then I shall be 'the attorney of record.'"

Enright gave her "whatever" hand swipe again, looking weary of the quibble. Then she said it. "Whatever. Of course, my client would prefer to settle this ugly situation without taking your cl . . . without taking the sheriff to court. He can't possibly win, and of course he will be held up to public ridicule—and that's not good for a political figure, now is it?" She glanced down at the files in front of her, selected a folder, and opened it. Looking back at Archie, she said, "Now Mr. Crane, my client is prepared to drop all charges under the following conditions: She requires that the offending party," she looked down at a sheet of paper in front of her, running her finger down the page until she found what she wanted, "that Deputy Carroll, be publicly reprimanded at a special meeting of all deputies for his remarks, that the sheriff make a public apology to my client at that same meeting, and that she be returned to her former position with all accrued pay and benefits."

She paused briefly to let her comments be digested, closing the file folder on the table. Then she smiled and said, "As you can see, my client is being very generous. She is not demanding that the offending deputy be terminated. Nor is she demanding a large cash settlement. The deputy is certainly guilty as sin of sexual harassment, and the sheriff is guilty of wrongful termination in retaliation for threatening to file a lawsuit—which, of course, she has every right to do. Through the kindness of my client, Mr. Crane, we can make all this go away right now."

Archie did not change his expression nor shift his gaze. "No, counselor, those conditions are not acceptable. If your client chooses to file suit, I'll simply file a motion for summary judgment on the sexual harassment and retaliation claims. And if you know anything about the law, you must know the plaintiff will lose. I agree that we need to make this go away because we have a lot of important things to attend to on behalf of the public and we don't need to be distracted by this trivial squabbling between a rather uncouth young man and a thin-skinned young woman. And now you come in trying to make much ado about very little. The sheriff has reprimanded the young man and made it clear that he will not tolerate such rude behavior from his deputies. But that's all it is—rude behavior. The young man apologized to your client and promised not to repeat his rudeness. And that should have been the end of it. But your client went ballistic, making Deputy Carroll's indiscretion seem like an annoying gnat to a raging banshee. She threatened a lawsuit against her employer, a lawsuit that would have had no merit; and the sheriff quite appropriately fired her. She refused to surrender her gun and badge and had to be forced to do so. The way we make this go away is for your client to go away."

Enright listened to Archie with growing irritation. "Are you a licensed attorney, *Deputy*?" she asked angrily, emphasizing "deputy."

Archie's tone and demeanor did not change. "I am," he said.

"Have you passed the bar examination?" she asked, turning her head and squinting aside at him.

"I have."

"Just where did you go to school, *Deputy*?" she asked.

"Austin," Archie responded quietly.

"*Where* in Austin?" she asked.

Archie smiled slightly. "Only one law school in Austin, counselor. Unlike Houston, where Our Lady of Good Hope holds night classes in company of several other law schools."

Enright was furious. "I have no apologies to make for my education," she sputtered. "I know enough to know the law, specifically..." she looked down at the papers in front of her, shuffling through until she found what she was looking for, "specifically Chapter 21 of 'The Civil Rights Equal Employment Opportunities Act,' which says that among the unlawful employment practices is, 'Discrimination for making charges, testifying, assisting, or participating in enforcement proceedings.' That's the law, *Deputy*! I know enough to be acquainted with Ferguson v. Chicago Housing, case law that upholds that law, *Deputy*! If you, by god, think you can get your client to slip off the hook because you are dealing with a couple of frail women, you've got another by god think coming!"

By now, Enright was standing, leaning with her hands on the table, glaring at Archie. "I will by god smack your client up side the head and hang his goddamned hide on the wall of my office! I came in here to try to deal with you in a civil manner, and you choose to insult my intelligence because you think you can just piss on two women and get away with it! Well, let me tell you, *Deputy*...."

She was so angry she had run out of breath. After a moment, Archie said quietly, "Well, breathe a while, and then to it again. But in the meantime, let me point out to you that...."

"You don't point out a goddamned thing to me, *Deputy*!" she continued, leaning further over the table, trying to control her anger. "For your goddamned information, *Deputy*, in Ferguson v. Chicago Housing, the United States District Court found for the plaintiff on sexual harassment and retaliation!"

Archie noticed that her arms were shaking slightly as they propped Enright up on the table. Just as he was beginning to worry that she might have a heart attack, assuming that lawyers had one to attack, the door to the conference room opened slightly, and Deputy Angie Wahlert peeped in.

Archie glanced over and said, "Yes, Angie?"

The young deputy opened the door more fully and stood in the frame.

"Everything all right, Archie?" she asked.

"Everything's fine, Angie," he said, smiling at the young woman. "Miz Enright is just explaining the law to me."

"She's pretty loud, Archie. You want me to throw her out?" asked Angie.

Archie laughed. "No, no, Angie, not a bit of it. That's just the way lawyers discuss things."

"Maybe some lawyers," Angie muttered as she withdrew and closed the door behind her.

Still trembling slightly, Enright sat down.

"Counselor," Archie began, spreading his hands a few inches apart and looking at them, "your client doesn't have a case. Yes, I am aware of Ferguson v. Chicago Housing Authority and I am aware that the district court ruled in favor of the plaintiff. But they did so incorrectly. If you will check the U. S. Supreme Court case Clark County School District v. Breeden, you will find that the Supremes ruled that the original incident, in this case, the alleged sexual harassment, did not constitute what they called "protected activity," and therefore firing the employee was not illegal. In Miz LaDeaux's case, as the sheriff tried to explain to her, the claim of sexual harassment was bogus. He pointed out that she did not have a case for sexual harassment. The guidelines we use are the same guidelines that the courts in this state and in the country have used for several years. They have been well adjudicated. I'll be happy to give you a copy of our department's sexual harassment policy. When the initial incident does not violate law—in this case, since Miz LaDeaux was not sexually harassed—the Supremes have ruled that the termination does not constitute actionable retaliation."

"That is...!" Enright began.

But Archie glanced up at her and held up his index finger, quieting her. "Just one other thing, counselor," he said quietly. "If you file a suit, not only will I seek and get a summary judgment based on the law, but I shall also bring charges against you for filing a nuisance suit. And, counselor, you will be found liable and held accountable."

That got her attention. Her face, which had been flushed with anger, was now pale. Her eyes spoke her anxiety. Slowly she placed her folders back in her briefcase, snapped it shut, and walked out of the room.

Chapter 21

Jerry had a long conversation with Anna Maria from his lonely motel room on the north side of Austin. He had not planned to spend the night away from home and had not packed extra clothes, sleep wear, or toiletries. But his clothes could tolerate a second day's wear, his underwear made acceptable sleep wear, and Holiday Inn was able to provide toothbrush, toothpaste, and shaving gear. He was up for an early breakfast and on his way by eight.

The drive from Austin to Denton was long and crowded. Jerry remembered nostalgically that when the Interstate from Dallas to Austin was first built, the way had been broad and fast and uncrowded. But now cars and trucks jammed the route between Austin and Hillsboro, and even when he diverted onto I-35W at Hillsboro to escape the traffic going to Dallas, he found the path only slightly less congested. The speed limit along most of the route was sixty-five, but seldom could he accelerate to that speed. And even when the traffic allowed him to drive faster, he noticed that when other motorists caught sight of his marked patrol car they would slow to five or ten miles per hour slower than the limit.

It was after eleven when he reached Fort Worth. The drive to Denton was easier, except around the new Texas Motor Speedway, where race fans were arriving extra early for the weekend races. Motor homes and travel trailers of every description were lined up on the far right shoulder both north and south bound, waiting to exit. Jerry was glad to get past the race fans, who ironically slowed the speed on the highway.

Jerry got a parking pass from a friendly co-ed at the gate near the Biology Building on the University of North Texas campus and found a space in visitor parking. Smaller than the UT campus in Austin, the UNT campus was nonetheless crowded. In the building, Jerry stopped by the Biology Office to ask directions to Dr. Haskell's office, and found the professor in a large office cluttered with books and papers scattered about.

When Jerry knocked lightly on the frame of the open door, the man sitting in the desk chair marking a student's paper, his feet propped on the desk in front of him, swung slightly to the right to look at his visitor. "Dr. Haskell?" Jerry asked.

The man languidly moved his feet from the desk and stood slowly to greet his guest. He was taller than Jerry, probably several inches over six feet, and big as well, probably weighing two-fifty. He had a full head of sandy blond hair, which he brushed back as he stood. A large handle-bar mustache decorated his upper lip and served as a lintel for the bright white teeth of his grin. "Sheriff Valdez, I presume?" he said with a slow West Texas drawl, holding his hand out.

"Yes," Jerry said, stepping the two paces across the room to shake the professor's hand. "Thank you for seeing me, Professor."

"Glad to, Sheriff," Haskell said, waving Jerry to a chair beside the desk. Then seeing that the chair was loaded with books and papers, he stepped over to remove them so Jerry could sit down. He looked around for a moment, trying to find where he might put the material. There seemed to Jerry to be no place on his desk or on the floor nearby uncovered. But the professor found a place on top of an uncovered glass aquarium on a shelf to his left. As he dropped the stack of books and papers on top of the aquarium, one of the books and about half of the papers dropped into the rectangular tank. Haskell kept his hands reaching toward the stack, waiting to see if they were going to stay put. Believing after a moment that stasis had been achieved, he dropped his hands and shifted his attention to his caller. "Now, what can I do for you? Emil said something about some botanical matter you need identified—Mary Warner, is it?"

"Mary...?" Jerry began, and then understood. "Oh, no, Dr. Haskell, at least I don't think it's marijuana. I've seen enough of that around the county." He reached in his jacket pocket and withdrew the plastic bag. "Well, this stuff might be marijuana, but it doesn't look like it to me."

The professor put his hand out, and Jerry gave him the bag.

"Nope," Haskell said, turning the bag from one side to the other as he gazed at the debris. "The stems might be cannabis of some sort or another, although I don't think so; but the leaves are certainly not." He opened the bag and, with a pair of long tweezers, pulled one of the larger pieces of leaf out of the bag and placed it on a piece of typing paper lying on his desk. He looked at it intently for a moment, then turned it over and gazed at it again. "Where'd you say you found this, Sheriff?"

"In the pant cuffs of a murder victim," Jerry responded.

"No, I mean, geographically. Where might the corpse have picked it up?"

"Oh, well, I don't really know. He's not telling us much. But we found him on a ranch in Kendall County, down northwest of San Antonio."

"Okay," Haskell said, "that's a place to start." He looked at the piece of leaf again before he stood up and shuffled his way past Jerry's chair through the cluttered office to a bookshelf on the north wall. He pulled a large volume off the shelf and trundled back to his desk, where he fell into his chair. He showed Jerry the title on the spine of the book: *Flora of North Central Texas*. "Wonderful book," he said. "I wish I'd written it. But then again I'm no taxonomist. And I'm glad I'm not. Damned dull work. But they in fact are right useful when they write books like this." He was thumbing through the book in his lap as he nattered on.

When he came to the section he was looking for, he picked up the piece of leaf with the tweezers and compared it to a picture in the book. He grunted and moved the specimen in front of another picture, then another and another. Turning the page in the book, he held the sample next to several more pictures on the verso of the sheet and the recto of the next. This procedure was followed until he was out of the appropriate section in the book. Then he placed the piece of leaf back into the plastic bag, closed the book and put it on top of some papers on his desk, turned to Jerry, and said, "Sheriff, your corpse fellow probably didn't pick that stuff up in Central Texas. Or if he did, it is an anomaly. This stuff is not native to the area. Let me expand the area a bit," he said, returning the one book and taking an even thicker one off the bookshelf. "This here is *Manual of the Vascular Plants of Texas*." He riffled through the thick volume, compared pieces of leaves to descriptions in the book, shook his head finally, and said, "Nope, not here."

"Okay," said Jerry slowly, not knowing really what he had expected to learn. "Any way you can tell me where it did come from?"

"Well, usually, Sheriff," the professor said, leaning back in his chair and locking his fingers behind his head, "usually you tell me where it came from and then I can find out what it is."

"Sorry to be abnormal, Professor," Jerry said, "but where it came from is what I'm trying to find out. Well," he continued, rising resignedly to leave, "thanks anyway, Dr. Haskell."

The professor unlaced his fingers, rocked forward in his chair, and said, "Now, not so fast, Sheriff. Just because I don't know what this stuff is doesn't mean no one else does. As I said, I'm no taxonomist. I know a lot about Texas plants because I was born and raised in Texas, and I've walked amongst them since I was two. But let's don't give up so damned easy on this. It's a plant and now all we've got to do is find the catalogue that lists it. There's enough stuff in that debris to determine how many leaves on a node and whether they are opposite or alternate—and somewhere we'll find some sweet old boring taxonomist has listed it. Sit down, Sheriff," he said, reaching for the phone. Jerry sat.

Professor Haskell pulled a small notebook from his shirt pocket, looked at a dog-eared page, punched some numbers into the phone, and leaned back in his chair. "Hey, Stanley!" he said, enthusiastically into the phone. "How's it going? Listen, Stanley, I've got a lawman in my office who has a few pieces of botanical matter he'd like to identify. I've looked in my copy of Reeves, and I know it's not from around here and won't be in Shinners & Mahler's—oops, sorry, *your* book. And it's not in Correll and Johnston."

Haskell said nothing for a few moments as he thought or rested or gathered wool or forgot what he was doing. After a while of dead air, he continued, "Soooooo, I thought we'd maybe just mosey down to Cowtown"—he picked up the plastic bag and looked at the contents again, as though the drying debris might come to life and speak to him— "see if you taxonomist-types can figure out what it is." He put his hand over the mouthpiece and said to Jerry, "You okay with a quick lunch and then we go down to Fort Worth to talk with this guy about two this afternoon?"

Jerry, having no idea who he was going to meet, nodded.

"Okay, Stanley," the professor said. "Wyatt Earp and I will see if we can find some edible food here in Denton, and then we'll drive down to the BRIT and see you about 2 in the p. m. Okay?" He nodded and, lurching forward in his chair, hung the phone up.

As the professor gathered his energy to heave himself out of the chair, Jerry asked, "Um, Professor, where exactly are we going? I don't have time to go to Great Britain—at least not right now."

The professor relaxed back into his chair but looked puzzled. "Great Britain?" he asked. "Why would you go to England right now?"

"Well, I wouldn't," Jerry responded. "I just heard you mention Brit on the phone...."

Haskell chuckled and heaved himself up and out of the chair. "BRIT, my dear Sheriff, is the Botanical Research Institute of Texas. Nothing to do with Engle-Land. If this plant's from Texas, these guy's will know about it. And even if it isn't, they'll probably know. They're the guys who wrote the latest edition of that book I was mentioning."

Jerry had no idea which book the professor meant. "Well, many thanks, Professor Haskell. I hate to take up your time to do this. I'll be happy to go down there by myself—as a matter of fact, it's on my way home, now that I know I'm not going to England."

"Naw, you got me curious, now, Sheriff. I'd sorta like to go along to see what this is." He handed the plastic bag back to Jerry. "But tell me, Sheriff: even if you find out what it is and maybe where it came from, how is that going to help you identify the body?"

Jerry sighed. "I really have no idea, Professor. I can't find anybody in the county so far who can identify him. Now you tell me the stuff in his cuffs did not come from Central Texas. So, where do I go to see if someone can identify him? If your BRIT colleagues can tell me the plant stuff comes from, um, Vermont, then maybe I can send his picture up there to see if anyone can identify him."

"It didn't," the professor said, shaking his head.

"Didn't what?" Jerry asked.

"That stuff didn't come from Vermont. Too cold up there for that kind of plant."

"Oh, well, okay, now I know not to send the picture to Vermont. I'd just sort of like to know where to start."

"Maybe you'll never identify this guy," the professor said, pulling on a jacket and moving toward the door.

"Maybe not," Jerry responded, following the professor.

Chapter 22

Professor Wiley Haskell had announced that he would drive his own vehicle to Fort Worth, although Jerry had offered to bring him back to Denton after their trip to the Institute. "Naw," the professor had said. "Fort Worth is on your way home, and I need to stop by the Denton Airport on my way back anyway."

They had decided that Jerry would follow Haskell to the Denton Town Square for lunch and then on down to Fort Worth. Jerry had thought the botany professor would likely drive a pickup truck, but as he pulled his patrol car around the parking lot to where Haskell had told him his parking place was located, he was surprised to find the professor waving at him from behind the wheel of a handsome vintage Lexus.

As the Lexus neared the small hut at the entrance/exit of the parking lot, the professor stopped to chat briefly with the young female attendant, whose job it obviously was to greet and direct guests to the campus. And to allow old botany professors and somewhat younger sheriffs to ogle her trim body clad in white shorts and green, form-fitting shirt with an eagle on it.

The greeting and ogling done, the professor turned right on Avenue C for a couple of blocks and then right on a one-way street, Hickory Street, to drive along the north boundary of the campus. The bookstores and fast-food shops near the campus on Hickory Street gave way to historical old houses as Jerry followed the Lexus east. Just past a major north-south thoroughfare, the professor pulled the Lexus over to the left curb and parked on the street in front of what appeared to Jerry to be an old theater. Jerry pulled in behind the Lexus and got out, looking for a parking meter to feed.

"Parking's free here, Sheriff," the professor shouted, crawling out of his car. "Walk down here a few steps. Let me show you our Court House."

Jerry followed the professor east past the old theater toward the square. Haskell waved generally at the theater without looking at it. "Used to be a movie house," he said, "The Campus Theater. Now It's used by the local arts folks to present live theater, like musicals and such. But let's step across the street so you can see the Court House," he said, pulling himself across a deserted intersection. In the center of the downtown square sat a large, ornate, domed courthouse made primarily of cream-colored limestone.

"That limestone," Haskell said, stopping on the walk and facing the building, "came from north Denton County. The Teamsters hauled it down in horse-drawn wagons in 1895 to construct the building. That red granite in the columns is from Burnett County. That clock up in the tower has four faces and was made in Michigan. We think that's one of the most interesting structures in the state." The professor stood, hands on his hips, head tilted back, admiring the building.

"It is a remarkable building," Jerry observed. "Built in 1895, you say?"

Haskell nodded. "Began construction in 1895, finished in 1897."

"County keeps it in good repair," said Jerry.

By then Haskell had continued walking east, still looking at the building and gesturing at several of the features as he described them to his visitor. Just in front of the courthouse on the south side was an arch memorializing Confederate veterans of the Civil War. The structure had two drinking fountains incorporated into the design. Jerry looked closely to see if one was marked "colored" and the other "white," but neither was so marked. Not now, anyway. The grass on the square was green, and old men and a few women of various races sat on the benches generously provided around the building. The Civil War seemed to be over in Denton, Texas.

After the historical tour completely around the courthouse, the professor led Jerry back west on Hickory Street to a restaurant near the Campus Theater. Jerry had thought he'd have maybe chicken-fried steak and a beer for lunch, but no such thing was on the menu. Quiche and soups and salads and sandwiches were offered in this off-the-square restaurant in the heart of North-Central Texas. What would John Denton, Indian Fighter and frontier preacher think of his namesake? No chicken-fried steak? No barbeque? No Tex-Mex? No beer? Are we in Texas? Jerry suffered pangs of homesickness for Kendall County, in this high-intellectual northern town with its two universities, and he ordered a Caesar Salad. He would hide it if anyone he knew happened in. But the food was good and the people friendly.

Chapter 23

Jerry followed Professor Haskell south along Interstate 35-W out of Denton, through Argyle, to Fort Worth. On the north side of the city, Haskell exited the Interstate and wound his way to Pecan Street just past 4th Street to what looked like a large, old warehouse. A handsome sign outside the south entrance to the building announced that this was indeed the Botanical Research Institute of Texas. The BRIT.

Haskell led Jerry into an attractive lobby, where he greeted the receptionist, a middle-aged woman busy shifting files of papers around.

"Hi," he said, not looking directly at the woman, his eyes resting first on a stack of books on the counter and then moving across the woman to glance down the hall to his right. "I'm Wiley Haskell, here to see old Stanley Kelley."

"He expecting you?" the woman asked, friendly, as she picked up the phone.

"Well, hell, I hope so," Haskell replied. "Unless he forgot in the last hour."

"He may have," she said. "He's old, you know?"

"Now wait a minute, young lady," Haskell jested. "He's some years younger than I am."

"Oops, sorry, Professor," the woman said with a grin.

In a few minutes a slender man, who looked to Jerry to be in his late forties, came down the hall and greeted Haskell. The professor introduced him to Jerry as Stanley Kelley, a botanical researcher at the BRIT and one of the authors of one of the books Haskell had mentioned in Denton. Jerry could not remember which of the tomes. Kelley led them down the hall and through a door into a very large warehouse-type room. But the floor was a polished hardwood, the walls were brick in some places and wood elsewhere, and the ceilings were vaulted modified barn ceilings with exposed wooden rafters and supports. The columns for the ceiling supports were 8 by 8 solid wooden beams. The building may well have been originally designed as a warehouse, but Jerry thought that it was a perfect setting for a botanical research center.

Along the walls were hundreds of cupboards and shelves loaded with folders. Other cabinets and shelves were arranged in rows the length of the large room. Kelley led them to a long conference table, one of dozens throughout the room. Kelley sat on one side, while Jerry and the professor walked around to the opposite side. Haskell took a seat in front of a microscope sitting on the table and began toying with the dials.

"Wonderful research area you have here, Mr. Kelley," Jerry said, gesturing broadly around the room.

"Yeah," Kelley said, hardly glancing at the familiar surroundings. "One of our brochure designers called it 'convenient and inspiring.' I really wouldn't quibble with that. It's also climate-controlled and gives us plenty of room. We've got nearly half a million dried plant specimens from around the world. We've also got a wonderful library of books on botany."

"And I bet you print all your brochures on recycled paper," Jerry said.

"Yup, we practice what we preach," he said. "So, Sheriff, uh, sorry, Sheriff Earp?"

Haskell laughed. "Yeah, Wyatt Earp," the professor said.

The taxonomist knew some joke was there, but he had no idea what the gag was.

Jerry noticed the discomfort of his host and quickly responded, "No, Sir, not Wyatt Earp. My name is Jerry Valdez, and I am sheriff in Kendall County."

"You're not from Texas, are you, Stanley?" asked Haskell, still amused.

"No, Wiley, I'm from the northeast. Why?"

"Well," Haskell replied, shifting in his chair, "Wyatt Earp was just about the most famous sheriff the west ever spawned. So every sheriff in the west somehow becomes Wyatt Earp."

"I assure you, Mr. Kelley," Jerry said, "I am nothing like the legendary Wyatt Earp, who seemed to shoot people for recreation. I have shot *at* some people, but I have never killed anyone, at least not while I've been sheriff. And I hope I never have to."

The taxonomist smiled slightly and said, "So, Sheriff Valdez, what can the BRIT do for you?"

"I'm some embarrassed to take up your time, Mr. Kelley," Jerry began, taking the plastic bag out of his jacket pocket and passing it across the table to Kelley. "We have an unidentified corpse down in Kendall County, and nobody seems to know who he is. I found a Las Vegas token in his cuff and thought that somebody out there might know him, but that turned out to be like trying to find whether a needle might have at some time or other been in a very large haystack. The only other evidence I have right now is this stuff in the bag I found in his trouser cuffs. It might be just some sort of common weed, but I thought I'd better check it out."

"Nope," said Professor Haskell, looking through the microscope at a piece of a plant he picked up from the table. The microscope was unusual looking to Jerry. It had a heavy base that kept it firmly on the table, with a vertical metal rod rising some eight inches from the base. Another metal rod was attached to the first one and ran horizontal for nearly two feet. On this horizontal rod were gears to adjust the eyepiece attached by a mechanism on the end of the rod. Extending from the horizontal rod and swooping like embracing arms down to a point near the lower lens of the microscope were two lights. Jerry could see that the lights were used to illuminate whatever objects were placed under the lens to be magnified. While Jerry was examining the instrument, Haskell turned a switch and illuminated the lights on the ends of the two arms. "That's not a common weed you have there, Sheriff; it's some kind of hawthorn. It's just not one I'm familiar with."

Kelley pulled a sheet of white paper in front of him and dumped the contents of the plastic bag onto the paper. Taking a mechanical pencil out of his pocket, he began to sort through the pieces. Jerry noticed that the body of the mechanical pencil was made out of a very handsome wood. "Yeah, Wiley, it's clearly a *Crataegus* of some sort. This one leaf is, at any rate."

"What's a *Crataegus* ?" Jerry asked.

Both men answered at once, neither looking up from what occupied their attentions: "Hawthorn."

Jerry was a bit confused. "Why do you call it *Crataegus* ?"

Haskell looked over at him the way he might look at a mentally deficient child. "Because that's what it is," he said simply and continued to look at the sheriff.

"Then why do you call it 'hawthorn'?" Jerry persisted.

"Oh," said Haskell. "*Crataegus* is the genus name; it's from the rose family, the Rosaceae. 'Hawthorn' is the common name. The 'thorn' part is simple enough, because the plant has some pretty potent thorns on it. I don't know where the 'haw' part comes from."

Kelley looked into the air about a foot over Jerry's head as though he were reading a sign. "'Hawthorn' is from the Old English word 'hagathorn.' 'Haga' means 'fruit,' and 'thorn' means—well, it means thorn. It became 'hawthorn' in Middle English, and that's still what most folks call it."

Jerry looked around, but found no poster with information on it.

Haskell looked slightly bemused at Kelley. "Where the hell did you come up with that information, Stanley?"

"I know everything," Kelley said cheerfully.

"Okay, can you tell me where hawthorn grows?" Jerry asked.

"Damn near everywhere," said Kelley, glancing at Jerry and smiling.

"Well, that's what I was afraid of," Jerry said, rising to leave.

"Now, just hold your horses, Sheriff," said Kelley, waving him back into his chair. "There's hawthorn and then there's hawthorn. Some species grow here and some grow there. There were at last count about two-hundred and eighty species of the genus *Crataegus*. The good news is that they grow only in northern temperate regions; the bad news is that they are found in North America, Europe, and northern Asia. But some of the species are pretty rare with a tight area of distribution. Let's see if we can find out for a first step what species this is." He continued to push the debris around on the paper. "Most *Crataegus* are well armed and have beautiful rose-like flowers in the fall, and rather attractive fruits—these small, rather pear-shaped red things that are about the size of a blueberry. You've got a piece of thorn here, several pieces of flower, some leaves—one of them whole, and a couple of fruits."

"Well armed?" Jerry asked, looking at the scientist.

"Yeah," Kelley answered, "as their common name suggests, hawthorns have these nasty spines protecting the trunk. The trunk itself is pretty formidable, though. The name *Crataegus* comes from the Greek word *kratus*, which means 'strength.' Now, here's something."

Jerry gazed intently at the samples, having no idea on earth what he was looking at.

Kelley reached to a shelf behind him and picked up a pair of long tweezers and a steel probe and turned back to pick up pieces of plant to look at. "Hmm," remarked Kelley, turning a small leaf he had lifted from the paper with the tweezers. He dropped the probe on the table while he looked at the specimen. "Looks like we've got a calyx lobe here, Wiley."

"Yeah," the professor said, still engrossed in whatever he was looking at under the microscope. "I saw it earlier. It's not like any hawthorn calyx I'm familiar with. This is a damned needle from a Norfolk pine!"

Kelley, still holding the leaf in front of him, looked over at Haskell. "What?" he asked.

"This sample I found on the table. It's just a plain pine needle. Who would be studying a pine needle?"

"No one, probably," Kelley said, looking back at the leaf in his hand. "Probably someone had some samples on the table and a needle fell off. You're the only one I know has been examining it."

Haskell looked disgusted. He wiped the needle away from the microscope and blew it onto the floor.

"You want to look at this calyx lobe under the herbarium microscope?" Kelley asked Haskell.

"No," Haskell responded. "I could see it well enough with my nude eyeball. It has a usual calyx base where it attaches to the fruit on the adaxial surface, but it has unusual serrated edges ending in a point. Looks sort of like an Indian arrowhead. Except the serrations point forward instead of backward."

Another man had walked up behind Kelley while Haskell was describing the leaf-like structure. "You know what I think that is?" he said. "That looks like that species Phipps found in that canyon in Mexico. You stood there and looked at it, Stan. You took notes on it."

Jerry stood and, leaning over the table, stuck his hand out and said, "Hi, I'm Jerry Valdez."

The newcomer was taller than Jerry by a couple of inches, had a shock of black hair, a craggy face, and seemed surprised to find Jerry standing with his hand out. But he took the hand and shook it gently without saying anything.

Haskell had glanced up at the man and then went back to looking through the herbarium microscope. Now he was examining the thumbnail on his left hand. He said, "This here is Dr. Gary Nettles. Gary, this here is Sheriff Wyatt Earp. He's trying to identify a plant he took off a corpse after he shot him in a gunfight. Gary's on the staff here at the BRIT."

Nettles had a quizzical look on his face. "Wyatt Earp?" he asked.

"Jerry Valdez," Jerry said, wishing Haskell would forget all about Earp. "I'm the sheriff down in Kendall County." He waved his hand at the leaf-like structure. "These good people are trying to see if this leaf can point me to some geographical starting point where I might can find out the identity of the corpse. I didn't shoot him."

Nettles took the tweezers from Kelley, held it in his left hand while leaning his right hand on the table, and looked closely at the specimen. "Well, Sheriff, first off, it's not a leaf. It's a calyx lobe. It comes from the fruit of the *Crataegus*. And this one is unusual. Stan, you got those drawings on the *Crataegus* of Northern Mexico? This calyx looks like one we found down there."

Kelley slid out of his chair and walked out of the room, his soft-soled shoes squeaking on the hardwood floor. Dr. Nettles sat down in the chair vacated by Kelley and picked up the metal probe. Holding the calyx with the tweezers in his left hand, he separated and lifted the serrated edges with probe, engrossed in the sample.

In under a minute Kelley returned, leafing through a thin book. As Kelley sat next to Nettles, Jerry saw that the title on the cover was *Crataegus of Northern Mexico*. *Damn*, he thought, *a book devoted to hawthorns that grow in Northern Mexico!* He was on the brink of commenting that even the esoteric must have its practical limits. But he figured such a comment would not set well with his botanical benefactors.

Dr. Nettles looked on as Kelley paged through the book. Even Professor Haskell abandoned the examination of his thumb, stood, and leaned over to look at the drawings in the book.

"Whoa," said Nettles. "Go back a page."

When Kelley had flipped back one page, he ran his finger down the page over a drawing of a plant. Jerry saw that the plant depicted had large leaves like the leaf he had found in Nobody's cuff. The drawing also had a thorn about four centimeters long below the leaves protruding from a stem. The drawing also presented a cluster of three fruit-like pods. They looked like tiny pomegranates, maybe a centimeter in diameter.

Under the drawing of the leaf-thorn-fruit which dominated the page were details of a leaf, the fruit, and the stems and leaf-like things shown growing from the fruit pods. Kelley's finger slid down the page to rest just under a figure marked "A," a drawing of one of the leaf-like structures. It looked to Jerry like what they had been calling a calyx lobe.

Nettles moved the tweezers with the specimen down to place it next to the drawing. Kelley reached over to take the probe out of Nettles' hand and used it to lift one side of the sample and then the other, shifting his eyes from the sample to the drawing.

"Um," Nettles concluded, moving the sample back to place it on the table. He placed the tweezers on the table, slid out of his chair, and walked away.

"Yup," said Kelley, looking up at Jerry. "It's a *Crataegus johnstonii*."

Dr. Haskell nodded and returned to looking through the microscope, this time examining a liver spot on the back of his right hand.

Jerry looked at the inexpressive faces of the two scientists. "Okay," he said. "Is that good or bad?"

Kelley shrugged. "It's neither good nor bad. It's just what it is. It's not poisonous, if that's what you mean."

"Um, no, I mean do you know where it comes from?"

Kelley's eyes opened wider. "Oh, yeah, sure," he said, reaching over to page through the book once again. When he came to a simple line map decorated with open and solid squares and lozenges, he picked up the probe and pointed to two lozenge shapes near the top of the map. The symbols were in sector of the map designated "Coah." "The *Crataegus johnstonii* was found by a colleague named Phipps in a canyon right about there in the Mexican state of Coahuila. I've been there and looked at this very species." He pronounced the place "Qua-wheel-uh."

Jerry looked at the simple map. "That's Coahuila?" he asked.

"Yup, you know it?" Kelley said.

"Well, yeah," Jerry began. "Not much to know, really. There's nothing there. I guess if you look up 'nothing' in the dictionary, you'd find a map of Coahuila, Mexico."

"Well, one thing that's there is the *Crataegus johnstonii*, right there in this canyon just across the border from Big Bend National Park in Texas." He tapped the symbols on the map. "Another thing was there are these specimens you brought in."

Jerry pulled the piece of paper with the samples on it over to him and looked at the fragments. "Is Coahuila the only place these could have come from?"

"Not just Coahuila," Kelley answered. "This one canyon in Coahuila, specifically in Sierra del Carmen. The *johnstonii* distribution is very tight. Whoever your guy is, he walked in this canyon and brushed against some of these plants."

Jerry thought for a minute. "What would he be doing there? I mean, there's nothing there. It's a desert."

Kelley shrugged. "Dunno. Maybe he was looking at plants. I've been there dozens of times."

Jerry tapped his finger on the map. "Any drugs grow there?"

"Nope," answered Kelley. "You called it right. It's all desert, not a good place to grow a cash crop of drugs. But whatever your guy was doing there, he was there."

"Well, I'll just be damned," Jerry said, shaking his head. "You guys are wonderful, and I thank you more than I can say. The good news is that I know considerably more than when I came in. The bad news is that I still don't know who Nobody is."

"Nobody is?" asked Haskell, looking up from the microscope.

"Yeah," Jerry explained. "We've taken to calling the corpse 'Nobody,' since nobody knows his name. Now I know where he was, but I still don't know who he is or, more important, who killed him. I'd rather hoped that we could place him in San Antonio or Austin or Dallas or Monterrey so I could show his picture around and maybe get an identification. Who can I ask in Coahuila? Prairie dogs? Scorpions? There's no one there."

"Maybe he was a botanist," suggested Kelley.

Jerry unbuttoned the right front pocket on his shirt, pulled a piece of paper out, unfolded it, and showed it to Kelley. "You recognize him as a botanist?"

Kelley took the drawing, looked at it, and shook his head. Haskell held his left hand out and wiggled his fingers. Kelley passed the drawing to him, and the professor studied it. He handed it back to Jerry. "If he had been doing botanical research in that area, either Stanley or I would know him. Stanley certainly would."

"Any guesses what someone might be doing there other than looking at plants?" Jerry asked the two men.

Both men shrugged. Kelley shifted in his chair and offered the only other information he had about the place. "There are people in northern Coahuila, Sheriff. There are some small villages—really small villages. We sometimes go to a place called Hacienda Piedra Blanca. As a matter of fact, we found a specimen of the *johnstonii* in the Cañon de Centinela on the Hacienda Piedra Blanca. There are lots of prairie dogs and scorpions there. But there are people there, too."

Jerry felt somewhat encouraged by the information. Yet he had no idea how it might lead to anything useful. Still, the only clue left to him had not led him to a dead end. As he rose to leave, he asked the two scientists generally the question that was on his mind: "You guys know an enormous amount about what seems to me a rather insignificant plant, and pretty obviously many others have spent a good deal of time studying the hawthorn, enough time to distinguish between over two-hundred varieties."

"Over two-hundred and eighty," Kelley corrected, smiling.

"Yeah," Jerry acknowledged. "Question is, why?"

Professor Haskell now abandoned the microscope and stood. "Easy answer is that God put them here and we like to know as much as we can about how things work. They are also just plain pretty plant life. If they are there, we'll study them. All that aesthetic crap about the wonders of the universe ain't wholly insincere, you know. Ol' Wordsworth can write poems about the beauty of a violet or daffodils, but a botanist who studies those plants sees the beauty, too. I know what Wordsworth meant when he said, '*To me the meanest flower that blows can give/Thoughts that do often lie too deep for tears.*' But to be less poetic, probably the main reason the scientific community knows so much about *Crataegus* is that it exerts a simultaneous cardiotropic and vasodilatory action on the body. It can be safely and effectively utilized for cardiac conditions for which digitalis is not yet indicated."

Jerry looked blank.

Kelley explained, "A tonic can be made from the flowers and berries to lower blood pressure. It has pharmacological benefits."

Both pretty and useful, Jerry thought. He thanked the two scientists enthusiastically for their help, asked them to convey his gratitude to Dr. Nettles, and left the BRIT to drive back to Kendall County.

It was nearly four o'clock when Jerry left the BRIT. On the way home he called Anna Maria to tell her he would be home for a late dinner. Then he called Professor Emil Brunner in Austin to report on what he had discovered and to thank him. But he still did not know who Nobody was or who killed him.

Chapter 24

Deputy Angie Wahlert smiled at Jerry when he walked through the lobby toward his office. She gave him a piece of paper and a slight curtsey.

"Good morning, you delightful ladies," he said to Angie and Miriam. Holding up the sheet of paper, he asked, "What's this, Angie?"

"You asked me to check with the BFI to see if they had any missing personas. That's my report to my most high sheriff." Another curtsey and a dazzling smile.

BFI, Jerry thought. "FBI, Angie?"

"Yep, Sheriff. Those FIB guys."

"Thank you, Angie. Um, you know where Willie Ward is?"

Angie looked over to Miriam Smith, who was responsible for communications. Without having to consult her record book, Miriam answered, "He's on patrol, Sheriff. He's checking up on all the patrol units to make sure they're where they're supposed to be."

Jerry nodded. Deputy Ward did have a patrol car assigned to him, and his territory in the county was general and undefined. As the deputy with most time on the job, Jerry let him devise his own patrol duties. No one had ever made Ward a supervisor, but the deputy had rather assumed the responsibility to oversee the patrol units. Since he often worked twelve hours a day, and since no one paid any particular attention to him, neither Jerry nor Archie had ever disabused him of the notion that he should check up on other patrol units. Ward was the senior deputy and a well-intentioned man but, insofar as talents were concerned, he was a firefly in a world of greater lights: He was pleasant and harmless but provided little light.

"Miriam, call Deputy Ward and tell him to stop by to see me when his orbit brings him close," Jerry said and turned to walk to his office. He stopped and turned back to his communications deputy. "But, Miriam, tell him to make it sometime today." It was better to be specific with Willie Ward.

He had time just to get to his office and glance at Angie's report—the FBI had no one on their missing-persons list remotely similar to Nobody—when Miriam called to tell him that Anthony Wragg was on the phone for him.

Wragg was a relative newcomer to the county, having been none-too-successful as a real-estate salesman in Houston. He was a somewhat larger fish in the smaller pond of Kendall County. He was a rather pudgy, short, not very handsome man past middle age; but the rural folks in the county did not require their real-estate hacks to have high-society looks. Wragg had done relatively well in the eight or so years he had lived in the county, and a few months ago he had been elected chairman of the Boerne Boosters Association.

"Sheriff Valdez, this is Anthony Wragg," the man said.

"Tony," Jerry responded. The man was "Tony" when he first arrived in the county and remained so until he finally sold enough real estate to be able to afford to join the country club. His wife, Hazel, had apparently decided that "Tony" was not elegant enough for the country club, not sufficiently distinguished for a gentleman rising by his own innate qualities to positions of grand importance. At his economic and societal ascension, she had begun referring to him always as Anthony, which she pronounced "On-tinie." At the same time, she began introducing herself as Marlene instead of Hazel. Anna Maria had explained to Jerry that Marlene was her middle name— Hazel by any other name. Jerry figured that folks could call themselves anything they wanted. He grinned at their pretensions, but he hid his thoughts as best he could. Still, whenever he thought of this guy trying to wrap himself in the presumed gloss of "Anthony," he thought of the emperor's new clothes. Now, he was calling Jerry, "Sheriff Valdez."

"What's up, Tony?" he asked familiarly.

"Sheriff Valdez," the real-estate salesman said seriously, "I need to broach an important issue with you. I wonder if you could come by my office at, say, eleven o'clock this morning."

The invitation seemed more like a command than a question. And Jerry was momentarily surprised into silence. He moved the receiver from his head and looked at it, as though to make sure it was really Tony Wragg ordering him to report to his office. Returning the phone to his ear, he said, "Um, Tony, what the hell are you talking about?"

"I need to talk with you, Sheriff."

"Well, goddamn it, Tony, it may have escaped your attention, but you ARE talking with me right now."

"I think, Sheriff, we need to talk in person and in private."

"Okay, then why don't you call Angie Wahlert and arrange for a time at your convenience when I'm in and stop by to see me. Why are you summoning me to your office?"

"Sheriff," Wragg said importantly, "I need to talk with you about important business, county business. And I don't think it is too much to ask an elected official of this county to come by the office of the chairman of the Boerne Booster Association."

"Goddamn it, Tony, the chairman of the Boerne Booster Bunch doesn't have an office. Nor do you have a building. You want to talk with me, call my deputy and make an appointment. Good-bye, Tony." He hung up the phone and dismissed Tony Wragg from his thoughts.

Jerry pulled the road atlas from the shelf behind his desk and opened it on his desk to the Texas map. Coahuila, specifically the Sierra del Carmen area, was not easy to get to. He'd really like to fax Nobody's picture over to police officials, as he earlier had done to Las Vegas; but there were no police in the desert of northern Coahuila. In that neighborhood, law was an individual thing. Cactuses arm themselves, as do scorpions and rattlers. And hawthorns. And they did not have fax machines. He'd have to go over there.

Driving west on Interstate 10 to Fort Stockton was probably the best way to go. Then south on 385 through Marathon, through Big Bend National Park, down to Boquillas. Or he could drop down from Boerne to pick up Highway 90 and then west over to Marathon. He ran his finger across the red line indicating Highway 90 and tapped the map at Del Rio. He could cross the border at Del Rio and cross the Mexican desert south of the Rio Grande. Shorter that way, but the line on the map indicated more of a trail than a highway. *Nope,* he thought. *Best way would be the Interstate to Fort Stockton and then south. Now....*

Angie Wahlert appeared in the door of the office, like a wraith with her angelic smile. "Mr. Wragg, chairman of the Boerne Booster Association, has asked that Sheriff Valdez make himself available for a conference in twenty minutes." Angie curtsied and pirouette to leave, her short khaki skirt flaring out and up a couple of inches. Jerry watched the harmony and magnificence of the phenomenon, silent with admiration.

Forcing himself to more mundane matters, he said, "Um, Angie, may I assume that Tony will come here to see me?"

Another swirl of skirt and girl, another dazzling smile, "Yes, Sir." Another curtsey and twirl and she was gone.

He looked back at the map, trying to determine how long the trip would take and where he might need to spend the night.

A knock on the doorframe disturbed Jerry's concentration on the map. He looked up to see Deputy Willie Ward.

Ward saluted, but did not wait for the sheriff to return the gesture, knowing he would not, but he still stood at an approximate attention. "You wanted to see me, Sheriff?"

"Come in Willie," Jerry sighed, folding his hands across the map on his desk. He had forgotten about asking the deputy to stop by, and he regretted the interruption. Jerry had learned to attend to several chores at once long ago—multitasking, his computer-scientist friend Ollie Johnson called it—but he much preferred to lend his full attention to one important thing at a time. He rarely had that luxury.

"Willie, two things. One, I want to congratulate you on a job well done at the crime scene. You took control and did a professional job."

"Thank you, Sheriff." Ward relaxed his more formal stance and smiled at the compliment, showing the gap left by a missing upper tooth in the front of his mouth.

"Second, Willie, I want you to cease and desist from making statements to the press, any press anytime."

The smile disappeared from the deputy's blushing face, and he straightened up like one of the jointed soldiers connected by strings. "But, Sheriff," he said plaintively, "that reporter, Ms Thornton, she asked me. What was I supposed to do? I tried to just give her the facts."

Jerry interlaced his fingers, looked a moment at his thumbnails, sighed, looked up, and said, "Willie, I know you did, but we can't have anyone, not anyone, speaking for the department except me or the chief deputy. I don't want you talking to reporters."

"Sheriff, Angie sometimes is quoted in the paper," the deputy said defensively.

"Angie knows what she can say and what she cannot say, Willie," Jerry answered. "She's the office manager, and she can answer certain factual questions by the press. But you are quoted as telling the reporter that we would have the case cleared right away. Now, that raises unreasonable expectations among the citizens. I have no idea who killed this man, and the evidence that might lead to his murderer is slight. I don't know when—or even if—we'll solve it. You also told the reporter that we were looking at the Mexican ranch hands on Harvey Phelan's place and would be bringing them in for questioning."

"Well, aren't we?" the deputy asked, surprised.

"No, I do not intend to bring them in," Jerry said.

The deputy rolled his eyes and shoulders, relaxing his more rigid posture. "Well, should," he said *sotto voce*.

Jerry knew that bellowing at Ward would not solve the problem. The deputy had no real notion about evidence or the law. Quietly, he said, "Look, Willie, just do not talk about departmental business with anyone outside the department. Don't talk about departmental business when anyone might overhear you. And don't ever, never ever talk to reporters about departmental business."

"Well, Sheriff," the deputy said pleadingly, "what am I supposed to do when they ask me?"

Jerry sighed. "Willie, if anyone asks you, just memorize this response: 'You'll have to ask the sheriff.' That's all I want you to say to anyone outside the department. Even if the county judge asks you, tell him, 'You'll have to ask the sheriff.' Now, let me hear you say it."

The deputy smiled and said, "You'll have to ask the sheriff."

"Very good, Willie. Now, get back to work."

At that moment the radiant figure of Angie Wahlert appeared at the door. She smiled at the deputy and said, "Hey, Willie."

"You'll have to ask the sheriff," Ward said and almost fell to the floor laughing. When he had himself under control, he wiped the tears from his eyes and left.

"Sheriff," Angie said quietly, "if Willie gets any dumber, we're going to have to take to watering him twice a day."

Jerry smiled, but did not respond to the entirely accurate estimate.

"Um, 'Wragg is in custody,'" she said, and looked at the sheriff intently.

Jerry had to think for a minute. "Matthew Arnold?" he asked.

She smiled. "I took sophomore literature this semester at San Antonio College. Learned all about criticism. I remembered Wragg because he sold Miriam a house. Anyway, he's here."

"Ask him to come on back, please, Angie."

She pivoted, twisting her skirt on her magnificent frame, paused, looked back over her left shoulder, said, "'K," and left.

Chapter 25

Anthony Wragg was a short man, wearing a light-brown suit with a matching vest. The material had a shine to it, like sharkskin. The vest had a gold chain stretching from pocket to pocket, with a key of some sort dangling from the chain near the right-hand pocket. It rather resembled a Phi Beta Kappa key, but since Wragg had not finished high school, Jerry figured he probably had not been inducted into ΦBK. Wragg walked in, closed the door, and stood in front of Jerry's desk.

He said, "Sheriff Valdez, I represent the membership of the Boerne Booster Association. I hope you take my comments seriously."

Jerry waved at a chair in front of his desk, and Wragg slid himself into it. Jerry had an area to the right of his desk with a couch and several comfortable chairs for a more informal setting. He would certainly have invited Tony to sit in the more relaxed setting, but Anthony Wragg did not quite deserve the intimacy implied by the setting.

"Okay, Tony, what's up," Jerry said, leaning back in his chair and folding his hands on his belly.

The salesman had a frown on his face. His thin brown hair was combed from the left over to cover the bald middle section. His expression was the one he always wore when he had to explain to someone he had sold a house to that the cracked foundation was not the responsibility of either the seller or the agent. "Sheriff, the membership of the BBA is much concerned that the person or persons responsible for the grisly murder have not yet been brought to justice. Murder is not, Sheriff, good for business. This is our busiest part of the year, business wise, and if people think that a murderer or murderers are roaming around the county killing honest citizens, they won't come here. And if they don't come here, they won't spend money here. And, may I remind you, your salary comes from the good people of this county. We need for you to do your job."

"Well, thanks, Tony, for reminding me I need to do my job. As a matter of fact, I was doing my job when you walked in here and interrupted me. I'm not sure why you call it a 'grisly' murder. The victim was shot as neatly as any man can be shot with a small caliber weapon. I've seen some grisly murders, and this is not one of them. Second, what exactly would the knowledgeable members of the BBA have me do that I am not doing?"

Wragg wiggled his butt to the edge of the chair, readying himself to instruct the sheriff. "The newspaper report said that you'd have this crime solved within the week. That comment was made almost exactly one week ago. Furthermore, the report said that you had some suspects, some Mexicans who were known to have been in the vicinity. I understand that you do not have these suspects in custody and that you have not even brought them in for questioning. Is that true?"

"Tony, I'm not going to discuss the details of the case with you...."

"Well, Sheriff Valdez, you'd better discuss the details of the case with me." His "bad news about the cracked foundation" look had given way to a stern "explain reality to a stupid Mexican" expression. "Why have you not arrested the Mexicans who were known to be in the vicinity?"

"I have not arrested anyone yet because I have absolutely no idea whom to arrest. If you can tell me, Tony, who the murderer is and give me the evidence District Attorney Peter Delgatto will need to prosecute, then I'll be very much in your debt. I'll arrest the sonofabitch and throw him in jail If you can't do that, I wish you'd get the hell out of here and let me do my job."

Wragg's expression grew more intense. "Sheriff, let me tell you something. I am getting a lot of pressure on this matter. A lot of pressure. We want you to arrest these Mexicans and bring them to justice. It just stands to reason. These men have already broken the law by coming here illegally. And now another Mexican turns up dead within spitting distance of the hovel they live in. We need closure on this. I represent a great many business people in this county." By now, the salesman was leaning over the desk, punctuating his remarks by stabbing his finger on the map. "We want these criminals punished, and we want closure on this heinous crime." He pronounced the word "hē - nē- us."

Jerry sighed. He found himself doing that more often recently. He'd like to take Anna Maria and the kids on vacation—to Key West, maybe, where he could do nothing more stressful than try to avoid the barracuda while fishing for large game fish that populated the warm and wonderful waters off that laid-back island. Instead, he was probably going to have to go to the cold Mexican desert by himself tomorrow, and today he had to put up with this real-estate twit, who knew no more about police work than a jackass knows about raising orchids.

"Look, Tony, I'm sorry you're getting pressure. Tell whoever is leaning on you to come see me, and I'll try to get you off the hook."

"I'm the chairman of the BBA, Sheriff," Wragg said proudly. "It is my duty to represent the business interests of this county, and I shall do so. I took time out of my busy day to tell you that we want these Mexicans arrested, prosecuted, and punished for the murder. And we want it done without delay." The finger stabbing had grown more intense.

"Tony, I'm not going to arrest anyone without adequate evidence, not right now and not next week. I doubt I'll ever arrest those men out at Harvey Phelan's place. I am persuaded that they had nothing to do with the murder."

The look on Wragg's face was one of outrage. He was standing now, leaning with both hands on the desk. "Are you mad, man? Or is it that you don't arrest Mexicans? What did they do, bribe you, Mexican style, to look the other way while they commit murder? Let me tell you, Valdez, you'd better get your...you'd better get out there and arrest those wetbacks today if you know what's good for you! This is America, not Mexico! And we will not let you destroy this great nation by letting cheap trash get away with murder!" Wragg was red in the face, breathing hard, his body trembling, as he stood upright and pulled his vest down.

Jerry thought for a moment before he picked up the phone and asked Angie Wahlert to come back. When Angie opened the door and showed her gentle face, Jerry said, "Deputy, do you want to throw this rag out of my office, or are you too busy right now?"

With a twinkle in her eye, she said, "Oh, please let me, Sheriff. And thank you." She grabbed Wragg's collar with her left hand, his belt with her right hand, and, holding him so that only his toes touched the ground, conducted him out of the office.

Chapter 26

The cold north wind tried to blow Jerry's patrol car off Highway 10 as he drove west toward Fort Stockton. He had had an early breakfast with Anna Maria before he left his home about four hours earlier. The two children, grateful for the opportunity to sleep late on a Saturday morning in late November, had done so.

Breakfast with Anna Maria in the garden room had been wonderful. Not only did the glass on three sides of the room overlook the small garden on the south side of the house, but the room itself had trees and flowering plants in every corner. In the northeast corner of the room, where the room was connected to the large family room, Jerry had built a fountain that pumped water from the small pond up to gurgle down over native hill-country granite into the pond below. Around the pond were water plants, and in the pond was a good collection of colorful fish. The room was beautiful, peaceful, quiet. It was Jerry's favorite room in the house—except for maybe the bedroom.

Jerry had prepared breakfast while Anna Maria packed a bag for his quick trip. The eggs were poached lightly, adequately salted and lightly peppered, and placed on honey wheat berry toast. Crisp shredded potatoes fried with a hint of onion, along with pork and venison sausage, bacon, and sliced tomatoes graced two of the large china plates Anna Maria's mother had given them many years earlier. English breakfast tea filled the eggshell china cups set at each end of the small glass-top wicker table near the fountain. A basket of biscuits covered with a cloth napkin was on a side table, along with lightly salted butter and three different sorts of fruit jam: red raspberry, peach, and apricot. By the time he had finished, Jerry had eaten everything on his plate and tried all three of the jams. He knew better than to drink the three cups of tea, but figured that stopping to pee every thirty minutes for a while was little enough to pay for so wonderful a brew as this tea. Best of all, however, was the company of the delightful woman who had sat across the table from him.

He was already missing her as he pulled into Fort Stockton. The kids were scheduled for a variety of school and church events over the weekend, and Anna Maria had felt obligated to serve as mother as well as mom. Their son was Juan Alexandro Valdez, but no one except his sixth-grade teacher called him Juan. To everyone else he was Alex. He looked like his mother, but his personality was that of his father: physical, outgoing, thoughtful, and sometimes unsettlingly witty. Young Maria, age eight, was four years younger. The copy of her mother, with sparkling eyes and a bright smile that enhanced an already beautiful face in the same way that a rainbow adorns a bright sky, young Maria Margarita was adored by her parents. Anna Maria needed to have at least one eye on her charges at almost all times. Four of Maria's friends had spent the night at the Valdez house, and Anna Maria had shifted her attention from Jerry to the giggling girls as soon as they woke. Jennifer and Rebecca McCallum and Katie and Kelly Chermack—and Maria—had all slept in Maria's small room, talked most of the night, and were up and ready for a soccer game. Two older Chermack sisters, Amy Lucy and Leslie Andrew, were coming over to help transport the girls to soccer, but Anna Maria kept close watch over them all, including the older girls.

Besides, while Anna Maria would have enjoyed the trip with Jerry, she did not care to wander about the desert of northern Coahuila, Mexico, in the winter. Jerry, therefore, pulled off Interstate 10 by himself when he found a sign that directed him toward Highway 385, that would take him south to Big Bend National Park and to the state of Coahuila, Mexico.

But because Interstate 10 had taken him north of Fort Stockton and he would have to drive through the small town on his way south, he thought he might as well stop for lunch. Besides, there was a barbeque place at the exit to Highway 385. He was almost stopped anyway. *Might as well kill two birds with one stone—along with a plate of ribs, onion rings, one beer, and peach cobbler. God, I'm efficient.*

With the wind at his back and the traffic not heavy, he made the trip from Fort Stockton to Boquillas Canon Overlook on the Mexican border in a bit over three hours. His near 100-mph speeds attracted the attentions of two state troopers, but they had merely waved when they noted his marked patrol car. The National Park Service personnel at Big Bend, having less power than law-enforcement officers, were more officious in dealing with Jerry. But he was able to get through the park and to the border without damaging too many egos.

At the border with Mexico, Jerry left his pistol, shotgun, and model 94 Winchester rifle, along with all ammunition, with the border guard on the Texas side. His marked patrol car would get some stares from Mexican citizens, but probably he would not run into any Mexican police types. And if he did, he had no weapons with him. A patrol car without weapons is just a car with blinky lights. They can't put you in jail for blinky lights. At least not legally.

Just across the border into Mexico, Jerry pulled to the right off the narrow macadam highway to park in front of a rather dilapidated cantina set some thirty yards off the road. The building was faded plaster over some kind of stone, the stone substructure plainly visible in many places where the plaster had chipped off. Some kind of name had obviously been painted above the door, but the paint was so weathered that Jerry could not make it out. In back of the tavern were several outbuildings, pole barns with rusted corrugated-metal sides and roofs. No one appeared to be about.

As Jerry stepped inside the cantina, he saw a couple of old men playing dominos at a table near the back door. Behind the chipped and scarred laminated-plastic bar was a somewhat younger man, maybe in his early forties, smoking a cigarette. The man was a couple of inches over six feet, thin, and stood with shoulders slumped. His face was dark and hollow, his eyes sunken and squinted against the smoke rising from the cigarette. He wore dark pants that might have been wool, but were wrinkled and stained. His belt wrapped around his thin waist, lolling out of the belt loop by a good three inches—like a tic-hound's tongue. His *Guayabera* shirt was too small for him and missing the two bottom buttons. It was perhaps once white, but now was a dingy gray and stained. The two old men at the table glanced at Jerry briefly and then returned to their clacking game. The younger man squinted one eye against the smoke of the cigarette dangling from his lips and watched Jerry approach.

Jerry fixed his eyes on the man as he removed a picture from his pocket and unfolded it. "*Señor*," Jerry said, "*¿Usted conoce a este hombre?* Sir, do you know this man?"

The man pulled the cigarette from his mouth, loudly expelled a lungful of smoke, and squinted at the drawing. While he was looking, Jerry noticed that his right hand was nervously chafing the paper. The man glanced over at the table of domino players, then back at the drawing. Handing the paper back to Jerry and reinserting the cigarette in his mouth, he shook his head.

Jerry was not convinced. The nervous rubbing, the glance over at the old men were unusual traits. He tried again. Handing the paper back, he said, "*¿Usted ha visto alguna vez a este hombre por aquí?* Have you ever seen this man around here?"

Without looking at the picture, the man said, "*No.*" He had begun to sweat. And it was a cold day.

Jerry tried again: "*¿Puede usted decirme el nombre de este hombre?* Can you tell me what this man's name is?"

Again without looking at the picture but growing more agitated, the man answered, "*No sé quién es este hombre.*"

Jerry stared at the man for a moment, knowing full well that he was being lied to, before he picked up the picture and walked over to the two old men. He got more agitation from them, but no identification.

These guys recognized Nobody, but Jerry had not figured how to get them to talk. He walked outside the cantina and, seeing no one else around, got in his car to drive down the road.

In a few miles he came to a happier settlement on the left side of the road, a white stucco building that looked like some kind of resort. Not an opulent resort, but certainly better than the no-name cantina he just left. This place had trees and grass, a swimming pool, and a legible sign swinging from a white wooden frame. The sign said, "Cañon of the White Stone." In English.

Jerry pulled left into the near parking lot and looked around. This place also seemed dead. No one was around. The main structure was separated from the parking lot by a small white wooden fence, all in good repair. Jerry opened the small gate and walked inside, up the stairs, and into the large open door.

On one side of the large room was what looked like a registration desk. No one was behind the counter. On the left was a bar with a thin, gray-haired man standing behind it polishing a glass. He looked to be young, not over forty, but his hair was totally gray. He smiled at Jerry and said, "*Buena tarde, amigo. ¿En que le puedo servir?*"

His accent was good, but he was not Mexican, nor did he look it. "You American?" Jerry asked, walking over to the bar.

"I am for a fact, *amigo,*" he said in a friendly manner, putting the glass and drying cloth down and extending his hand. "Name's Sam. Sam Alton."

"Howdy, Sam." Jerry shook his hand. "I'm Jerry Valdez from Kendall County, Texas."

Sam gestured toward Jerry's badge and said, "You the law up in Kendall County, Texas?"

Jerry smiled. "Part of it, Sam. I'm down here trying to get a lead on a body we found in my county. We don't have an identity on him."

Sam looked puzzled. "Well, okay, Jerry, sounds like a good thing to do. But what the hell led you to this godforsaken place?"

"It's a long and complex story, Sam. We found some plant parts in the guy's cuffs, and some really neat scientists up in Texas were able to tell me that the plant we found on the body came from this canyon right back of your place. This is your place?"

"Yeah, mine and the bank's," Sam agreed.

"Sam, I don't mean to be nosey, but this is a nice establishment and you seem to be a nice guy...."

"What's a nice guy like me doing in a nice place like this in the middle of the miserable Chihuahuan Desert?"

"Yeah, something like that."

"Tell me the name of the scientists who helped you identify this plant, Jerry."

Jerry was a bit taken aback by the switch in direction the conversation had taken. "Okay, well, it started with my old botany professor at the University of Texas, Dr. Emil Brunner. He sent me up to the University of North Texas to see a Dr. Wiley Haskell. Haskell took me down to the Botanical Research Institute of Texas, where I met several people, but mainly a Stanley Kelley, who, it turns out, had been in this very canyon and seen the actual plant that I found on the body in Kendall County. How's that for convoluted?" Jerry had been ticking off names on his fingers as he remembered them. When he looked up, he saw Sam smiling.

"The BRIT," he said fondly. "People like Stanley Kelley and Gary Nettles are why I'm here—or part of the reason I'm here. When I got out of the Marine Corps, I didn't care to be around people too much, not most people. I was down here walking the desert, which I find to be restorative of soul, when I met Stanley and Gary and half a dozen other botanists who come down here from time to time to find, identify, describe, and document plants. Seemed like a worthy thing to do. And they were all bright, together people. I liked them. This place was for sale, so I bought it. Now, when folks come to walk into the desert, they usually stay here." He kept his eyes on the glass he was polishing.

"Vietnam?" Jerry asked, guessing at the man's age.

Sam nodded. He glanced up. "You?"

Jerry shook his head slightly. "Korea," he said simply.

Looking back down at the glass he was worrying, Sam said, "Frozen Chosen. I've heard stories. Maybe a bit more conventional than 'Nam, but not a good war. You in the Corps?"

"Maybe some wars are less bad than others, but no such thing as a good one. No, I was army."

"See action?"

Jerry nodded. "I danced with the North Koreans for a while. And then the Chinese. The Chinese led."

"You at the Reservoir?" Sam raised his eyes, looking at Jerry more intently.

Jerry nodded again.

"God-damn!" The sound seemed to have been forced from the man's body, as though he had been squeezed hard.

"Yeah," agreed Jerry. "Goddamn."

Jerry had Sam's full attention. "Glad you're still alive, man."

"Glad to still be alive, Sam. I lost most of my men."

"You an officer?"

"Captain. Company commander."

"Heard it was cold as a witch's tit there."

"Words are 'way inadequate."

Sam nodded, uncomfortable as Jerry with the conversation. Jerry had met a number of Vietnam veterans who talked incessantly about how bad their experience was in that war and how no one had appreciated the great sacrifices they had made, blaming their subsequent dissolute lives on what the war had done to them, as though no one had ever undergone hardships but them.

The Vietnam War was different in many respects, Jerry knew. Not only had it separated men from their families and friends, put them in harm's way, exposed them to nature red in tooth and claw as War One, War Two, Korea, and all wars from time immemorial had done; but 'Nam had put immature young men in villages where they had no idea who was a good guy or a bad guy. Jerry was never able to answer for himself whether or not, if faced with the presence of a young indigenous female who might or might not kill him, he could pull the trigger. Could he burn a village populated with old women and men and young children because it might support enemy activities? The war had obviously affected Sam Alton—as war changed any sentient creature—but he had dealt with the experience as an aberration to be relegated to a footnote. His life now seemed concentrated upon polishing that damned glass.

"Sam," Jerry said, "I'd like to ask you if you will look at a drawing of the man we need to identify." He pulled the drawing out of his pocket, unfolded it, and held it out.

Sam put the well-polished glass on the bar, lay the cloth aside, and took the paper. "Captain, you can ask me anything."

"Sheriff," Jerry said.

Sam smiled. "You *are* the law in, what was it? Kendall County, aren't you?"

"Such as it is, Sam. You recognize this guy?"

Sam Alton looked closely at the drawing. "How tall was this man?"

Jerry pulled a small spiral notepad out of his pocket and consulted it. "The medical examiner put his height at about five eight and weight at about one eighty."

"Yeah, I've seen the guy," Sam said, handing the drawing back to Jerry and picking up his glass and polishing cloth. "Business he was in, he was just looking for a place to die. I guess he found that place in your neck of the woods."

Jerry felt a rush of adrenalin course briefly through his body. He flipped to a blank page in his notepad and asked, "You know his name?"

"People called him 'Jorge,'" Sam replied. "Don't think I ever heard his last name. Guys up at the cantina north of here can tell you."

"Maybe they can, Sam, but they haven't so far. I showed the picture around up there and got *nada*."

Sam nodded. "Yeah, well, they know him. Let me tell you about this guy, Captain." He put the glass down on the bar and placed the cloth beside it. "He was one of eight who stopped in not long after I bought this place with a proposition for me. I've got eight guest rooms here. They wanted me to rent them all eight rooms for at least ten weeks out of the year, wanted me to guarantee that the rooms would be available on a week's notice."

"Why'd you turn them down? You that busy?"

"No, I'd have probably doubled my income by taking the deal. But there were three reasons I wouldn't do it. One was that I always want to have rooms for my botanist pals when they come down. I enjoy their company.

What they do is really interesting stuff, and it's probably important science too. Second, I don't favor knowingly climbing in bed with rattlesnakes. I don't want anything to do with their business. Third, I just plain don't like these sonsabitches. Can't say I'm sorry he's dead. I'm sure not surprised."

Jerry was scribbling in his notepad. "What business, Sam? Was he smuggling drugs?"

Sam picked up the cloth and the glass once again. He held the glass up to the light and looked at it. Jerry thought the damned thing probably had a hole worn in it by now from so much rubbing. But Sam apparently found a spot, and he began his polishing again. "Nope, not drugs. Well, probably drugs, too, Captain. I mean, he and his cohorts are scum. They'd sell their sisters if they got a profit. So, I guess yeah, they probably sold drugs, too. But that was not their primary business, from what I saw around here."

"If it wasn't drug smuggling, what was it?" Jerry asked.

"People smuggling," Sam replied, setting the immaculately polished glass down. "He was a coyote. That's what they call guys down here who smuggle illegals across the border into the States."

"Yeah, I know about coyotes," Jerry said, thinking about how this information might help explain Jorge's presence in Kendall County. The county had its share of illegal Mexicans working on construction crews, garbage details, and on ranches. They would all work for much less than minimum wage and be glad to get it. "These coyotes make much money for their work?"

Sam snorted. "Damned straight, Captain. A while back the mayor of a border town in Arizona was down here for an INS conference. He told me that people smuggling in his area is much bigger than drug smuggling—and more profitable. In the first place, if the coyotes get caught smuggling their cargo across the border, they just blend in with the crowd. Then all the border patrol officers do is send them back across the border. With drugs, the cops confiscate the product and imprison the traffickers. With people, the cops return the product *and* the traffickers. Then they just start all over. I don't see much evidence of drugs going across the border around here anymore. People smuggling is damned profitable, and the penalties if they get caught are minimal."

"You have any idea how much each illegal pays a coyote for his services?" Jerry asked.

"Depends on where they come from and where they want to go," Sam said. "See, the way this works is that some of the coyotes are what they call *polleros*."

"Whoa," said Jerry. "That's a new one on me. *Pollero* means something like 'chicken farmer.'"

"Yeah, maybe 'chicken wrangler' is a better translation for what they do. These *polleros* recruit clients all over Mexico and South America—like rounding up chickens and herding them north to the border. The farther the *polleros* have to herd the chickens, the more the coyotes charge per head. Some of the illegals from South America pay as much as ten thousand, but three thousand is as little as I've ever heard of anyone's paying."

Jerry whistled in surprise. "So, was Jorge a *pollero?*"

"No," said Sam, "Jorge was a scout. He had a team of *polleros*, *brincadores*, and scouts working with him. They all worked for a honcho coyote.

Jerry shook his head again. "*Brincadores?*" he asked.

"'Fence-hoppers,'" Sam said, amused. "When the *polleros* bring their chickens into this area, they put them in some corrals. Did you see those outbuildings back of the cantina up the road?"

Jerry nodded.

"When the *polleros* bring their chickens up here, they put them into one or another of those barns, depending on where the chickens want to go in the States. Then the *brincadores*, who are specialists in knowing where and when to cross the border, lead a flock of chickens across the border."

"Do the *polleros* help smuggle them across?" Jerry asked.

Sam shook his head. "Naw, that's not their specialty. After they herd their flocks up here and into the corrals, they go on back to their areas to round up more chickens and sign them to contracts. The *brincadores* and the scouts are responsible for getting the clients across."

"Doesn't the Mexican government interdict the chickens coming north?" Jerry asked.

"*Hell* no!" Sam said. "In the first place, the Mexican government doesn't consider people crossing into the States illegal. I've heard the *federales* argue that the coyotes are providing a valuable service. They say that the aliens are going to cross anyway, and they might get hurt or killed if they didn't have a professional coyote to help them out. 'Course, they never mention the times when the coyotes abandon the chickens when things go wrong or how many illegals die when they're left locked up in trucks. Second, there's too damned much money involved. The *polleros* never get into any trouble a small bribe can't get them out of. I've even heard of *polleros* raping and murdering their

130

chickens without consequence. There's *beaucoup* money involved here."

Jerry smiled. Different era. He would have said, "*Tak'san* money." He asked, "Don't the U. S. border guards give them trouble?"

Sam shook his head. "They try, but they obviously don't catch many. They tell me that about a million and a half illegals enter the U. S. each year. Anyway, there's a dozen or more places within walking distance of the cantina where you can cross the river on foot into Texas, places in the canyons so hidden that you'd have to be watching that particular crossing to catch them. And the *brincadores* know all these places. Their scouts are out ahead of them telling them which crossings are safe. What's weird is that the more pressure the U. S. border guards put on illegals, the more need there is for coyotes to get them across safely."

"Ironic," said Jerry.

"If you say so, Captain."

"Okay, Sam, when the coyotes get their clients across the border, what then?"

"They take them to trucks or vans, depending on how many they have scheduled for a certain location. Usually one or two other members of the coyote team will go with the honcho coyote, usually scouts. I understand that when they cross here, they have to walk maybe twenty miles to meet the trucks. Then they haul the chickens to relocation centers—like, they send them to safe houses throughout the U. S. until they can get them to their final destinations—usually get them to a sponsor or family member who's already in the States. 'Lotta times some builder or rancher will contract with a coyote to deliver a certain number of illegals. And, of course, the coyotes hold the chickens until they make the final payment to the coyote. The illegals are held hostage until they pay. Then the coyotes come back to Mexico and start all over."

"Sam, isn't 'honcho' a Japanese word? Why is a Mexican coyote called 'honcho'?"

Sam dropped his head, shuffled his feet, and smiled. "Naw, Captain, that's just what I call him. It's what we called whoever was in charge of something in the Corps. I didn't know it was Japanese. Just means leader, so 'honcho coyote' sounded right to me."

Jerry nodded. Sounded right to him too. "Does it seem like to you, Sam, that there is some one person or group who controls all the people smuggling in this area?"

"You mean like are they controlled by the Mexican equivalent of the mob?"

Jerry nodded, his pen poised over his notepad.

"Naw, Captain, these guys are too damned independent. There are several honcho coyotes working in this area, and sometimes they get in fights among themselves. Jorge's honcho coyote once killed a *pollero* from another team who had tried to put his chickens in one of the barns he had already spoken for up at the cantina. Sometimes a *pollero* will try to steal chickens from another team, and that almost always leads to violence. Several times scouts from rival teams have gotten into it with each other when one of them picks out a safe crossing and another scout tries to run his chickens through there. And sometimes there'll be a group of OTM's—that's 'other than Mexicans'—will come through on their way north. I don't see any evidence that there's any mob coordination, no Mr. Big."

"Can you tell me who else worked on Jorge's team?"

Sam answered, "Not all of them. I probably never heard their names. His honcho coyote was a guy named Marco."

"You see him recently?"

"No. In fact, there has been no activity in this area for a week. That happens sometimes. If things get too hot, the coyotes just shift their activity to another area." Jerry was hurriedly taking notes, amazed at how much he had learned about something he thought he understood. "Sam, I owe you big time," he said, closing and pocketing his notepad. "I think I know pretty much what Jorge was doing in my county now. All I have to do is to figure out how it got him killed and who did it."

"Killing him was no great crime, Captain. As you Texans sometimes say, 'he needed killing.'"

"Maybe," said Jerry. "But it sets a bad tone for the county. Couple of other things, Sam. I'd like to have Jorge's full name, if I can get it. You say that skinny fellow up at the cantina knew him?"

"His name's José Galena. I don't know who owns the cantina—maybe José, maybe one of the honcho coyotes—but those outbuildings are used to warehouse the chickens when the *polleros* bring them in. So, José was the local agent for Jorge's team. He runs the cantina and warehouses."

"Any thoughts on how I can get him to tell me what I want to know?"

Sam smiled. "Easy, Captain. The guy's only tough when it's safe to be. About a month after I bought this place he tried to appropriate some booze from me when a bunch of the coyotes and their clients were there. Came swaggering in here with a mean look on his face demanding I give him several cases of hooch on credit. Well, hell, I wouldn't have *sold* him anything, much less advance him credit. He got a bit uppity, and I admit, Captain, I lost my patience with the fellow."

"Had to tune him up, Sam?"

"Yes, Sir, I did. Now, I'm a peaceable man under ordinary circumstances, but that man provoked me."

"Did *Señor* Galena understand your point?"

"Sir, *Señor* Galena is, as I say, a pussy. If you even indicate that you will be angry with him, he'll rat on his mother. He'd rat on his father, too, but I doubt he knows who that is. Hey! Tell you what." Sam pulled a pencil from behind his ear and wrote on a bar pad. "Give old José this note and then ask your questions."

Jerry took the note and looked at it. It said, "Tell Captain Valdez everything he wants to know or I'll come up there tonight and stomp your sorry ass into the ground." It was signed, "Gunnery Sergeant Alton, USMC."

Sam said, "You said you had a couple of things, Captain. What's the other?"

Jerry had to think for a moment. "Oh," he said after a moment, "actually two other things. One, may I buy you dinner tonight?"

Sam smiled, "Hell, I own the place. Let me buy you dinner. I've got a steak that is as tender as old Sam's heart. And I employ the very best cook in the whole state of Coahuila, Mexico. Me."

"The steak sounds wonderful, Sam, but I'm buying dinner for you and me. I hope you have a good bottle of Merlot to go with that steak. Or two bottles."

"Chilean okay?"

"Some of the best reds available," Jerry said. "And the second thing is, do you have a room available in the inn? I hope I don't have to sleep in the stable again this close to Christmas."

Chapter 27

Jerry had risen early on Sunday and had breakfast with Sam Alton before heading back to Boerne. The two men had felt an immediate affinity, a sense that had grown stronger with association. Both men had belonged to a military company, a unit that demanded devotion to certain inviolable rules. It was a community that tested people before they were admitted to membership, to make sure they could be trusted. Then you trusted them. Mr. Samuel Johnston Alton was a good member of the community. *Semper fidelis*: always faithful. And he was only marginally crazy, whereas most Marines were thoroughly and pridefully so. Jerry was happy to have met him.

Dinner had been great, and Sam's breakfast was even better. He had spooned chorizo and scrambled eggs on a large flour tortilla, melted several varieties of cheese on the eggs, and topped the dish with fresh salsa. With the eggs Sam served fresh biscuits with butter and honey. Jerry tried to limit himself to one cup of coffee, knowing that he had a long drive ahead of him. But he had four. *Good thing I'm not a woman*, he thought; *I'd be pregnant all the time. I'm just too easy.*

The night before, he had driven back to the cantina to visit with *Señor* José Galena. Sam was right. The guy was a pussy. Jerry had entered the cantina to be met with a scowl from Galena. Without a word, Jerry had handed the man Sam's note. The frown on Galena's forehead was replaced with sweat. With his hands shaking, he said, "*Si, Señor*, what is it you wish to know?"

Jerry now knew Nobody's name: Jorge Mendez. And he knew why he had probably been in Kendall County. He still did not know who killed him. But he had some leads to follow. José had also provided the last name of the honcho coyote: Marco Morales. He just had no idea where Morales was. Maybe dead too.

On Monday morning, Jerry was in the office early to catch up on what had been going on in the county and to begin tracking the path of Jorge Mendez. No sooner had he walked into his office, however, when Deputy Angie Wahlert appeared at his door with a newspaper in her hand. Jerry could tell that she was angry by her posture, almost defensive in her step and stance. Her face was clouded, unsmiling. She was small, unambiguously feminine, and soft in appearance. But Jerry knew he did not want this beautiful young woman angry at him.

"Sheriff," she said, holding the newspaper out with her right hand, her left hand upon her hip, "have you seen the editorial in this morning's paper?"

"Why, no, Angie, I haven't," he answered, reaching out for the paper. "I hardly ever read the paper on weekdays until after dinner. What's up?"

"Well," she said, giving him the paper and pivoting quickly, her nose held high, "I'm ashamed to admit I live in Kendall County." She stormed back down the hall.

Flounced, Jerry thought. He'd never seen Angie in such a mood. He did not know she could walk like that. She flounced. If he tried it, he'd break something.

He opened the *Boerne Bugle* to the editorial page and folded the paper back. On the left side of the page, he found a short article:

Protective Non-Custody

Kendall County does not have many serious crimes. We like it that way.

And when we have the rare serious crime, we expect our law-enforcement officers to solve crimes and punish the perpetrators—without regard to bias or prejudice.

But Kendall County Sheriff Jerry Valdez does not seem to share that view.

On Friday last, a citizen was murdered and his body left hidden in the wilderness of a canyon, as though he was a gut-shot deer. After a promise by the Sheriff's Department that they had suspects and that they would bring the murderer to a quick justice, the good citizens of this county still have no resolution.

Is it because the suspects are Mexicans and the sheriff is Mexican? Is the sheriff running a biased investigation?

From this desk, it looks like the age-old Mexican tradition of bribery of law-enforcement officials may have infected and destroyed justice in Kendall County.

Wake up, citizens of Kendall County. Demand a quick and sure justice.

When Jerry finished reading and looked up, he saw Archie Crane standing in the door to the office, smiling. "You have been libeled, Sir. I have drafted a plaintiff's petition." He waved a file folder at Jerry. "Shall I file it in the District Clerk's Office?"

"What the hell got into Kenny?" Jerry asked. Kenny Sellers was the long-time editor of the *Boerne Bugle*, one who usually wrote thoughtful, perceptive editorials on local and national issues.

"Couldn't have been Kenny," Archie said, walking in and taking a seat in a chair in front of Jerry's desk. "That insulting 'wake-up' cliché is something no good writer would ever use. And Kenny is a good writer."

"No one else could have gotten it in the paper. Kenny wouldn't give any of his reporters carte blanche on the editorial page."

"No one but Albert Lane," Archie replied, raising his eyebrows. "I guess the owner trumps the editor."

Jerry thought for a moment. "Sounds like Lane, doesn't it? But he usually stays away from running the paper, mainly because he isn't a journalist. He inherited the paper from his grandfather."

Archie nodded. "Yeah, but sometimes he meddles. Remember a couple of years ago he wrote that editorial favoring tearing down the Catholic cathedral and replacing it with a modern structure?"

Jerry smiled. "You'd think the backlash he got on that would have taught him to tend to his insurance business and leave running the newspaper to Kenny." Jerry pondered for a moment. "Wonder what's behind this editorial? Have you heard any great hullabaloo around about the murder or the investigation?"

"Nope," Archie responded. "'Course, people are talking about the murder. But I haven't heard anyone blaming anyone. I don't think a lynch mob is going to show up out at Harvey's to string up his ranch hands."

"That's what I thought," Jerry said. "But something is biting on somebody's butt." He shrugged. "File the suit, Arch. Name Lane personally. Even if he isn't the source, he's the owner. I want a retraction of the editorial and an apology. An even ten million ought to pay damages."

As Archie rose and walked to the door, Jerry said, "Oh, by the way, Anna Maria told me to ask if you and Jo Anne would like to come to dinner on Friday evening." Archie had been dating Jo Anne Matthews for over a year. In her early thirties, some ten years younger than Archie, she had been widowed five years ago when her husband, Timothy Matthews, died when the Army liaison aircraft he was piloting crashed in a vertical dive from two-thousand feet. Jo Anne had moved to Boerne to be near Timothy's parents and to teach first grade in the local school while Tim was in Army flight training in Alabama, and when he died she made Boerne her home. Jo Anne was a beautiful young woman, tall and shapely and blonde, but what was most attractive about her was her gentle good nature. Archie, Jerry often thought, was a fortunate young man.

Archie turned, his eyes staring down, not at Jerry. "I'd like to come to dinner, Jer, if I can come by myself."

Chapter 28

After calling Harvey Phelan to set up a time to interview the Mexican ranch hands, Jerry drove by his home to have lunch with his wife.

"Why can't Archie bring Jo Anne to dinner?" Anna Maria asked as she set a platter with two beef and cheese chalupas in front of him at the small glass-topped table in the garden room. "Are Archie and Jo Anne having a fight? Do you want a beer?"

"Nope, better not. I've got some sheriffing to do this afternoon. A beer'd put me to sleep. Iced tea?"

Anna Maria nodded and walked through the door into the kitchen. When she returned with a large glass of iced tea and put it on the multi-colored place mat in front of her husband, she asked again, "Are Archie and Jo Anne having a fight?"

With a mouth full of chalupa, Jerry mumbled, "Dunno. Din' ask."

With a frown on her face, Anna Maria sat down opposite her husband. "I just can't imagine Jo Anne doing anything serious enough to cause Archie to get angry. And I can't imagine Archie getting angry about anything except something serious."

Jerry shrugged. "Only half a lemon?"

"It's all we had, Jerry. Get some on your way home tonight, okay?"

Jerry nodded, his mouth full of the last of the second chalupa.

"I'm going to call Jo Anne," she said, having made up her mind.

"And say what?" Jerry asked, wiping the tortilla crumbs from his mouth.

Anna Maria looked surprised. "Why, I'm going to ask what's wrong."

Jerry got up, kissed his wonderful wife just at the edge of her left eye and said, "'Bye, dear."

As he walked out, Anna Maria shouted at him, "And tell Archie that of course we want him for dinner on Friday."

At the Phelan ranch, Harvey had told his hired hands to stay around their house. When Jerry and the rancher knocked at the door, Eduardo answered the door, dipping his head deferentially to Jerry.

"I need to talk to you and the others," Jerry said. "May I come in, or do you want to meet me under yonder live oak?" he asked, pointing at a large tree in the front yard.

Eduardo backed away and swung the door open wide, gesturing for the two men to come in, then motioning them to come into the dining room, where Jerry saw the three other men finishing up their lunch—something wrapped in large flour tortillas. The men stood as Jerry entered, worried expressions on their faces.

Jerry waved them back into their chairs, but they stood until Jerry and Harvey sat. Jerry pointed at each of the men in turn: "Miguel, Victor, Juan, Eduardo?"

The men smiled and nodded their heads.

Jerry pulled the drawing of the dead man out of his pocket and passed it to the men sitting across the table from him. Eduardo took it, glanced at it, and looked up questioningly. "I need you to look at this picture again, please. His name is Jorge Mendez. He was a coyote."

The men looked back at the picture, examined it carefully, and looked up at Jerry as they shrugged.

"Did you men use a coyote to get across the border?" Jerry asked.

The men were obviously uncomfortable. They were in the county illegally, and they were faced with the law asking them questions that could get them deported. Jerry noticed the anxiety and said, "Look, guys, I'm not the INS; I'm not going to send you back to Mexico. As long as you don't break any laws, you have nothing to worry about from me."

The four men looked over at Harvey Phelan. The rancher said, "You can trust him, boys. Just tell him what he wants to know. You'll be okay."

Eduardo, the oldest of the men, and obviously the leader, shifted in his chair, handed the drawing back to Jerry, and said, "*Señor*, we don' know this man. My friends and I, we din' use no coyote. We come across the border many times. We don' need no coyote."

Jerry took the drawing and thought for a moment. "How about the two women? Did they pay a coyote to get across the border?"

Young Miguel and Victor looked even more uncomfortable and looked pleadingly at Eduardo. The older man shrugged and said, "*Digale lo que él desea saber.* Tell him what he wants to know."

Miguel dropped his eyes and nodded his head.

"I need to talk to the two women," Jerry said.

The men sat motionless, their eyes fixed on the tabletop.

"Miguel, Victor, NOW," Jerry barked.

Startled into action, the two younger men jumped up and left the room. The women must have been just in the next room, the kitchen, for Jerry heard the muffled whisperings of the two men and the high-pitched protests of the two women. The men prevailed, however, and in less than a minute the two men ushered the women into the room. Jerry stood when they entered and motioned for them to sit. The two younger men, having no chairs, stood along the wall behind the women. The women glanced nervously behind them from time to time, uncomfortable having to face the sheriff without their husbands to shield them.

Jerry took his seat and began by apologizing to the young women for interrupting their day. But, he told them, he needed to ask them some very important questions. He tried to speak to them in English, but it was immediately obvious that they had absolutely no understanding.

"Ladies," he said in Spanish, "I need for you to look at this picture and tell me if you know the man."

The two women did not look at Jerry, but one of them took the drawing when it was pushed across the table and positioned it so that both she and her companion could see it. The women's eyes grew big when they looked at the drawing. They looked up at Jerry and then back down at the drawing.

"Do you recognize this man?" Jerry asked.

Both women nodded.

"By what name do you know him?"

After a moment's hesitation, the braver of the two women, muttered, "*Señor* Mendez. Jorge Mendez."

"What is your name, *Señora?*"

"Merita, *Señor*. I am the wife of Miguel."

"Was the man one of the coyotes who got you across the border?"

Both women nodded.

"Was he the honcho coyote?" He hoped she would understand "honcho." She did.

Merita answered: "No *Señor*. He was a scout. He take good care of us."

Jerry knew he was a scout, but he was surprised that the women thought well of Jorge.

"Who was the honcho coyote?"

Merita responded, "*Señor* Marco Morales. He is not a good man."

"Tell me how you got here, to this ranch."

The two women looked at each other with confusion. Merita said, "*Señor*, we came to be with our husbands."

"I'm very sorry, *Señora* Merita, I did not make my question clear. Tell me, please, the route you took to get to this ranch. Where did the *polleros* pick you up, where did you cross the border, how did they transport you to this ranch?"

Merita nodded her understanding and told Jerry that she had arranged in Monterrey, Mexico, with a *pollero* to be taken across the border. The price was three thousand dollars, with one half due before they left Monterrey and the other upon delivery to the ranch. Along with twenty-three others, she was taken in the back of an open truck to the area near Boquillas del Carmen, where Jerry had visited. After staying in the holding sheds for two days, a group of twenty bound for Kendall County was led at night up the canyon, across the Rio Grande, and into Texas. After walking most of the night, led by the honcho coyote, the *brincadores*, and two scouts, the illegals were loaded into a box truck and taken along bumpy back roads to a safe house near Boerne. The honcho coyote phoned Harvey Phelan, who told Morales that the rest of his fee was ready for him. Jorge Mendez had brought the two women at night out to Phelan's ranch, where Miguel and Victor had paid fifteen hundred each to the coyote.

Jerry looked at the two younger men. "So you saw this Jorge Mendez when you gave him the money? Why did you tell me you didn't recognize his picture?"

The men both had frightened expressions on their faces. "*Señor*," responded Miguel, "it was dark when the man brought my wife and the wife of Victor to the ranch. We gave him money and he left. He never got out of the truck. We did not see him well."

The answer sounded plausible to Jerry. "Okay," he said to Miguel, and then, "*Señora* Merita, tell me where is this house where you were kept?"

The young woman spread her hands in confusion. She said, "*Señor*, I do not know. It was night when we arrived and night when we left. And we were not allowed to leave the house while we were there."

Jerry was disappointed, but he told himself he should have known better.

"Okay," he said, "were all the others in your group taken away from the house when you were?"

"No, *Señor*," Merita said. "We were the first. The others had to wait until they paid their fees."

Jerry thought for a moment. "How many in your group were women?"

Merita said, "Only two men, *Señor*. All the rest were women."

That would be eighteen out of the twenty. With Merita and Victor's wife free, that would leave sixteen women.

"How many *young* women?" Jerry asked.

Merita thought. "All women about our age. Two were younger, maybe fourteen."

"Did the honcho coyote tell them how they were going to have to pay the rest of their fees?"

"*Si, Señor*," Merita said abruptly, some anger showing. "He said they have to steal or whore if their sponsors did not pay. Rosita and I," she said, nodding toward the other woman, "we ask *Señor* Mendez if the other women have to whore, but he say he would protect them until their sponsors pay the rest of their fee. Or, he say, they could be released and work out a payment schedule."

Yeah, right, thought Jerry. He'd bet a bundle he'd found Glad Ass's whores. "Okay, *Señora* Merita," Jerry said, "tell me everything you can about the safe house where you were kept until you were brought here."

With careful suggesting, nudging, and urging, the young women were able to come up with some information about the safe house. It was in a rural area about a half-hour drive from Harvey Phelan's place. But which direction, they had no idea. The house itself was set back and slightly down hill from a dirt road. Along the road had been bushes and briars so thick that the house could not be seen from the road. Merita had noticed a metal sign lying on the ground beside the drive leading into the property, but she had no idea what it said. The house had one bathroom inside the house, and water was pumped into the house. She thought the water came from a shallow well. When she turned the water on to wash her hands, she heard an electric motor switch on, and off when she turned the water off. And the water was hard, full of minerals. Out back of the house was a dilapidated barn, where the coyotes kept the box truck. A smaller truck, a pickup, was also kept in the barn. Merita and Rosita, they told him, had been brought to Phelan's ranch in the pickup.

Jerry thanked the women, nodded his thanks to the men, and left the Phelan ranch to get on with their business, while he drove back to his office.

Chapter 29

Monday afternoon was pretty well spent by the time Jerry got back to his office. Angie Wahlert was still miffed at the editorial, but she was somewhat mollified after she learned that Archie had delivered the legal petition to the District Clerk's office. Jerry had stopped by the office of Boerne Real Estate. Joshua Kunkel, the broker, had lived in Kendall County all his life and had probably walked over each square inch of the land at some time or another. He listened to the details the women had given Jerry, made notes, and promised to consider likely sites.

Angie handed Jerry a "while-you-were-out" phone memo as he walked back to his office. It read, "McGarrett. Please call." And a phone number. McGarrett was FBI Special Agent Walt McGarrett, who was assigned to the San Antonio office. Jerry had worked with McGarrett on several cases in the past three years and had found him to be friendly, honest, and not afflicted with the hubris that he had seen in other federal agents. McGarrett had been especially helpful in bringing to justice the drug dealers responsible for the murder of Deputy Jesse Mueller almost a year earlier.

"Hey, Jerry, thanks for returning my call," McGarrett said, when Jerry had identified himself. "Um, Jerry, your Deputy Wahlert faxed a missing-person inquiry to our office last week."

"Yeah, Walt, we had an unidentified body over here and we were covering the usual bases."

"Tell me what you know about your John Doe."

"Nobody," Jerry corrected.

"I beg pardon?" McGarrett asked.

"We called him Nobody, since nobody knew his name."

"You run a weird shop over there, Jerry. Okay, tell me what you know about Nobody."

"Well, he's not Nobody any more. Turns out he was a coyote, one of those guys who runs illegals across the border from Mexico."

There was a moment's silence. Jerry asked, "You there, Walt?"

"Yeah, I'm here," McGarrett said. "Can you tie the body directly to the coyotes?"

"I can," Jerry said, puzzled. "I traced him back to Mexico, the state of Coahuila. He worked with a coyote outfit running illegals across the border in the Boquillas Canyon area."

"You got evidence you consider conclusive?"

"Yeah, I do, Walt. Way I found the area is that the guy's pants had some botanical residue in the cuff. Some really bright botanists were able to isolate the plant to that one canyon in Mexico. It grows nowhere else."

"That sounds incredible, Jerry."

"Did to me, too. But I drove over to that area where these guys said the tree grows—it's a hawthorn, by the way—and found some reliable witnesses who recognized the drawing of the victim."

"And these witnesses identified the victim a member of the coyote team?"

"Definitely, Walt."

"Did they know what part of the team he was? —I'm asking that badly, Jerry. It is our understanding that different members of the team have different duties. Did your witnesses know what duties your victim had?"

"Yeah, he was a scout. They even knew his name. He was Jorge Mendez."

McGarrett sighed audibly. "Not exactly, Jerry. When we received the inquiry from your office, we didn't know our guy was missing. He was an INS agent working undercover. Our office has been involved in a cooperative undercover operation with INS to try to stop the bigger of the coyote groups. We call the operation 'Rio Stop.' This man, who was working under the name of Jorge Mendez, was an INS agent working out of our office. He was building a case against a people-smuggling group run by a Mexican mob family named Morales, working out of Monterrey. This particular cell was run by the oldest son, Marco Morales."

"Yeah, that's the name I got from two different sources," Jerry offered. "Morales was the honcho coyote."

"We had things pretty well set, both here and in Mexico, to shut this operation down. Our man had checked in when they had a truckload of illegals on this side of the border. He was to check in again when they got them to the safe house, but we never heard from him again. When your office made the missing-person inquiry, we didn't know the INS guy was missing. Now we do, and the drawing looks like him."

"Is him, Walt. I've had several people identify him as Jorge Mendez."

"I'll need to get access to the body for a DNA test. Will you call your medical examiner and clear that for me?"

"Sure, Walt."

"Know who killed him?" McGarrett asked.

"Still working on that, Walt. Can you give us any information on that?"

"No, Jerry, he was undercover and on his own most of the time. I can only speculate that someone found out he was an agent and killed him for all the obvious reasons."

"Do you know where the safe house is they were taking the illegals?"

"No idea, Jerry. The INS had an assault team available waiting for their guy to give us the word. A couple of our agents were set to go with them. Needless to say, we never heard from our undercover."

"If his name was not Jorge Mendez, Walt, what was his name?"

"Um, I guess I never knew, Jerry. I know it wasn't Jorge Mendez. We always used his undercover name. Anyway, can I come over tomorrow with the lead INS guy to liaise with you on the murder?"

"Sure, Walt. Anytime. Just let Angie know when you'll be here and I'll make sure to be around. I'm working on finding the location of the safe house. Maybe that'll lead to something, though at the moment I have no idea what."

"Thanks, Jerry. I'll let Angie know."

"Okay, Walt. And, Walt, I'm sorry as hell about the agent. Please pass my condolences along to the INS people."

"Thanks, Jerry. Will do. See you tomorrow."

"Whoa, Walt, you still there?"

"Yeah."

"Um, Walt, along with the botanical stuff I found in the clothes on the body was a Las Vegas token. It was stuck in his cuff. Can you tell me anything about it?"

"Not a thing, Jerry. I'll check around. See you tomorrow."

Archie was obviously hovering outside Jerry's office for his friend to get off the phone. As soon as Jerry hung up the phone, Archie entered.

"Hey, Jer, I filed the petition this afternoon. They'll have a constable serve Lane with a citation and a copy of the petition. My guess is that we'll hear from him soon."

"Thanks, Arch. We'll probably catch hell for having you act as my lawyer, since by law you work for me. But what the hey, let them yell. By the by, old buddy, I think I stumbled upon the answer to the mystery of the missing prostitutes."

Archie raised his eyebrows. "Did you for a fact? You want to be careful stumbling upon prostitutes. Anna Maria will have you stumbling for right certain."

"I didn't stumble across prostitutes, dummy. I stumbled across the answer to who they were. But speaking of Anna Maria and such, she told me to tell you dinner on Friday at six, with or without Jo Anne. And then she told me to ask if you are having a fight with Jo Anne. She also said she was calling Jo Anne. So you might as well tell her what's wrong. Anna Maria is not patient not knowing things."

Archie looked pained and diverted his gaze. "Well, Jer, I wish I could tell Anna Maria what's wrong. I don't rightly know. Jo Anne treats me, well, like a brother."

Jerry looked surprised. "That's it? What's wrong with her treating you like a brother?"

"Anna Maria treat you like a brother?"

"Sometimes, yeah."

"Jo Anne treats me like a brother all the time."

"Oh. Why?"

Archie shrugged. "I have no clue. God knows I've made my intentions clear to her. Her response is kind, sweet, gentle, loving, and unyielding. First base is ever and always the extent of my progress."

Jerry was astonished. Both Jo Anne and Archie were normal, seemingly healthy, handsome heterosexual adults. Any definition of normal would have put them in bed together no later than the second date. "First base?" Jerry asked.

"And that on a walk. The bat was never in play."

"Damn," Jerry said, otherwise speechless.

"Something too much of this," said Archie, changing the subject. "Let me tell you about Glad Ass. I thought her reaction to the reported sightings of prostitutes was more than a little strange, so I thought I'd check up on her comings and goings, so to speak, when she left the county to go to New York.

You know, by the way, how many sheriff's offices there are in the city of New York?"

Jerry thought a moment. "No, can't say I do."

"Five. One for each of the five boroughs, or counties, that make up the city. Anyway, I called all of those offices and asked them to run Glad Ass's record through their files. I got a fax from the Manhattan Sheriff's Department. They had a file on her. She was arrested one time on charges of solicitation."

"Our Glad Ass a prostitute?" Jerry said, stunned.

"Yep. I talked to the detective who handled her arrest. He said she, and about a million young women like her, came to the big city to become big stars on the stage. After a few minor jobs in the chorus of off-off-Broadway shows, she ran out of money and prospects. She evidently didn't want to come back to Solace a failure. She worked in various restaurants and bars while she auditioned for every show in town, but that income didn't pay for her apartment. She didn't have an agent up there; the detective told me that there are so many wannabes trying to break into the arts that no matter how good you may be, you've got to be or do something spectacular even to get an agent. So Glad Ass was hustled by a pimp who told her he was an agent. He suggested that she take one trick to pay her rent, and then she was hooked. After her arrest, she climbed on a bus and came back to Solace. The detective who worked her case said she was just a good girl who stumbled into a bad life. He said she hated her life and hated herself for living that life. I told him about her crusade against prostitutes down here, and he said he'd seen that behavior dozens of time. The guy was really bright, Jer. I invited him to come to work with us. I don't think he's ready for life in the slow lane, though."

"Too bad. Sounds like a perceptive fellow." A thought struck Jerry suddenly. "Arch, we know now that prostitution and the murder are somehow connected. You don't suppose that Gladys was angry enough at the coyotes for forcing these girls to prostitute themselves that she killed him?"

Archie smiled faintly. "Not hardly, Jer. Our Glad Ass is a pain, and she may have once violated her moral principles by renting out her body. But can you imagine her shooting someone in the back of the head? Twice? Or cutting off his hands?"

Jerry shook his head. "No. You're right. Not Glad Ass. Why don't you call and tell her that the rush of prostitution was caused by some coyotes forcing young illegals from Mexico to sell themselves to pay off the debts they owed to the smugglers who brought them across the border. Tell her that we're working on making sure that nothing like that happens again. Anyway, tell her the girls were innocents, being forced to sell themselves."

"Yeah, I will. We need to go over and make nice to Glad Ass. In a way, she was also forced to sell herself. And she's hated herself for it. 'Course, I'll shred the file I got from NYC. At least now we know what got her so damned involved in all this."

"Yeah, good," Jerry agreed. "Turns out, by the way, Nobody appears to have been an INS agent working undercover with the FBI. Walt McGarrett is coming over tomorrow to talk with me about the case."

"Oh, damn. I'm sorry to hear that. We any closer to knowing who killed him?"

"I can't tell for sure. Closer, yes; but close, no. Walt McGarrett speculates that the coyotes found out somehow that the guy was a fed and killed him. I'm trying to find the safe house where the coyotes held the illegals. Maybe that'll tell us something. Maybe not. How about you? Anything more from the sexual harassment case?"

"Yeah, when I threatened to bring Miz LaDeaux's lawyer up on charges for filing a nuisance suit, she vanished like a trailer house in a tornado. She's withdrawn the suit. When I called her office to confirm, a secretary told me that Miz Enright is no longer Miz LaDeaux's attorney. So that's done with."

"Good. Enright showed good sense. So, with the sexual harassment issue and the prostitute scandal over, you're relatively freed up."

"Yep."

"Okay, take some time off and get this thing straight between you and Jo Anne."

The smile on Archie's face was only partially mirthful. "'Tain't funny, McGee."

Chapter 30

The realtor had called Jerry on Monday night to give him eight pieces of rural property in the county that might meet the description Merita and Rosita had given him. Jerry was up early on Tuesday morning and in his office before seven to plan his exploration. He had three of the locations on a list marked "C" to look at last, if need be. These places were occupied by their owners, all long-time residents of the county. Two other properties he put on a "B" list, a secondary file. These places were owned by individuals who lived out of county and used on an irregular basis. The three properties on his "A" list were unoccupied and for sale. Jerry remembered that Merita had noticed a metal sign lying on the ground near the front of the property, and he was assuming that it might be a "for sale" sign. Josh Kunkel had warned Jerry that the list was old and suggested that he check with the original listing agents.

As he walked to the lobby to check the properties against the large map of the county framed on the wall behind the lobby counter, Jerry noticed Dorie LaDeaux walk through the door into the deputies' locker room.

"She asked if she could go in to clear out her locker, Sheriff," Deputy Miriam Smith said. "Angie don't come in 'til about eight, and I din't think it was important enough to call her. Or you. I hope it's okay."

"Sure it is, Miriam," Jerry responded. "How is Miz LaDeaux?"

"Real down in the face, Sheriff," she responded.

Jerry nodded and turned to the map. After he had located the properties and numbered them on his list in geographic order, he waited around a moment for the young woman to finish up in the locker room. When she came out, he saw that she was wearing jeans and a plain white T-shirt. No aphorisms or mottos in defiance of anything.

When she noticed Jerry behind the counter, she stopped, blushed, and lowered her eyes. Hesitatingly, she walked the few feet to the counter and, with her eyes still diverted, said quietly, "I asked Miriam if it would be all right for me to clean out my locker, Sheriff Valdez. I tried to come in early so I wouldn't bother no one."

"No problem, Miz LaDeaux," Jerry replied. "You find all your stuff okay?"

"Yes, Sir, thank you."

Jerry looked at the young woman for a moment with compassion. She looked up briefly to glance at him and gave him the hint of a pained smile. "Well, Sheriff, I'll just be going...."

"You got a minute right now, Miz LaDeaux?" he asked.

She looked up at him fully now, her expression frightened. "Uh, Sheriff, I dropped all the, uh, complaints, everything. Oh, God!" She dropped the bag she was carrying and covered her face with her hands as large tears come to her eyes. "I'm sorry, Sheriff," she said through her sobs. "I never wanted to...God...I'm sorry, Sheriff."

Jerry walked around the counter to the young woman. He picked up her carryall and said, "If you have time, come back to my office for a minute, please." His first impulse was to put his arm around her shoulders protectively as she cried, but he knew, sadly, that these chaotic times put bars between what should be and what might be. Trying to perform a good deed in a naughty world could get a man sued. Carrying the young woman's bag, he walked back to his office with her following.

Jerry motioned her to a chair in front of his desk rather than to the sitting area in his office. He left the door open, knowing that Miriam would eavesdrop for all her ears could hear, and walked around behind his desk to sit down. Dorie LaDeaux had controlled her sobbing and was drying her eyes and face with a shredded tissue.

"Miz LaDeaux," Jerry began, "I hope you understand my response to you during the recent unpleasantries. I had no intentions to do you any harm or to be unkind to you."

The young woman was shaking her head sadly. "No, no, Sheriff," she interrupted. "God, the way I acted, you had every right to hate me." She shook her head again and looked off to the side, as though looking for some oracle to give her an answer. "I did everything wrong." She looked back at

Jerry. "All I ever wanted to do was be a good deputy. When I got that job, I felt like a success in life. It's what I had always wanted. My ma and pa always told me I wouldn't never amount to anything. But then I got to be a deputy, and it was what I wanted in life, all I ever wanted." Tears started again, but with determination she forced herself to control her emotions. "I screwn it up big time, Sheriff, and I apologize. God, I'm really sorry to have caused so much trouble, Sheriff." This time she could not stop the tears.

Jerry never knew what to do when an unfamiliar adult female cried in his presence. When his young daughter cried, he would pick her up, dry her eyes, sooth her. On the rare occasions when his wife cried, he would embrace her, stroke her hair, comfort her, tell her he loved her. But with Dorie LaDeaux, he was helpless. He turned around to grab a box of tissue off the credenza behind his desk and put the box on his desk where she might reach it. If she wanted to.

She did.

"Um, Miz LaDeaux, again I am sorry for your unhappiness; and I want you to know that neither I nor anyone in this department wanted to hurt you. It's just that in our jobs we have to be sort of a family, we have to be able to work together with as much real concern for the welfare of each other and as little friction as possible. Now, when you decided to file suit, that was not, in my estimation, what one family member does to another."

The young woman was nodding her head at every remark. "I know, Sheriff, I really do. It's just that I never had a family like that before. I've had to fight my brothers and my pa all my life. My ma was, well she still is, scared, sorta chicken-like. I swore I would never be like her. But you and Avon and Archie and the others, you warn't like that. You all supported me in almost everything. Then I just pushed too far and lost everything. I'm really sorry, Sheriff." She slumped in the chair, weak, tired from emotion.

"And those sayings or quotations you've been wearing on your shirts, Miz LaDeaux." Ever since that Larry McMurtry novel that had all the white trash wearing shirts with cutesy sayings on them came out, the wannabe chics around the county had taken up the fad, had worn their clichés on their chests. Jerry generally liked McMurtry's novels, had met the fellow Texan and mostly liked him. He usually told a good story and told it well. But Jerry never finished any of the novels about the dissipated recent rich characters McMurtry wrote about in some of his novels. Wasn't enough about them, good or bad, to keep the mind alive. Dorie's inane shirt mutterings were in the same category.

"I never said anything to you, because you have every right to broadcast those views if you choose to do so. But I believe when you wear sayings on shirts like, 'Men have only two problems: Everything they think & Everything they do,' well, that's really offensive, Miz LaDeaux, and it's just plain stupid. Or you had another shirt that said, 'Do Not Start With Me. You Will Not Win.' Now, that attitude carried over into your work. Your last two efficiency reports had been unsatisfactory, and frankly your behavior toward Deputy Carroll and me did not promise improvement. You cannot browbeat everyone you come into contact with, Miz LaDeaux, not the suspects, nor the citizens, nor your colleagues in the department. And that's what you have been doing."

The young woman toyed with the tissue, alternately pulling it apart and balling it together. With an audible sigh, she said, "God, I know, Sheriff. I became everything I hated about my family. I just wanted…well, hell, I just screwn it all up." As she slowly and resignedly began to stand, she said, "I'm really sorry, Sheriff. You took a chance with me, and I let you down."

Jerry replied, "Just a minute, please. Sit back down for a moment."

The young woman, cowed, as a child being reprimanded, returned to the chair and sat, ready to accept more censure.

Jerry turned to the credenza behind his desk, unlocked a drawer, and took out a large document envelope, which he put on his desk and re-locked the credenza drawer. "I'm going to invite you join our team, Miz LaDeaux, as a probationary deputy sheriff. If you accept, I will require you to serve a probationary period of six years, and you will be evaluated by a supervisor and the chief deputy and me every year, or more often if we deem it necessary."

The young woman looked at Jerry in shocked silence, her eyes wide, her mouth open. Then abruptly tears streamed from her eyes and her homely face contorted grotesquely as though in pain.

"May I take that as an affirmative answer?" Jerry asked, not really sure.

With flooding eyes still large and distorted mouth still open, seemingly using all her strength, she nodded.

"Okay," Jerry said, opening the envelope and removing her gun and badge and sliding them across the desk to her. Then he roared, "Angie, you out there yet?"

He heard Angie Wahlert giggle, and in a moment she appeared in his doorway, her right hand on her shapely hip. "You roared, Sir?"

Jerry smiled at the extraordinary young woman. "Angie, Deputy LaDeaux has agreed to rejoin the department as a probationary deputy. List her on the regular six-year track, and set up annual reviews. I want Deputy Patricia

Patton assigned as her first training officer. Make a note that I will reappoint her mentor every year. I want her to work with a variety of senior deputies."

Angie smiled broadly. "Sure thing, Sheriff. Welcome back, Deputy Dorie. We've missed you around here. Why don't you go on out and put your things back in your locker and then we'll get all the paperwork done. Okay?"

The deputy slowly rose to her feet and shifted her gaze from Angie to Jerry. She tried to give words to her emotions, her mouth working to frame proper language; but no sounds came. Instead, she walked around the desk and embraced Jerry, burying her face in his chest. This time, Jerry put his arms around his new deputy and held her close for a moment. Still unable to speak, looking first at him and then at the smiling Angie, she picked up her bag and walked tentatively out of the office and down the hall.

With a sparkle in her eyes, Angie walked around the desk and embraced Jerry, kissed him on his cheek, and said, "You're an old softie, Papa Bear."

Jerry pulled her close and said in his most severe voice, "If you and Miriam don't drop that 'Papa Bear' stuff, I'm going to spank both of you."

Angie squeezed him and kissed him again. "Yeah, you scare us to death. You are our Papa Bear." She moved away from him, walked to the door, and said, "And that's all there is to it." Then she was gone.

Jerry had to sit down quickly to keep from being embarrassed as Archie walked in. "Hired old Dorie back, did you?"

"Yep," Jerry said. "That okay with you?"

"Yeah, hell, I'm as big a wimp as you are. Papa Bear."

"You can kiss my Papa Bear butt," Jerry said, self-conscious.

"Yeah, well, I'll pass on that, thank you," Archie responded.

"You freed up right now, Arch?" Jerry asked.

"Yep."

"I gave old Josh Kunkel all of what those women out at Harv Phelan's could remember about the safe house, and I have a list of places he thought might be likely. How about going with me to scout them out?" He explained to his friend how he had classified the sites.

"Sure," Archie nodded. "Let me get my coat."

Angie Wahlert stopped Jerry on his way out of the office to tell him that Walt McGarrett had called and asked to meet him at two o'clock.

Chapter 31

Archie navigated while Jerry drove. One property mentioned by the realtor, the first on Jerry's geographically ordered list, was north and east of Boerne off of Highway 474, about twelve miles out of town. When they passed Ammon's Crossing, they turned left onto a dirt road, heading north as 474 bore slightly east. They drove down the dirt road for two miles to where Josh told them an unoccupied ranch was for sale. They easily found the realtor's sign near the entrance to the property. The metal gate across the dirt driveway was closed and padlocked, "Do Not Trespass" and "No Hunting" signs wired to the gate. Jerry and Archie climbed over the gate and walked the hundred yards to the house, a small, rectangular, mail-order type house. The doors, both front and back, were locked; but the windows bore no shades, blinds, or curtains to hinder a clear inspection of the interior. The house contained no furniture to hide the layer of dust on all the wooden floors. Dust also lay undisturbed on the countertop in the kitchen. A small pole shed occupied a patch of ground fifty feet behind the house, but spider webs decorated the opening, and weeds carpeted the earthen floor.

"No one has been here for months," Archie said, looking around at the rocky land.

To get to number two on the list, they had to go back through Boerne and drive southwest on Highway 46. About seven miles out of Boerne, near the county line where Bandera County takes over from Kendall, Archie directed Jerry to turn right on a winding dirt road tumbling over rough country. On the left two miles off Highway 46, Jerry slowed as he came to a driveway almost hidden by thick bushes that stretched for nearly a hundred yards along the road. "This it?" he asked.

"Dunno," said Archie. "Josh say it was for sale?"

"Yeah. Well, it was on an old list."

"I don't see a sign."

Jerry turned into the drive and stopped. The gate had a thick chain and padlock on it, but it was standing wide open. As Jerry opened the door and got out of his patrol car, he saw a sign, displaced and partially obscured by weeds. He quickly removed his Colt automatic pistol from his holster and looked to see if he could locate the house. He saw Archie striding openly through the gate. "Arch!" he called sharply. "Com'ere!"

Archie turned and moved quickly back toward the patrol car, looking quizzically at his friend. When he got close, Jerry said, "I believe this is the place where the coyotes held the illegals. Let's assume that they are still there and that a murderer is among them."

Archie moved off the drive and behind the shrubs as he pulled his Browning automatic from its holster and worked the slide to chamber a round. He and Jerry crept quietly to the edge of the shrub near the drive. Signaling Archie his intention, Jerry moved quickly across the drive to take a position behind the shrub on the other side. When he was in place, he chambered a round in his Colt. Then he and Archie peered around the hedges, guns ready, to inspect the house.

The house was about fifty yards behind the shrubs, downhill slightly from the county road. It appeared to be rather large, but in poor repair. It had once been painted white, but little of the paint remained clinging to the bare wood siding. A large branch from the huge elm tree in front of the house had broken and fallen onto the ridge of the roof, the ridge now sagging like a sway-backed nag. The two lawmen looked carefully and thoroughly at the house and what they could see of the surrounding land.

Jerry signaled his friend with his hands and got a nod from Archie. Crouching low, Jerry ran across the drive and took position behind the elm tree in front of the house. He brought his pistol to point at the house and peered carefully around the tree to get a closer look. Archie raised his pistol as his friend ran in front of him and lowered it to the ready position as soon as Jerry was past. When Jerry nodded to him, Archie dodged around the hedge and zigzagged his way to the corner of the house. He took cover where he could see both the front and the side of the house. After a moment, when he neither saw nor heard anything, he nodded to Jerry, who dashed to the other side of the house, where he stopped with his back against the house, his Colt ready. After a moment's careful attention, he dropped to his knees to look underneath the house. The beams of the house were almost two feet off the ground at the front of the sloping site, maybe three feet near the rear, resting on what appeared to be six by ten concrete piers imbedded into the ground. Debris littered the ground beneath the house, the broken and abandoned dreams of families who had tried to make the place a home. But among the pipes and broken utensils and toys and tools there were no coyotes poised to attack.

Catching Archie's eye, Jerry signaled his friend to watch the front while he circled the house to check the back. Archie nodded, and Jerry moved down the side of the house toward the back, looking into the two windows on that side, pausing at the edge of the house to listen before he moved around the corner to the back. Falling quietly to his stomach, he crawled forward until his pistol and his eyes could point around the corner. No one. He rose and walked down the back wall, looking into the windows and door. Thick curtains covered all the windows, and the glass in the rear door had been replaced with solid plywood. He noticed a dilapidated barn in back of the house, its sagging doors standing open. He could see nothing inside. As he moved around the house to join Archie near the front, he saw that the windows on that side of the house were also covered.

After a muted conversation with Archie, Jerry climbed up on the porch and moved quietly over to the front door. He waited for a moment to give Archie time to get into position in back, and then he summoned all his strength and kicked the door near the latch, shattering the frame and knocking the door twanging around on its hinges and into the wall inside.

"Police!" he shouted as he swept into the room, looking in as many places as he could at once, moving his Colt as though it were mechanically fixed to his eyes. He heard Archie crash through the rear door, heard him yell, "Police!"

"Clear in here Arch," Jerry said and moved to his right to check the rooms on that side of the house. He knew Archie would search the rooms on the other side. When Jerry reached the kitchen and saw the broken back door, he shouted, "Clear, Arch!" and got the same in response from Archie. They met in the front room before parting again to conduct thorough searches of each room.

The house had obviously been occupied recently. No canned food was in the kitchen, but several opened boxes and packages of food were still in the doorless cabinets, and spoiled milk and several unidentifiable foods remained in the refrigerator. No trash of any amount remained, however: a piece of gum wrapper here, a bit of chip package there. A search of the barn showed tracks from two different types of tires and several empty, plastic motor-oil containers.

Jerry and Archie stood in back of the house, hands on hips, looking around to see if they had missed anything; but neither could think of anything else to do. There probably had been coyotes there—and their chickens. But they were all gone, and no evidence presented itself to suggest that they would be back. Jerry gestured toward the car, and the two men walked around the house and to the patrol car.

When they reached the car, Jerry reached through the window to pull the radio microphone to him. He spoke with Miriam to ask her to send Deputies Hilton O'Brian and Barry Jordan out to lift whatever prints they could from the house. They probably would not come up with anything useful, but Jerry worked on the Lawrence Sanders' maxim that "One never knows, do one?"

"Want to check with the neighbors?" Archie asked.

Jerry looked around. "Nearest neighbor is ten miles away."

"Is that a 'no' then?"

Jerry shook his head. "You're getting as bad as Willie Ward," he said, opening the car door. But then he stepped over into the bar ditch to look at the sign, lifting it out of the weeds. "For Sale" in large, faded letters was written across the top of the rusting metal sign. Jerry brushed muck off the sign so that he might read more. "Bank Repossession," he read, "North Towne Bank and Trust, Boerne, Texas." He could make out a phone number, and he wrote it down in a spiral notebook from his shirt pocket.

On the way back to the office, Jerry and Archie discussed all the possibilities they could think of regarding the illegals that Merita and Rosita reported still at the safe house when they left. The two men hadn't gotten very far in their analysis when they stopped by the Boerne Burger Bar for a quick lunch. Archie used the Burger Bar's napkins to make his notes, while Jerry used a page from his notebook. When they had considered every possibility that came to mind, Jerry made a composite list, with the heading INPO:

"In No Particular Order."

Moved to another safe house.

Paid their fees and released to their sponsors.

Escaped

      a. Slipped away

b. Killed their guards
Returned to Mexico or otherwise left the county
Sold off as whores.
Killed en masse and buried.

After much debate, the two men decided they could ignore none of the possibilities, but some were more immediate than others. He would send Deputies Billy Joe Smith and Jesus C. Ortiz out to the safe house to look for fresh grave sites. Archie volunteered to write and distribute a directive to all deputies on patrol to visit businesses and ranches in their areas to see if any new illegals had shown up looking for work in the past few days, or if any illegals they had contracted for with the coyotes had been ransomed in the last few days. They would also double check the truck stops and rest areas along major highways to see if any evidence of recent itinerate prostitution could be found. Archie would also ask the patrol deputies to check on all known vacant houses in their areas to see if a flock of illegals were living there.

Those measures would cover most of the possibilities. If the illegals had left the county, either to return to Mexico or to look for work elsewhere, Jerry was not sure how he would proceed. If they were just innocent women and men caught up in a bad situation, then he would be satisfied to have them safely away from the coyotes.

But he still had to find out who killed Nobody. Or Jorge Mendez. No, Walt had said that was not his name, after all. Not Jorge. Not Nobody. Somebody.

Chapter 32

Special Agent Walter McGarrett provided some answers when he met Jerry in his office at two o'clock on Tuesday afternoon. The murdered INS agent's name was Santiago Madrazo.

"Are you sure?" Jerry asked.

"Yeah," McGarrett said, lifting his eyebrows in mild surprise. "Why wouldn't I be sure?"

Jerry waved off the concern, smiling. "No, Walt, it's just that for a long time, nobody knew his name. We even called him 'Nobody.' Then I thought I had identified him as a coyote scout named Jorge Mendez. Now I've got to get my mind attuned to calling him Santiago Madrazo. One more name change will overload the circuits and cause a short."

The FBI agent nodded thoughtfully. "His sisters called him Popo."

"I don't need to know that," Jerry responded quickly.

"And that Las Vegas token you asked about: his INS pals told me he always carried it with him as a good-luck piece. He won a few thousand in some game or other in Las Vegas at an INS convention. And he kept one of the tokens as a memento of his good luck."

"Some good-luck piece. I thought you were going to bring the INS with you today."

McGarrett shook his head. "Guy we're working with is Marvin Wells. He went down to the valley to be with Madrazo's family for a while. So," McGarrett continued, "where are you on nailing down what happened to our guy? Jerry, I don't have to tell you that the loss of one of their agents has the local INS guys really shook up. Everybody liked Madrazo. The bureau, too. We feel in large part responsible for him. We're of course conducting our own investigation, but if you find his killer first, I don't have to tell you we want him."

Jerry thought a moment. When a drug runner had gunned down his young deputy, Jesse Mueller, earlier in the year, Jerry had uttered almost the same words to McGarrett. And McGarrett had fought tough to make sure that Kendall County got justice. Now the shoe was on the other foot. "You'll get him, Walt," Jerry promised.

McGarrett just nodded. "Now, what have you got?"

Jerry went through every step of the investigation up to that point. He showed McGarrett the list of possibilities regarding the missing illegals and explained what he and Archie were doing to investigate the leads. McGarrett studied the list carefully and nodded, but offered no suggestions.

"You follow the Sir Arthur Conan Doyle investigative maxim, I suppose," McGarrett said in an attempt at a British accent. "'When you have eliminated the impossible, whatever remains, however improbable, must be the truth.'"

"Hey," said Jerry, "it works for Sherlock Holmes, it works for me."

"Excellent!" said McGarrett.

"Elementary," said Valdez.

"You got a line on the honcho coyote?" McGarrett asked.

"Marco Morales," Jerry offered. "No, we'll be looking around the county, but so far we have nothing on him. It's very possible he found out that Nobody, um, Madrazo was a plant and killed him himself. So, I'd like to find him. Would the bureau know if he turned up in Mexico?—in Monterrey, I believe you said he was from."

"Yeah, Monterrey," McGarrett agreed. "And yeah, his family is being watched…"

"'Is being watched?' Does that mean that it is not the FBI that is watching him?" Jerry asked.

"Well, yes and no," Walt responded with a grin. "Our surveillance techniques are so arcane that we have to have a powerful computer to follow the permutations. Reason I use the passive voice 'is being watched' is that describing exactly who is doing the watching is really Byzantine. Anyhoo, we'd probably know. His family is being watched, but they are pretty good at the shadow arts. We'll keep trying to find him, but for all we know, he's lying dead in some shallow grave in Kendall County right now."

"True," said Jerry. "Well, we still have a few leads. We'll chase them down and keep in touch with you."

"One other thing," the agent added. "We believe that there is someone local involved in this."

Jerry wrinkled his brow at McGarrett. "Who is 'we' and what do you mean 'involved'?"

"The 'we' is the INS and FBI agents involved in this 'Rio Stop' program, and we are pretty sure that some local manager arranges with ranches and businesses in the area to have a certain number of illegals brought in, bankrolls the whole system that brings them in and delivers them, and then launders the money."

"Why can't the coyotes do all that themselves? I thought that people smuggling was incredibly profitable."

"It is. But much of the money comes in only after delivery is made, and there are expenses prior to that. Somebody local needs to secure safe houses, pay for transportation, and such-like stuff. And the money paid by the illegals is almost always cash, and that has to be washed. When the INS catches a smuggling operation, the coyotes need to blend in with the chickens if they hope to be sent back without prosecution. They can't be carrying large sums of money with them. All our mock-ups of their activities suggest that someone local runs sort of an employment agency, putting prospective employers together with illegal workers, and handles the financing of the whole scheme, including laundering the cash."

One more thing for Jerry to worry about. "Anything else? You got a profile on the murderer?"

"We don't, Jerry. There's not really enough information in yet for us to have much of an idea. It was probably someone our guy knew. The perp would never have been able to get him in a position to shoot him in the back of the head unless our guy was either tied up or he knew his murderer. Now, I know that the hands had been severed from the corpse, but there were no other signs of his being bound, were there?"

"Couldn't really tell," Jerry said. "But I don't thinks so."

"We also don't think drugs are involved here. Madrazo had reported in when they had the illegals on this side of the border, and he had never said anything about drugs. And he would have."

"He ever said anything about sex, about prostitution?"

McGarrett looked him surprised. "No, why do you ask?"

"Seems the female illegals, girls, really, were forced by someone, the coyotes I guess, to prostitute themselves for a while."

McGarrett shook his head. "That's news to me. I read the transcript of Madrazo's telephone call. He said it was a straightforward chicken run into the county. The illegals were consigned to employers or to their families in the area. If any prostitution was planned, he wasn't aware of it."

"Okay, Walt. Let us know if you find anything. And by all means, if you have any suggestions, with all your high-powered brains and connections and technology, be sure to let me know."

"Yeah, smart ass. You're not going to let me forget about 9/11, are you?"

"Big sins cast long shadows," Jerry said philosophically.

"He that is without sin, let him cast a stone," said Walt smugly.

Jerry shook his head. "People who live in glass houses shouldn't throw stones."

"Sticks and stones may break my bones," Walt continued, "but words will never hurt me."

Jerry shrugged. "You buy land, you buy stones."

Walt laughed and got up to leave. "Okay, Jerry, I've gotta go. A rolling stone gathers no moss. Keep up the good work."

"A constant dripping of water wears away the hardest stone," Jerry said thoughtfully.

McGarrett groaned, waved, and walked out, saying, "Keep up the hard work."

Jerry walked to the door and yelled after the agent, "You cannot get blood from a stone, you know."

As he walked into the lobby, McGarrett said, "Fling but a stone, the giant dies," and left.

Jerry walked back into his office frowning. "I don't know that one," he said aloud. *Sounds biblical*, he thought, *but most things do*. While he was thinking about where he might look up that proverb, his phone buzzed on intercom.

Angie Wahlert said, "Sheriff Valdez, there are some men here asking to see you: Mr. Albert Lane and Mr. Kenny from the newspaper, and a Mr. Martin Golden, says he's a lawyer."

Jerry was surprised. "Did they have an appointment, Angie?"

"No, Sir. I asked them. They just showed up."

Jerry was sorely tempted to tell them to call and make an appointment and to stay away until they had done so. But such behavior would serve no purpose except to feed his desire for revenge—a craving Jerry worked hard to control. He and Archie had not planned on meeting the defendant so soon,

162

and they would not have chosen this location. But he and Archie had no need to plan strategy; their plan was uncomplicated. He wanted a retraction and an apology, and he wanted to approve the language. Newspaper people hated prior approval—"prior restraint" is what they called it. But it was either that or an even ten million. "Angie, hold on a second, please." He put the phone down and stepped around to Archie's office.

Archie looked up from a couple of reports coming in from patrol deputies in response to his directive. Jerry said, "Arch, Albert Lane and Kenny are here with a lawyer wanting to meet. Any reason we shouldn't meet with them now?"

Archie was caught unawares. "I didn't know we were scheduled to meet with them," he said.

"We weren't," Jerry responded. "They just showed up."

"Tell them to just go away," Archie said.

"I'm sorely tempted. But I was thinking, we need to get this behind us. Any good reason, other than the fact that Lane is a sonofabitch, that we shouldn't go ahead and meet with them?"

Archie thought a moment. "No," he said. "I guess now's as good a time as any."

Jerry walked back into his office followed by Archie. Into the phone, he said, "Angie, please ask the visitors to wait in the conference room." Then to Archie, "Any advice to me as my lawyer?"

"Yeah," Archie responded. "Don't kill Lane. Let me."

Jerry laughed, clapped his friend on the back, and followed him out of the room.

When they walked into the conference room, Jerry and Archie found the three men already seated, Albert Lane and Kenny Sellers on one side of the conference table and Martin Golden at the head of the table. They all stood and shook hands.

Archie and Jerry sat opposite the men from the newspaper, Jerry across from Lane and Archie across from Sellers. Golden took a seat back at the head of the table.

Jerry and Archie sat silent. No one said anything for a long moment. Then Golden laughed broadly and said, "Sheriff Valdez, we had asked to speak to you. May I ask who this is with you?"

Jerry remained silent. After a moment, Archie said, "I am Archie Crane, Sheriff Valdez's attorney."

Golden nodded knowingly, with a bit of a smirk on his face. "Am I correct in believing that you work for Sheriff Valdez, Mr. Crane?"

"I am the chief deputy sheriff of this county," Archie answered. "I am also a licensed attorney. And I am Mr. Valdez's attorney."

Golden grinned broadly, as though he had scored a point. "Let me ask again, for the record. Do you work for Sheriff Valdez?"

Archie repeated, "I am the chief deputy sheriff of this county."

"Well, you see," Golden began. But Jerry interrupted him.

"What record?" Jerry asked quietly.

"I beg pardon, Sheriff?" Golden asked, puzzled.

"You said you asked for the record. What record?" Jerry persisted.

"Well, Sheriff," Golden said, smiling largely and spreading his hands expansively, "it's just an expression."

"No," said Jerry. "In the law, 'for the record' is not 'just an expression.' It has legal meaning. If you intend to advertise a meeting on legal matters, use precise language."

Golden nodded without speaking and without smiling. He opened a folder lying on the table in front of him and withdrew a paper.

"One other thing, counselor," Jerry said. "Move over to the side of the table with your client."

Golden looked at Jerry with a puzzled expression on his face. He looked at Lane and then back at Jerry.

"You're not the chairman of the board here. Move over to the side of the table. Sit across from my attorney."

His face glowing red, Golden picked up the folder from the table, stood, and moved around to sit to the right of Albert Lane after Kenny Sellers moved down a chair. He glanced at his briefcase still resting on the floor at the head of the table but did not get up to retrieve it.

No one said anything for a while, Jerry and Archie sitting quietly and comfortably in their familiar room.

Golden fidgeted for a while, looking at Jerry and Archie to see if they were finished. When they remained mute, he spoke again. "Sheriff…"

Jerry held up his hand. "Please direct your comments to my attorney."

Golden sighed, shaking his head. But he shifted his gaze to Archie. "Deputy…."

Archie held up his hand. "Please refer to me as 'counselor' or 'Mr. Crane.' I am not acting here in my capacity as chief deputy."

Golden's face was growing dangerously red, and it took him a moment to calm himself enough to speak. "Very well, counselor," he said, emphasizing the word sarcastically, "I have before me a Plaintiff's Petition filed on behalf of your client alleging libel and naming my client as culpable." He looked up at Archie, who sat mute. Golden continued, "Now, counselor, I assume you are aware of first amendment rights and that my client, as owner of a major newspaper, has the right to speak and to write freely." He looked up at Archie again. When Archie said nothing, Golden shuffled through his papers and continued, "And I warn you, counselor, and warn your client, whether he wants me to or not, that not only can you not win this suit, but that both of you will be held accountable for your actions. Especially you, counselor. Filing frivolous lawsuits can bring you strong sanctions and maybe even disbarment. I warn you that if the suit is not dropped immediately, we will counter-sue for damages, and I will personally see that you are disbarred."

Archie had held his eyes fastened on Golden during the oration and for a while longer. After a few moments, Archie said, "You finished?"

"I am," replied Golden, folding his hands on the table before him.

Archie, without taking his eyes off Golden, said, "Then while warnings are being distributed, let me advise you to review the laws involving libel. My client was accused by your client of malfeasance in office, of accepting bribes, and of acting in a prejudicial manner in pursuit of his official duties. These allegations were published in your client's newspaper, and they are categorically and verifiably false."

"These allegations had been made to my client," Golden interrupted, warming to the argument. "He had every right, he had every responsibility to print them. Your client is a publicly elected person, and the public has a right to know!"

Archie responded, "If your client had practiced even the most elementary conventions of journalism by checking into these allegations sufficiently, as the law requires, then he would have found no support for them. You must know, Mr. Golden, that case law consistently has required that a newspaper must check out allegations adequately before publishing them. The facts in this case are clear and uncomplicated. Your client rushed into publication without checking his sources adequately. I know that, Mr. Golden, because I know that there is absolutely no foundation for such a claim. And the courts do not take gossip as a defense against libel. If we go to court, your client is going to lose and my client is going to own a newspaper. And I suggest you explain the facts of the case to your client so that we can get on with the business of settling this mess. Now, you can string this out, file your General Denial. That will waste twenty days. And then you can hope for a delayed court date. And then you can drag your feet on jury selection and ask for rescheduling at some later date. But finally, at some point, after you have thoroughly angered both my client and me into not giving one iota of relief, we will go to trial, and your client will lose."

"Why didn't you arrest the damned Mexicans?" Albert Lane shouted.

Golden put his hand on his client's shoulder to restrain him, and Archie, without looking at Lane, put up his hand in a stop motion.

But Jerry spoke. "I'll answer, Mr. Crane. Do you mean the Mexican nationals who work and live on the Phelan ranch?"

"That's exactly who I mean, goddamn you. They were right there, and even your own office admitted that they were good suspects."

Jerry nodded slightly. "I did not arrest the Mexican nationals because they did not kill the victim."

Lane snorted, "Bullshit!"

Archie turned to Golden. "That your evidence, Mr. Golden? Bullshit?" You going to take that to a jury? Bullshit?" He turned to Jerry. "You'll soon be ten million dollars richer, Mr. Valdez."

"Let me talk to my client for a moment," Golden said.

Archie looked at Golden, trying to read him. He said, "All right, Mr. Golden. But first I want to ask a few questions before we proceed."

Golden looked at his client, who shrugged and said, "Ask away."

"Not of you. I want to ask Kenny."

Kenny Sellers, who had not said a word, nodded.

"Kenny," Archie began, thoughtfully, "Did you write the editorial?"

"Don't answer that question!" Golden interjected quickly.

Archie shrugged. "This meeting is over, gentlemen. We will see you in court."

"Answer the question, Kenny," Lane said.

"No," Kenny Sellers said, "of course... No, I did not."

"Did you review the text before it was published?"

"Yes."

"Did Mr. Lane write the editorial?"

Golden exploded again. "Do not answer, Kenny!"

Lane, without expression, said, "I wrote the editorial."

Archie continued, "Kenny, did you advise Mr. Lane not to publish the editorial?"

Golden leaned forward as though to object, but Lane merely held his hand up. After glancing at Lane, Kenny Sellers answered. "Yes, of course I did. But he is the owner."

Archie shifted his gaze to Golden, whose face bore an expression of resignation. "Mr. Golden, my client and I will leave the room for ten minutes. At the end of that time, we will reconvene this meeting to see if we can avoid further involvement of the court. What we will require to settle this right now is simple. First, we require that the paper print a clear and unambiguous retraction. Second, we require that the paper print an absolute and detailed apology. We require that Mr. Sellers write both the retraction and the apology and that Mr. Lane sign both articles. We require that it be published in next Sunday's paper on the front page, above the fold, under the general headline, in forty-eight point type, 'Bugle Guilty of Gross Libel.' We require that in the same issue Mr. Sellers write and print an editorial explaining the responsibilities of a newspaper to examine evidence to make sure it is accurate, typical, relevant, and adequate before making allegations."

Kenny Sellers had pulled a notebook out of his shirt pocket and was making notes, nodding at the points Archie was making.

"That it?" Golden asked. "How about money?"

"No money," Archie replied.

Jerry nodded, but added, "One other thing. I require that your client give me a list of names of those who made the allegations against me."

Lane looked up sharply. "That you will not get!" he said decisively. "I will not reveal my sources."

"Gossip is not a source," Jerry said. "And I will get a list, a complete list, if there is to be a settlement. Talk it over. That is the best and only offer you are going to get prior to going to trial."

Jerry and Archie stood and left the room. When Jerry asked Angie to take coffee in to the men, she wrinkled her nose and asked if she could pour hot coffee down Lane's collar. Jerry thought a moment before shaking his head.

Exactly ten minutes after Angie had left the conference room, having delivered a carafe of coffee, three cups, spoons, and condiments, Archie and Jerry reentered the room.

Golden rose and said to Archie, "If you would care to draft an agreement containing the requirements you stated, my client will sign it. The document must stipulate that the suit now filed will be withdrawn, with prejudice."

Archie nodded. "We accept. But no document is necessary. If your client agrees to the conditions we articulated, then we will assume he will abide by his word and we will drop the suit." He looked over at Kenny. "Kenny, did you get all those requirements down?"

Kenny nodded. Archie knew that Kenny would not have missed any of the stipulations, nor would he have altered them. He was a thorough and accomplished newspaperman.

Golden said, "For the protection of my client, I will insist on a signed document."

Lane, looking morose, waved Golden off. "No," he said, "his word is enough. He takes my word, and I take his."

"That's not wise," Golden said to him.

"Yeah, well, no one has accused me lately of being wise," Lane muttered.

"Are we in agreement?" Archie asked.

Lane nodded.

Archie said, "Kenny?"

Kenny nodded.

"I want the list now," Jerry said, looking at Lane.

Albert Lane exhaled noisily, and signaled his attorney to comply. Golden reluctantly pulled a handwritten note from the folder and handed it to Archie, who gave it to Jerry without looking at it. There were three names on the list.

"This all of them?" Jerry asked.

Lane, head down, nodded.

"This is very important, Mr. Lane. If there were others who urged you to bring pressure on me to arrest Harvey Phelan's hired hands, I want to know them all. Otherwise, we have no agreement. I want you to understand that I am dead serious about this."

Lane looked up at Jerry, a renewed fire in his eyes. "Listen, goddamn you, making me give you my sources is unethical enough. Don't accuse me of lying!"

Jerry leaned over the table so that his face was inches from Lane's. "Is this everyone?" he asked again.

Lane was breathing hard, his face turning red again. "It is everyone," he said.

Jerry handed him the piece of paper. "Sign it," he said.

Lane looked at Jerry with hatred in his whole demeanor. After glaring for a moment, he picked up an expensive pen from the table, signed the note, and hurled the pen across the room to crash into the wall.

When the three men had left the conference room, with no handshakes offered and none taken, Archie said, "I'm glad you didn't let Angie pour coffee down Lane's neck. He was hot enough without help. I don't believe Mr. Lane's paper will support you in the next election, Jer."

"I expect not," Jerry replied. "Good job, Archie. I'm glad to get that out of the way so that we can get on with more important things. Kenny was embarrassed, wasn't he?"

"Yeah, Kenny is a professional who has to work for a dilfod," Archie said. "By the way, speaking of dilfods, you never told me how you know Harvey's Mexicans had nothing to do with the murder."

"You calling me a dilfod, Deputy?"

"You are what you are, Sheriff."

"Yeah, I guess. Reason I knew those boys did not murder him is that they would never have left the body where it was. Harvey has a trash cave on his property, and they would have used it."

"A what?"

"A trash cave. A hole in the rock that opens down into a large cave where Harvey's family and workers have dumped trash and cow guts and deer entrails for years. Couple of times a year he dumps in some diesel fuel and burns the waste. Those boys use the dump every day. If they had had a body they wanted to get rid of, it would have gone into the cave. And it would never have been found. Whoever killed the guy went to a lot of trouble to cut the hands off and to hide the body. If Harvey's men had killed him, they would not have gone to that trouble."

"Damn," said Archie. "You'd make a good detective."

Chapter 33

Jerry sat at his desk looking at the list of three names: citizens of Kendall County who had wanted some Mexican illegals arrested and tried for murder. Why? He picked up the phone and asked Angie to connect him with the real-estate office of Tony Wragg. When Wragg came on the line, Jerry said, "Tony, I'll be in your office in five minutes. I need to talk with you."

"I'm busy, Sheriff Valdez," Wragg responded pretentiously.

"I'll be in your office in five minutes, Tony."

"I won't be here. It's late," Wragg responded defiantly.

"Well, if you aren't, I'll have you arrested and your fat ass thrown unceremoniously into one of my less comfortable jail cells."

When Jerry arrived at Wragg's small office, no one was at the receptionist's desk. Jerry opened the door to Wragg's private office and entered without knocking. The sullen, pudgy little man was obviously not happy at the sheriff's manner.

"Tony," Jerry said, sitting in a chair in front of the desk. "You told me that you were being pressured by people in your booster group to insist that I arrest Harvey Phelan's ranch hands. I asked you at that time to tell me who was pressuring you, and you refused to do so. Now I am demanding that you give me a list of every person who leaned on you to come to me."

Wragg scoffed at Jerry. "Why, I'll do nothing of the sort. Who the hell do you think you are, the Gestapo?"

"No, Tony, I am not the Gestapo. But a murder has been committed, and I am trying to solve it. Some people, including you, have insinuated themselves into the investigation, and I want to know who they are and what their motivations are."

"I'm a suspect?" Wragg asked incredulously.

"You are. You are one of three men who pressured Albert Lane to write an editorial demanding that I arrest the Mexican nationals who work for Harvey."

"How do you know that?" Wragg asked, suspiciously.

"Do you deny that you urged Lane to pressure me?"

Wragg, not knowing what to say, remained silent.

"That's why you are a suspect, Tony. Now I need for you to list everyone who has urged you to make your demands to me."

"No," said Wragg, seemingly proud to be defying authority.

Jerry sighed. "Okay, Mr. Wragg, stand up and put your hands behind your back." When he did not move, Jerry rose, walked around the desk, and pulled the smaller man to his feet. He snapped handcuffs on the man's right wrist, pushed him around to twist his left hand behind, and locked the cuffs on. When he finished cuffing Wragg, he spun the man around and began reciting him his rights.

By now Wragg's defiance had fled, replaced by deep and thorough fear. "Wait, Sheriff, what's going on? You can't do this to me."

"You are being arrested on suspicion of being an accomplice to murder. You have the right to an attorney, If you cannot...."

"God, Sheriff, I didn't murder anyone."

"I didn't say you did. But you are an accessory after the fact. And you sure as hell are not cooperating with the authorities."

"I'm cooperating, Sheriff. I don't know anything about the murder. I'm just the chairman of the Boerne Booster Association. I'm not involved in any murder. I don't know who murdered that man."

"You know who instructed you to pressure me, and you are protecting those people. That makes you an accessory to murder."

Wragg was in a panic. The smell of urine reached Jerry's nose, and he noticed that the front of Wragg's pants was wet. "No, Sheriff, I want to cooperate. Take these handcuffs off and I'll give you the names."

When Jerry removed the cuffs, careful not to appear to have noticed the wet pants, and returned to the chair, Wragg sat quickly and, taking a notepad from his drawer, wrote two names. He was pale and sweating, although the temperature in the office was cool. He pushed the notepad across the desk, and Jerry turned it around and looked at the names.

"Now, Tony, this is very important. And I want you to know that if I find that you are holding out on me, I will come back and I will arrest you. Is this everyone who sent you to see me?"

"Yes, Jerry," Wragg said, subdued. "They came to me and we talked about it. They said it was bad for business to have an unsolved murder, and what with so many Mexicans in the area we wanted to make sure we were safe. We talked about it, and they told me it was up to the chairman of the Boerne Booster Association to go see you. So I did. And then when you wouldn't arrest the Mexicans, we three went to see Albert Lane over at the paper, and he agreed with us and wrote that editorial to get you off the dime. That's all I know about the murder, Jerry. I was just trying to do my job as the chairman of the Booster Association. I didn't have anything to do with the murder. Honest."

"Okay, Tony. Now sign this list."

He did.

Next, Jerry walked three blocks to Shirley's Barber Shop, where William Barksdale Shirley ran a three-chair barbershop. Shirley was also the mayor of Boerne. Young Jeremiah Bentley was cutting Bill Smedley's hair in the middle chair of the shop when Jerry walked in. Bill Shirley and Harmon Shockel, the other two barbers, were sitting in their respective barber chairs watching ESPN on the color television set. Everyone greeted Jerry familiarly when he walked in. Shirley climbed out of his chair, picked up his cover cloth, and waved smilingly for Jerry to take the chair.

"Hey, Jerry," Shirley said. "Jeremiah just cut your hair, what? a couple of weeks ago, wasn't it?"

"Yeah, Bill," Jerry responded. "I don't need a barber. I need to talk with the mayor."

Shirley smiled and folded the cloth back onto the chair. "Oh, well then, no charge for that," he said, looking around to make sure his humor was appreciated by the others in the shop. "What can I do you for?"

"Let's go back to your private office, Bill," Jerry said, walking through some curtains into the storeroom in back of the shop. Shirley followed and suggested they go out the back door and stand under a large elm tree, where he could smoke a cigarette.

While Shirley lighted up, Jerry said, "Bill, you met with Tony Wragg and then later with Albert Lane to get them to pressure me to arrest some Mexican nationals for murder."

"Yeah," said Shirley, inhaling deeply and twisting his mouth to blow the smoke out.

"Why?" Jerry asked.

Shirley walked over to the trunk of the large tree, leaned his back against it, crossed one foot over the other, and said simply, "I was approached as Mayor and was told that you should be pushed to get this murder solved. I agreed, so we went to see Tony Wragg. He agreed to talk with you. When he struck out, the three of us went to see Lane to get him to use the paper to get you moving."

Jerry pulled the notebook and pen out of his pocket and handed them to Shirley. "I'd appreciate it if you would write the name of the person who came to you to suggest you should push me to arrest Harvey's hired hands."

Shirley paused for just a second, then pushed himself away from the tree and took the pen and notebook. As he wrote, he asked, "Why didn't you arrest the Mexicans, Jerry?"

As Jerry took the pen and paper back and looked at the one name written, he said, "Because they are not guilty."

"Okay," said Shirley.

Jerry gave the pen and paper back to Shirley. "Sign it, Mr. Mayor, if you please."

The piece of paper had one name on it. That same name had appeared on each of the other two signed lists.

Chapter 34

Two blocks away from the barbershop, Jerry walked into the North Towne Bank and Trust. At the loan counter, he asked the middle-aged woman if she could give him some information on land the bank had foreclosed on and was for sale.

She said, "Sure thing, Sheriff Valdez," and smiled at him, looking expectantly into his eyes.

"Thank you," he said.

"You don't recognize me, do you," she said, cocking her head, still smiling.

Jerry hated that. He was obviously supposed to know her, but he had no idea who she was. She had to be disappointed that he did not remember her, and he felt like a fool for being so damned imperceptive. Why couldn't people just reintroduce themselves?

Which is what she did. "I'm Melissa Morrow, Megan's mother. Wow, that's a mouthful, isn't it," she giggled. "Megan is in your daughter's class."

"Oh, sure, Miz Morrow. I'm sorry. My mind is pretty dull today. Melissa is a wonderful young lady. She's been over for birthday parties and such. Maria thinks highly of her."

The woman nodded her head and smiled. "I have a list of foreclosed properties for sale, Sheriff, if that's what you want."

"Please call me Jerry. Yeah, that'll help. Would the list tell me who owned the property, who had the loan that was called in?"

"No," she said, "that information would be confidential, not listed. I don't even have it here in the loan department. Once the note is foreclosed, the note goes into another department and I get new paperwork on the property. If you need that other information, you'll have to ask the president of the bank."

"Yeah, that makes sense," said Jerry. "Is the bank president in the building? Tritt, isn't it?"

"Yes, Monte Tritt is the new president. Been here about a year. And no, he's out. He spends most of his time out trying to get more customers for the bank."

Jerry nodded. "May I see the list of foreclosed properties that are for sale?"

"Sure," she said, "that's easy." She produced a stapled sheaf of papers.

Jerry read through the descriptions and locations of about thirty properties on the five sheets of paper. Then he looked through the listings again. "Miz Morrow," he said, "I ran across one of your signs a day or two ago on a piece of property out off of Highway 46 near the Bandara County line. I don't find it on your list."

Melissa Morrow frowned and thought a moment. "Well, you're right, Jerry. And it's Melissa, please. No property out that way is on the list. Are you sure it is still available?"

"No," Jerry admitted. "It is unoccupied and the sign is still there is all I know."

"Well," she said, "this list is new this week, Wednesday, to be exact. Either it's an old property that is no longer available, or it's so new it hasn't made it on the list. Or," she said thinking, "it has been pulled from the list for some reason. Maybe there is a legal complication. Or something else. If it has not been disposed of, it'll still be on the books. The bank examiners check these things very regularly and very thoroughly."

"Check your list?" Jerry asked.

"No, these lists are just for our use in the bank, so our loan officers can try to sell them. The examiners never look at these."

"Um," Jerry thought. "Can you check the books to see if that piece of property off Highway 46 is still owned by the bank?"

"Sure. It'll take a day or two, though. Only the bank president can access that part of the records. You interested in buying some land, Jerry?"

Jerry smiled. "No, I've got several hundred acres I inherited from my parents that I barely have time to take care of properly. I mean, I certainly take care of it, but I can't spend nearly the time on it I'd like. Anyway, my interest here is purely job-related. If you can get that information for me, I'll really appreciate it, Melissa." He gave her his card. "And tell young Miss Megan hey for me."

Chapter 35

Jerry arrived home at seven o'clock to find that Anna Maria had dinner prepared and ready for the table. "Oh, damn," he said. "I'm sorry, babe. I promised to be home early enough to cook dinner."

Anna Maria smiled as she drained a mound of fried shrimp from a large, iron frying pan and transferred it to a bowl lined with paper towels. "You don't fry shrimp as well as I do," she said simply.

"I wouldn't have fried it," he said. "I would have skewered it with onions and peppers and barbequed it."

She shook her head and handed him the bowl of fried shrimp while she took four baked potatoes out of a roasting pan and put them on plates. "I don't know why I bother," she said. "The blind man's wife needs no cosmetics. Get the salad, please, dear."

Jerry stopped on his walk to the table, trying to fathom the relevance of blind men and their wives' toilette habits. He figured it out, but refused to honor her by commenting on her jibe at his tastes. He prepared the salad instead.

Nor did he comment on how wonderful the fried shrimp was. He had just finished pulling one sizeable shrimp from its tail/holder, having dredged it through, first, a blob of tarter sauce and, second, a splotch of red sauce, when the phone rang. *Damn, Anna Maria can cook good fried shrimp,* he thought as he got up to answer the phone, wiping his mouth on a cloth napkin. A bit of garlic salt in the cracker-crumb breading made a world of difference. She was right. This was much better than barbequed shrimp. He wasn't blind. He knew his wife was beautiful. But he wouldn't mention it to her. "Hello."

"Hey, Jerry," Archie said. "I hope you've finished dinner."

"Now you mention it, I haven't," Jerry said, suspecting that he wasn't going to.

"Sorry," Archie said. "You need to eat earlier, Jer. Old people need time to digest their food before they go to sleep. Not that you're going to sleep tonight."

The trepidation Jerry had felt when he first heard his friend on the phone was confirmed. "What is it?" he asked seriously.

"I've been working on looking for our illegals all day, and I think I can now account for all of them," Archie said.

That's not bad, Jerry thought—unless. "They all alive, Arch?"

"Yeah, Jer, they're all alive. I had Joe and Jesus check out the land around the house for grave sites and, thank God, they didn't find any."

Jerry's relief was palpable. "You found all, what was it? Eighteen?"

"Yeah, that's what you told me the two women at Harve's place said. Twenty made the trip and two had been released to Harvey's ranch. The remaining eighteen were sixteen women and two men."

"And you found them all?"

"Yeah, well, the patrol deputies have been checking the ranches and businesses all over the county. First thing I got them to do was to check on all the vacant houses in their areas they knew about to see if the illegals had moved into them. They found nothing there. Then they started checking the ranches and businesses. We found the two men almost immediately. They had made their way to the ranch where their brother worked, where they were supposed to go anyway. That left sixteen, all the women. We found four of the women soon after that—all at different ranches. Two of them had found their ways to the ranches that had contracted for their work, and the other two had found ranchers who were willing to take them on. That left twelve. We didn't find them until an hour ago. Seems they didn't have any luck finding their ways to where they were supposed to go, nor did they find anyone to hire them. They were walking up and down the county roads together, trying to find a place to work when they stopped at a rest area on the Interstate to use the facilities. An Hispanic truck driver offered them transportation and jobs, and these poor dumb chickens climbed into his bobtail truck and set off with him. That was last week sometime—let me check my notes, Jer. No, it was Wednesday two weeks ago that happened."

"I had told Andy Barlow and Morgan Potts to check all the rest areas and truck stops, and today Andy pulled into the particular rest area the women had visited. One of the state maintenance workers had watched the negotiations between the driver and the women and knew that the women were doing something dumb. He got the license number of the truck, meaning to call it in. But he forgot. He gave it to Andy, and Andy called Johnson Washington back at the office. Johnson ran the plates and found that the truck was registered to a—let me see—to an Armando Cruz, who lives in an old house down off of the Interstate near Balcones Creek. Johnson called Darrell and Hilton, who were patrolling southeast county, and they both went out to find the guy. Hilton spotted the truck in front of the old house down by the creek and found all the women just sitting around the house. Anyway, Darrell and Hilton arrested Cruz for kidnapping and for promoting prostitution…"

"For WHAT?" Jerry asked.

"Yeah, prostitution. The women told Hilton that the guy had been one of the men at the rest area a couple weeks ago when they were caught up in a scheme to sell sex. They told Hilton that this guy remembered them and threatened to turn them in unless they went with him. He admitted that he had always wanted to open a whorehouse. Seems this Cruz guy was holding them until his brother could finish remodeling a house they owned in Houston. And here was a whole stable of young women available. It was a dream come true for him. He's just been holding them, feeding them, for all this time."

Jerry shook his head in disbelief. "That's the most unheard of thing I ever heard of. Where are these women, now?"

"I took our van down and picked them up. They're all here at the office. I had all the deputies bring in the others, the ones they found around the county, including the two women at Harvey's place. Soooo, we've got quite a party going on here, all twenty of them. I rather thought you might want to join us for the fun and games. We maybe need to sort these guys out and decide what to do with whom."

Jerry looked over at his smiling wife, his delightful children, at his plate of fried shrimp, baked potato, green salad with bleu-cheese dressing and thought seriously about resigning as sheriff.

"Be right there, Arch."

He called Peter Delgatto, District Attorney for Kendall County, and asked him to come over. When Peter agreed to meet him there, he asked the DA to bring a licensed Spanish translator along. Then he called Walt McGarrett in San Antonio to invite him and the INS officer involved in "Rio Stop" to the gathering.

Chapter 36

The Sheriff's Office was a madhouse. A dozen women, all looking frightened and vulnerable, were huddled in one corner of the conference room. The two women from Harvey Phelan's ranch were sitting together at the conference table, but their husbands, Phelan's two other Mexican workers, and Harvey Phelan himself had been required to wait in the lobby. Four other women sat in a cluster across the table from Phelan's group. Two Hispanic men sat together near the far end of the room. As Jerry glanced in, he was struck by the obvious fear that seemed to pervade the room.

The lobby was alive and noisy, with deputies trying to explain to the various groups of friends, families, and employers why their friends or families or employees were being held and what was likely to happen to them.

Archie smiled at his friend's dour expression and asked, "Have a good dinner, Jer?"

Jerry held his thumb and forefinger apart just the size of a shrimp and said, "Came about this close."

"What we gonna do with all these guys?" Archie asked.

Jerry shrugged. "Peter Delgatto and a translator should be here soon. Anything we suggest will have to be cleared through him, since a murder is likely connected to it all. And I'll want us to interview them all before we let any of them go. Even then, I don't want any of them to leave the county until we get the murder disposed of. 'Course, INS might have a different set of wishes. I called Walt McGarrett to come up from San Antone and asked him to bring the INS agent he's working with. I hope they'll let us keep them in county until we get all the information we're going to get."

"You mean at county expense? Or do you think we can send them back to their work?"

"No, I hope we can let them get on with their plans. Like the two young women from Harve's place, Merita and Rosita. I'd hate to separate them from their husbands."

"How about the tawdry twelve?" Archie asked.

"The what?" Jerry responded.

"The twelve young women who were going to be taken to Houston to staff—no, that's the wrong word—to crack into the escort service. You want to send them on their way?"

Jerry looked perplexed. After a while, he said, "You know, Arch, why don't you call Glad Ass and tell her we've picked up the young women. Ask her if she'd like to come down to help out. Tell her we need her advice."

"I think that'll do, Jer," Archie said, nodding his head. "I think maybe Glad Ass is just the thing."

"Meanwhile," Jerry said, "while we're waiting for the FBI and INS to show up to lend some dignity to this uncouth gathering, I want to draft some questions we need to ask every one of the twenty illegals involved with this particular coyote operation. We can split up the questioning. You and I know enough Spanish to get along, and I asked Peter to bring a licensed translator. If you or I get an answer we might want to take to court, we can ask the official translator to record and certify it."

What Jerry wanted to know from the illegals had to do with their backgrounds and their plans in the United States. He wanted to make sure that they were what they seemed: disadvantaged young women and men of good character, who wanted nothing other than a chance to improve their lives. But he also wanted to know all they could tell him about the coyotes: who they were, how many, who they talked to both in Mexico and in Texas, who came to the safe house while they were there. By the time the interviews were over, he was persuaded that all twenty were what they seemed. He still had nothing to indicate who the murderer was. But he had an idea where to look.

The two women from Phelan's ranch took little time, for they were away from the safe house early in the series of events. The other eighteen all told essentially the same story. The honcho coyote and one of the scouts told them that they were going to have to work to pay the money owed to the coyotes. The two men in the group were each given control of eight women.

The two groups of eight women, along with their male handlers, were to be taken in the large truck to different areas, sometimes to a rest area and sometimes to a truck stop, where they were instructed to approach men who seemed to be alone and to offer to trade sex for money. All the women and the two men refused, but after the honcho coyote had stripped one man and one woman and had beaten them with a whip, the others chose prostitution over whippings. One of the scouts, whose description by the illegals almost certainly identified the INS agent Santiago Madrazo, was away in the pickup truck, trying to locate the ranchers who had contracted to have the illegals brought in to work.

When the scout returned, the illegals all reported, he argued with the honcho coyote that his plan to prostitute the women was dangerous, would endanger the enterprise and themselves. He had quarreled so vehemently that the honcho coyote and the other scout had subdued him and bound him with duct tape while they trucked the women around to sell their wares car to car, rather like girl-scout cookies.

The women were told to charge sixty dollars for ten minutes. All the money received would go to the honcho coyote, but only fifty of the sixty would be used to pay down the contracted debt owed to the coyotes; the other ten per trick was "operating expenses." The two men were promised five dollars for every trick turned. The women were urged to work fast. The faster they worked, they were told, the faster they would pay off their contracts and be free. The women all admitted that they were too ashamed to work hard, and the two men had no heart to force them.

After two nights' work, the sixteen women had brought in under a thousand dollars. The honcho coyote was furious, they said, and threatened to whip all of them if they did not perform better on the third night. All admitted to being afraid of what the coyotes would do. When the honcho coyote and the scout wandered out back to drink and smoke, the INS agent asked the two men to unbind him. When they did, he urged them to leave quietly by the front door to get as far away from the house as possible. He urged them to go to any farmhouse, call for the police, and tell them to come to the safe house. The scout who had been tied up remained at the house.

Several of the illegals knew approximately how to get to the ranches they were bound for, and they left the group. The twelve young women, however, were lost, wandering around in the dark, until they found the rest stop and the accommodating truck driver.

When Jerry, Archie, and Peter Delgatto and his translator sat together to discuss their separate interviews, the stories agreed on all major parts. Santiago Madrazo had probably been killed, not because his identity as an INS agent had been discovered, but more likely because he had released a flock of chickens and thus deprived the coyotes of the profit they would have brought.

Santiago Madrazo had been shot and killed, as nearly as the medical examiner could tell, on Wednesday, November 13. The illegals had escaped from the safe house the preceding evening, Tuesday. So the INS agent had not been killed right away.

When McGarrett and an INS agent named Marvin Wells showed up, Jerry and Archie briefed them on the interviews, assuring them that they could detect no criminals in the group of twenty. The INS was concerned mainly about the twelve women who had no immediate place to go, except to a fledgling whorehouse. But Miz J. Maurice Hump, who had arrived earlier and had taken the "poor things" into her protection, told Wells that she would personally take care of them, see that they all had medical examinations, new clothes, respectable jobs, and all the benefits that her husband's wealth would provide.

Gladys Hump was in a new element, clucking over the chicks, wiping their eyes, speaking not a word of Spanish, but demonstrating with all her other communication devices of her concern for the young women.

Maurice Hump stood aside, smiling proudly as his wife pledged to spend large sums of money on twelve young women who had, at the very least, broken laws of his country. Jerry did not know whether or not Maurice understood the reasons for his wife's compassion for these women. He thought not. Gladys would probably not have admitted her transgression even to herself most of the time. Maurice was just the best of the good old boys. And Gladys, pain in the ass that she could be and usually was, had a core of compassion. And her husband recognized and admired it.

"Really nice people you got in this county, Sheriff," the INS agent said, marveling at the compassion displayed by Gladys and the beneficence shown by Maurice.

"Yeah, Gladys has a heart as big as her...well, she's got a big heart," Jerry said, meaning it.

None of the illegals knew the whereabouts of either the honcho coyote or of the other scout. Jerry assumed that when the chickens had flown, the two coyotes had fled the area. Leaving only the "local" person, the coordinator. Jerry was persuaded that he knew who had to be the prime candidate for the role. But he had no idea how to prove it.

Chapter 37

Early on Friday morning, Jerry called North Towne Bank and Trust and asked to speak to Melissa Morrow. When she came on the line, he asked her about the piece of property where the illegals had been kept.

"I asked Mr. Tritt, Jerry. He told me that the reason the property was not on the list is that it had been sold. I told him I figured you'd want to know to whom, but he said that it was to a blind corporation and that the transfer of title papers had not been filed yet. That's exactly what he said."

"What's a 'blind corporation,' Melissa?"

"Well, Jerry, I don't know. I never heard the term before. But he says that's why the property isn't on my list. It's been sold."

Jerry thought for a moment. "Can you give me a legal description of the property?"

"Well, I could if I had it. But, remember, it's not on my list."

"Yeah, that's right. And you can't access the computer file to get the information, right?"

"Only Mr. Tritt can, as far as I know."

"Thanks for all you've done, Melissa. Uh, would you transfer me to Mr. Ferguson?"

"Do you mean Wally Ferguson, one of the tellers?"

"No, the guy used to be president before Tritt."

"I'm sorry, Jerry, Mr. Ferguson retired just recently. I sure hated to see him go. I mean, he was old enough to retire, but I think he really enjoyed working here. Anyway, one day Mr. Tritt just out of the blue told us that Mr. Ferguson had retired."

Jerry knew that Monte Tritt had been hired as president by the bank's board of directors about a year earlier to build the customer base of the bank, to make the bank more profitable. He had come from Houston, where he had earned a reputation as a great salesman of bank services.

Jerry thanked the loan officer and hung up. On an impulse he looked up the number of Ephraim Ferguson and called. Ferguson greeted Jerry as an old customer of the bank and agreed reluctantly to meet with him.

Jerry drove over to Ferguson's house, a beautiful old Victorian home on a shady street in Boerne. Ferguson greeted Jerry politely, invited him into a formal parlor, and indicated a rather uncomfortable chair that felt like it was covered in horsehair. The grand piano at the end of the room, Jerry noticed, had a velvet skirt around the bottom to hide the "limbs." When Jerry expressed his sadness to learn of the man's departure from the bank, Ferguson reported that he had retired because of certain "innovative" attitudes at the bank.

Loans, for example, were made with only the security documents demanded by the bank examiners. Ferguson wanted local bank officers to inspect the physical collateral to make sure that the property, whether it be land or vehicles or grain in a silo, was as advertised. But the new president had rejected the notion as being "not good for business."

Ferguson was also greatly concerned about what seemed to him irregularities in some of the new business accounts. Tritt had undeniably increased the customer base for the bank, both in loans made and new business checking accounts; and he had delighted the bank's board of directors. But Ferguson was "uncomfortable" with some of the new accounts, many of them from outside the county.

When Jerry asked for particulars, Ferguson grew reticent. "Sheriff, I worked at North Towne Bank for many years and made many friends and acquaintances among the employees and customers. I will not sully a life I tried to make honest and orderly. Now, I admit that I think that my long experience in the principles of the business would have been useful to the bank. I worked for over thirty years to make the bank what I thought it should be. But others thought me too reserved, too hide-bound. It was just time for me to leave."

Jerry answered, "I appreciate your loyalty, Mr. Ferguson. And I certainly am not interested in provoking an argument about business principles, as long as they are legal. But..." Jerry did not want to tell the man that some connection might exist between the bank and the murder. "But, Mr. Ferguson, I just need to see all the pieces to know what might fit into the puzzle and what parts seem not to."

"I've known you for these many years, Sheriff. Even voted for you. I believe you to be an honest and prudent man. But I cannot allow what is little more than gossip to damage that bank."

"Sir," Jerry said, "I agree with you. But I promise that unless the pieces fit together to form a provable picture, they'll go no further than between you and me. I need to know the particulars of what bothered you so that I can see if those pieces fit some of the pieces I have."

"All right, Sheriff. Here are some of the things that concerned me. On the subject of property that had been repossessed by the bank. That property that had been repossessed before... well, when I was president—and that wasn't much, two businesses and two ranches—those properties recently ceased being recorded on the list of repossessed property to be sold. They were still carried in the assets inventory of the bank, they were still on the computer; but no one else in the bank ever saw anything about them."

"Did you ask about them, Mr. Ferguson?"

"Yes."

"Who?"

"The new president."

"Mr. Tritt?"

"Yes."

"And what did he say?"

Ferguson paused a moment before answering. "He told me not to worry about it."

"Why do you think the property was no longer listed?"

"I don't know."

"Can you speculate?"

"No, I cannot."

"Might these properties have been used for some illegal activity?"

"I do not know."

"Okay, Mr. Ferguson, what else?"

"On the subject of business accounts, and we had many new ones, I was troubled that many of the new ones were from businesses outside the county, just as many of the new loans being made were to individuals and businesses outside the county."

"Anything illegal or improper about that?"

"No, not per se. I just didn't know them and that, along with other things, concerned me."

"What other things?"

Ferguson paused before continuing. "We had a large amount of cash coming into our night depository from some of these new accounts, especially from three used-car dealerships in Houston."

"Houston?" Jerry asked.

Ferguson nodded and looked directly into Jerry's eyes.

Jerry asked, "Why would used-car dealers drive all the way to Boerne to put cash deposits in the night depository?"

Ferguson did not answer.

Jerry asked, "Did you ever check up on these clients?"

Ferguson responded, "I did not. I was assigned by the bank president to oversee transit, not customer relations. It was not my job to do so."

"Whose job was it?"

"Mr. Tritt took care of customer relations."

"Can you give me the names of these car dealers?"

"No, I don't work at the bank anymore."

"Who can?"

Ferguson was quiet for a moment. "Call Ms. Morrow."

"Isn't she in loans?"

"All those used-car businesses have loans at the bank. Every one of them. But I can tell you that all of them list post office boxes as their address, not street numbers."

"But if I have their names, I can locate them."

"Maybe," Ferguson said, without further comment.

Jerry thanked the former bank president and drove back to his office. Ferguson clearly suspected that some laws were being at least strained, but he would not speculate further. Jerry was not so reticent.

Back at his office, he called Melissa Morrow to get the names and addresses of the Houston used-car customers. He told her that he had spoken with Mr. Ferguson, and she was not reluctant to give Jerry the information he wanted.

She said, "Mr. Tritt came by about an hour ago to ask me if I'd heard any more from you."

"What'd you tell him?"

"I told him he'd just missed you, that you'd called and I'd passed on the information that the property was in escrow."

"What was his reaction?"

"He just gave me his usual grin. Like a...."

"An alligator?" Jerry suggested.

Melissa Morrow laughed. "I was going to say 'like a Cheshire cat,' but you're more accurate."

"Guy's got a lotta teeth, Melissa. If he asks you again, can you tell him that you haven't heard any more from me?"

Without hesitation she replied, "Okay."

When Jerry called Houston information to request telephone numbers for the car companies listed as customers of the bank, he was not surprised to learn that no such companies were listed with the telephone company in the Greater Houston area. He thought he might check with the Houston Chamber of Commerce, but he knew it would be futile. A used-car company without a telephone was like a snake without a slither: it wouldn't get very far.

He punched in Mr. Ferguson's number again and apologized for pestering the man. "Mr. Ferguson, I'd like to run a hypothetical past you to see if it is possible, okay?"

"As long as it is hypothetical, Sheriff. I shall not comment on bank business."

"Oh, no, Sir. Purely hypothetical."

"Very well."

"Okay. Say I have a lot of cash and I need to open a bank account. Say several thousand dollars."

"How many thousand?" Ferguson asked.

"Say, fifty thousand."

"Then the bank would report that cash deposit to the federal government, and they would require that you explain and document where you got the cash."

"Okay, Mr. Ferguson, I think I knew that. But I still need to put that money in a bank so that I can write checks on it and use it legally for all sorts of things. And I may need to make such deposits on a regular basis. So, say I tell the bank that I run a business that brings in lots of cash, something like a, maybe, whorehouse or gambling casino."

"Please, Sheriff. Those 'businesses,' as you call them, are illegal. No bank in this state can legally do business with them."

Jerry smiled at the banker's prudishness. "Okay, then maybe a grocery store? Or a used-car dealership?"

"Continue," said Ferguson.

"Say for example if I claim to own a used-car dealership in another city and no one at the bank ever checks up on it to make sure it is really there, then I could take the cash I have and deposit it as receipts from my business, couldn't I?"

"Yes."

"But stick with me now, Mr. Ferguson. Say I have fifty thousand, but before I got that cash I needed some start-up money to pay for inventory, you know, cars. Couldn't I get a loan from the bank where my new account is to use as start-up money?"

"Probably," Ferguson replied. "But the bank would hold the titles of the cars until the loan, or the appropriate part of the loan, is paid off."

"Do the titles have to be real? I mean, would the bank know if titles were forgeries? Or maybe titles of wrecks rather than saleable cars?"

"The bank examiners are not fools, Sheriff. A Houston company doing business with a bank in Boerne would raise flags."

"Unheard of?"

"Unusual."

"But if the loans were paid off in a timely manner and the titles shuffled in and out like a legitimate dealership?"

"That's mainly what the examiners would be looking for."

"So, it could work? Somebody could launder cash like that?"

"It would be very risky business, Sheriff. If someone found out, such behavior would lead to jail time."

"Even if the president was involved and controlled the situation?"

There was no sound for a moment. Then Ferguson said, "Good day, Sheriff Valdez." And he hung up.

Jerry opened his desk drawer and took out three small pieces of paper clipped together. On one sheet three names appeared: Tony Wragg, Bill Shirley, and Monte Tritt. On the second piece of paper were two names: Bill Shirley and Monte Tritt. And on the third, only one name: Tritt. Tritt had encouraged the mayor to bring pressure to arrest and prosecute the Mexican workers for the murder of Nobody. Tritt and Shirley had approached Wragg to get him to take the leadership position. And when that did not work, all three, probably at Tritt's urging, went to Albert Lane to increase the pressure.

If Tritt were involved, he would want Jerry to close the case without further investigation. If Jerry's suspicions about banking improprieties were provable, the bank examiners could probably find enough illegalities at the bank to get Tritt fired and maybe even sent to country-club federal jail— Club Fed—for a month or a year. But Jerry was persuaded that Tritt was implicated in people-smuggling and maybe even murder. But absent a witness, he could not prove it.

Chapter 38

It was late on Friday evening when Jerry remembered that Anna Maria had invited Archie and Jo Anne for dinner—and Jerry had volunteered to cook. He had remembered to get steaks out of the freezer, but during the day he had completely forgotten about dinner. Even when Archie had left the office earlier and told him "See you later," Jerry had just waved at his friend and continued writing a report on all that he knew about Tritt's seeming involvement with the coyote operation.

He did remember dinner when his stomach protested. Then he remembered the steaks. Then the guests. He shook his head at his forgetfulness as he phoned home.

Anna Maria was amused at her husband's preoccupation. "I'd blame it on advancing age," she said, "except that you've always had a poor memory."

"Yeah, babe, but I shouldn't have forgotten this. If you can scrub some potatoes and put them in the oven and throw a salad together, I'll get right home and put the steaks on. What time did you tell Jo Anne and Archie to be there?"

"Seven," she responded, "but I didn't invite Jo Anne. Archie should be here any time."

Jerry wanted to ask why she hadn't invited Jo Anne, but now was not the time. He was gathering up papers to put them in his briefcase as he talked to his wife, and when he hung up he locked up and left.

It was already dark when he turned onto his street and neared his house. Archie's marked patrol car was parked in the drive, leaving room for Jerry's

Chrysler on the side of the drive nearest the front door. Hurrying to get out of the car, Jerry banged his head on the low doorframe. Rubbing his head, he murmured about modern cars being made for children rather than men, and made a mental note to trade his patrol car for a vehicle he could climb up to get in, rather than have to fall down into. As he walked in front of the car toward the door, he suddenly remembered the briefcase on the front seat and turned back to get it.

At almost exactly halfway through his one-hundred-eighty-degree turn, a bright flash from across the street commanded his attention, and Jerry's eyes began to move to focus on the bright burst. Before his eyes could move the centimeter up to concentrate on the light, a massive blow hit his left shoulder and drove him into the garage door. He slid down the door and into a heap on the concrete apron, blood sketched in an irregular path down the garage door from a cut on his head and began to pool on the concrete from the shoulder wound. He did not move.

Chapter 39

Light glowed rather too strongly through his closed lids, as though the morning sun was chiding him awake. "Get up, get up for shame," the light instructed him; "Come, let us go while we are in our prime." He tried to lift first one arm and then the other over his eyes to block out the light; but, as though he had lain on them and cut off the circulation, his arms did not respond. So he tried reluctantly to open his eyes just a bit to look at the clock. But when his lids seemed not to open, as though they were stuck shut, he gave up the effort and tried to turn his back to the light. Try as he might, he could not get his body to roll onto his left side.

"Jerry," he heard a seraph, or at lest a cherub, speak gently. He felt a soft rubbing of his right eye, then the other, some moist solution bathing his lids. "Jerry," the voice whispered again.

A seraph, Jerry believed. Anna Maria. Definitely a seraph. And he opened his eyes to see the vision looking down at him. She had tears in her eyes. "The children?" Jerry croaked, trying unsuccessfully to get out of bed. Anna Maria rarely cried. If she was crying, he knew something must be wrong.

Anna Maria gently pushed him down. "They're right here, Jerry," she said.

Two other visions materialized on his left, Alex and Maria. Both were crying. Jerry tried again to sit up, but he could do no more than to tense his muscles. He could not rise. "Is it Archie?" he asked. Jerry moved his head slowly to try to look around. "Where is Archie?" he asked.

Anna Maria stroked his head with a wet cloth. "Archie is fine, Jerry.

He'll be in later."

"Why are you crying, babe? What's wrong?"

"You were shot, Jerry. We were just scared, that's all. You're going to be fine."

"Who?" he started to ask. But with his concern for his family resolved, his mind opened the right file. "Tritt," he said.

"What, dear?"

"Where am I?" he asked.

"You're at Methodist Hospital in San Antonio, Jerry," Anna Maria answered, her hand stroking his brow carefully. "The bullet shattered your left shoulder, and several orthopedic surgeons worked most of the night to put it back together. The good news is that it'll be fine. The other good news is that you can't get out of the house until after Christmas. There is no bad news."

"Dad," twelve-year-old Alex, his eyes dry after seeing his dad awake and responsive, said excitedly, "They flew you in a helicopter. Landed in the street right in front of our house. Archie called them. They wouldn't let me 'n Maria ride with you. Angie brought us down here."

Jerry smiled at his son, more with his eyes than his mouth. He tried to reach over to touch him, but he was still unable to move his arms.

At age eight, Maria could not regain her sense of well being as quickly as her brother. She still looked frightened, tears still in her eyes. Jerry wanted to touch her face, to brush away her tears. But he felt exhausted after moving his head to the left to look at his children. Maria, he noticed, had both of her small hands on his bed, touching his bandaged arm with just the tips of her fingers. He could smile a bit at the children, and did.

Turning his head to the right to speak with his wife seemed to take an eternity. "I need Archie, Babe. Where is he?"

"In Boerne, Jerry. When we heard the shot, we all hurried outside and found you lying on the ground...."

"Sweetheart, but I need to talk with Arch. Get him on the phone for me, please."

"Jerry, I will do no such thing! You've lost a lot of blood and are as weak as a kitten. Archie can take care of things while you just look after yourself for a while. I am not going to..."

Jerry tried to roar, without much success, and used all his strength trying to sit up. "Anna Maria, get me Archie on the phone NOW!" His strength drained immediately and he fell the few inches back to the bed, exhausted.

He was able to add in almost a whisper, "Please."

His wife looked at him a moment, irritated at her husband's insistence. Then she said, "Alex, do you remember the waiting room Angie is in?"

"Yes, Mama."

"Go ask her to come in. Alex, go straight there and come straight back here."

The boy left the room and was back in less than a minute with Deputy Angie Wahlert, an apprehensive look on her face, following. Jerry caught a glimpse of a uniformed deputy standing outside the door as Angie and young Alex came in.

When the young woman approached the bed, she looked down at Jerry's pale face and broke into tears. Leaning down, careful not to touch his bandaged arm, she kissed him lightly on the cheek, her tears wetting his face.

Jerry grimaced. "Angie, I need you to hold together now. Deputy Sheriffs don't cry."

"Well, I do, when you get yourself shot, you big poop!" she answered, trying to grin through her tears. Looking across the bed, she said, "Is he going to be all right, Anna Maria?"

"I think with some time for healing, he'll be fine, Angie."

"Angie," Jerry interrupted, "I need for you to get Archie on the phone for me. Use that one on the table. I need to talk with him now."

The deputy looked across the bed quizzically; and, when Anna Maria nodded, the deputy made the call. She found Archie at the office and handed the phone to Jerry. Seeing that his left arm was immobilized by a cast and straps and his right arm was being used as a pincushion by an IV needle, she nestled the receiver into the pillow near his ear.

"Arch," he said.

"Hey, partner," Archie said. "I hear that all the king's horses and all the king's men put Humpty together again."

"Yeah, maybe. I just woke up, and to tell the truth I'm not in complete control of my faculties. So, bring me up to date. I've obviously been shot. What do you know?"

"I was in the house at about fifteen after seven having a glass of wine when we heard you drive up. Anna Maria looked at her watch and said something about your being fifteen minutes late. She got up to do something in the kitchen when we heard the shot and all of us ran outside. We saw you lying on the ground bleeding and unconscious. Anna Maria yelled at Alex to call 911 to get an ambulance, and then she ran over to you. I asked Alex to call the department to tell Johnson Washington that you'd been shot and to get some help out to your house. Both Anna Maria and I checked on you to see your condition. I found the one wound—in your shoulder—and then I left you with her while I grabbed my flashlight out of the car and checked to see if the shooter might still be around. From inside the house, it sounded like the shot had come from across the street, so I ran over to see what I could find. When I got into your neighbor's front yard, I heard a motorcycle roar away on the next street. I looked around, but whoever shot you was gone. When Andy, Morgan, Avon, and Billy Joe got there a few minutes later, we checked more thoroughly, but we didn't find any signs. We came back this morning at first light, and I found what I guess is where the shooter stood. There's some bent grass and broken shrubbery near your neighbor's fence where someone or something has been. But I didn't find any bullet casings or other evidence there. How many shots did you hear?"

"None," said Jerry wearily.

"I think I heard only one," Archie said.

"You find the bullet?" Jerry asked.

"Yeah, well, no, I don't have it yet. I told the medical team that took you down to San Antone to ask the surgeon to collect it and save it for me. You didn't have an exit wound, so I figured it was still in you. I talked to the surgeon about an hour ago. He says it looks like a 30-06."

"Deer rifle," Jerry said.

"Yeah. I asked Angie to get it and bring it over, but she told me that she wouldn't leave until she was sure you are out of danger. I guess I'll get it soon enough."

"Is Deputy LaDeaux over here too?"

"Hell, Jerry, half the department was over there last night. I had to threaten to fire them to get them back over here. Dorie told me she'd been fired by better men than I am. She thinks that the shooter might try to get you again, so she's been guarding you ever since she got there. The doctors and nurses even have a hard time seeing you. She won't let anyone she doesn't know alone with you. I could have ordered her to get back here, but a little caution is not bad. Besides, she probably wouldn't have come back, anyway. Same with Angie."

Jerry smiled. "Okay, Arch. Do this. Get a search warrant for that rifle, for a .22 pistol, for a motorcycle, and for anything else you can think of and serve it on Monte Tritt. Search his home and his office at the bank. And arrest the sonofabitch."

"Why? You think he's the shooter, Jer?"

Jerry sighed, barely able to keep his eyes open. "Hell, I don't know, Arch. But I've been messing around in his watermelon patch, and now I get shot. It seems likely. But it could have been one of the coyotes. Or it could have been just some dilfod who doesn't like sheriffs. Don't question Tritt just yet till I've had time to think." *And energy*, he thought wearily.

"You talk with Walt McGarrett, Arch?"

"Yeah, I called him last night, just in case the shooting was connected with the smuggling case."

"He say anything about the other guys, the ones they've been keeping an eye on in Mexico?"

"All he said was that Morales still hadn't shown up at his family's home. Oh, and he said that the DNA test confirmed Nobody to be his INS guy."

After ending the conversation, Jerry motioned with his head for Angie to remove the receiver. He was very tired, struggling to keep his mind in gear. It kept trying to shut down. But he had to think. Maybe Morales was dead too. But he could also be the one who killed an INS agent and shot a sheriff. He said, "Angie, call on this phone, please, for, um, Sam Alton. He owns a place in Coahuila, Mexico, called Cañon of the White Stone. I need to talk with him." Jerry closed his eyes.

The young deputy looked puzzled for a moment, trying to determine how she was going to get the number. After a moment, she called Miriam Smith, who ran the Sheriff's Department communications office during most days, and asked her to find the place on the internet and give her the number. In less than a minute, Angie had the number and had placed the call. Jerry heard her say, "Mr. Alton? Will you please hold for Sheriff Valdez of Kendall County?" Jerry opened his eyes when Angie cradled the receiver into the pillow near his ear.

"Sam," Jerry said, his voice barely above a whisper. "I need to ask you— you remember we talked about a honcho coyote named, um, Morales, Marco Morales?"

"Hey, Captain. Yeah, I remember. Why?"

"I don't guess you've seen him recently, have you?"

"Define recently," the man said.

A smile tried to form on Jerry's face, but the muscles were too tired to respond even to nature. "Last few days," he muttered.

"You really sound tired, Captain. You okay?"

"Well, no, Sam. I had an altercation with a bullet last night, and I'm such a sissy that I let them put me in a hospital to recuperate."

"Well, damn, Cap. You going to be okay?"

"Yeah, fine, Sam. I've been shot before. This is just a shoulder wound."

"Who shot you?"

"I'm not real sure, Sam. That's why I called you. Have you seen Morales around for the last day or two?"

"Oh, yeah, Cap. He hasn't been by here, of course. But his *polleros* have been herding their flocks into the holding pens up the road, and a couple of days ago I saw Morales in a pickup driving north—up to the cantina, I'd guess. He's with his *polleros, brincadores*, and scouts, getting ready for another crossing, I'd guess."

"Any idea when, Sam?"

"No," the innkeeper responded. "I don't know whether or not they have all the flocks from the wranglers collected up there. Even when they do have everyone gathered, the *brincadores* will have to choose several crossing sites and send the scouts out."

Jerry understood the problems in determining when the illegals would be led across. And even if he could find out when and where they would cross, he had no ideas where they would be headed for in the U. S., or whether Morales would even cross into the U. S. with the paying customers.

"Sam," he said after a moment, "I need to ask a big favor. Can you find out if Morales is around there right now? I hate to...."

"Not a problem, Captain. I'll just drive up there for a beer and meter-meter the situation."

"No, look Sam, somebody tried to kill me last night, and somebody did kill a man over here a couple of weeks ago. I don't want you to put yourself in danger."

"Now, Captain, you've gotta know, I've found myself amongst much rougher *hombres* than this."

"Me too, Sam. But if I hadn't forgotten my briefcase and turned back to get it last night, I'd likely be dead now."

There was a moment of silence. Then Sam spoke: "You want to know if Morales is here now?"

"Yes," Jerry responded. "And if we can be sure that he was there last night, not over here. And...." There was something else, but Jerry's mind was running on very low voltage, and whatever else he wanted to ask the innkeeper had crashed. After a moment, "Well, I'd like to know if any of his scouts or *brincadores* have been away from the cantina area in the last couple of days And, oh yeah! I remember now. See if you can find out when they plan to cross, where the illegals are bound for in the U. S., and whether Morales is expected to cross with them."

"I'll find out what I can, Captain. Gimme your number."

"Many thanks, Sam," Jerry said. "My deputy will give you the number."

Angie took the receiver, spoke to the innkeeper briefly, and hung up. She turned to speak to Jerry, but saw his eyes closed. She looked over to Anna Maria, who mouthed "asleep." Angie nodded and sat in a chair to watch Jerry sleep.

Chapter 40

It was evening before Sam Alton called back with the information. Angie grabbed the receiver after only one ring, but Jerry's eyes opened. She answered the phone and after a moment placed it near his ear.

"Captain, it's Sam. How you doing?"

"Shoulder's beginning to hurt like hell," he responded. He watched his wife get up and walk out the door. Jerry knew what for. "What've you got for me on the smugglers?"

"Several things you wanted me to find out. Morales has been here for several days. Never left, except for short periods, never more than half a day. The fence jumpers have been out in the canyons several times, but only for an hour or two at a time. The scouts haven't left the cantina, and won't leave until the *brincadores* determine the area where they want to cross. The *polleros* have all left, all going south—and I'm guessing on this—to round up another flock to hustle."

"Morales going to cross with them?"

"Near as I can tell, Captain. The scouts—they're the ones I talked with— are pretty close mouthed about such details. But I asked them if Morales was going shopping on this trip, and they all figured he would. Morales likes to buy sophisticated electronic gadgets. Anyway, the guess is that he will cross with the illegals as he usually does."

"You find out when?"

"Couldn't ask that question directly, Cap. But from the preparations I see, I'd guess either tonight or tomorrow night—I saw the chickens packing suitcases and bags. I'd guess they'll go tonight, but if not then, they'll almost certainly go tomorrow night."

"Anyway you can let me know when they move out?"

"Sure. That many people moving make plenty of noise, even when they try to be quiet."

"I hate to ask you to do this, Sam. But I need the information, and it's too late to send one of my men over there."

"No need, Captain. I'm here and glad to help."

"Just one other thing, Sam: If you can spot Morales going with them, let me know, please. But don't take any risks."

"You remember reading about those tunnels in 'Nam?"

"Yeah, I do."

"Wandering through them in pitch dark is taking a risk. Drinking a beer in the cantina is not what I'd call a risk."

"We've got one down and one out up here, and our best guess is that the shootings are related to these coyotes. They kill folks."

"I don't kill too easy, Sir. I'll call you when they leave to walk across the river, and I'll keep an eye out for Morales. You want me to use this number?"

"Well, I hope to get out of here in the morning, so..." He glanced at his wife as he spoke and saw her smile and shake her head slightly. He had not known she had come back into the room. A nurse carrying a hypodermic needle and a small bottle of drugs was with her. Jerry continued, "No, just call here, please, Sam. Any time of the day or night. And I'll owe you big."

When Angie reached down to get the phone, Jerry said, "Angie, please get Special Agent McGarrett on the phone for me."

"Jerry Valdez!" his wife said threateningly. "You need to rest!"

"Just one more thing, babe. Then I'll rest." At Anna Maria's direction, the nurse injected a drug into the IV tube. Into the phone Jerry said, "Walt? Jerry. Some illegals are set to wade the river out in the Boquillas Canyon area either tonight or tomorrow night. Morales is with them, and my source thinks he will cross with the others. My information is that he was in Mexico when I was shot, but we still really need to talk with him. I thought you guys might like to pick them up on this side. Especially Morales. I expect my source to call me to tell me when they will cross and whether Morales will cross with them."

"Really good, Jerry. Many thanks. I appreciate the info. I'll go ahead and put a welcoming committee together and into the area so that we'll be ready when they do come across. Just gimme a call."

Jerry nodded and, relaxing his grasp on consciousness, went to sleep.

In less than an hour, an annoying electronic sound pushed his mind out of the comforting fog. He heard Angie answer the phone and opened his eyes when he felt the receiver being placed next to his ear. "This is Jerry Valdez," he said softly. After listening for a long moment, he said, "I owe you big time." Then, "Angie, please hang up and get Special Agent McGarrett on the phone—call his cell phone number. It's on his card."

Angie Wahlert looked over at Anna Maria.

Jerry chaffed without much power at his fetters and tubes. "Angie, don't look at her. Call McGarrett!"

"Hush, Papa Bear," the young woman said. When Anna Maria nodded her head, Angie picked up the card and punched in the number for Walt McGarrett's phone.

"Walt," Jerry said weakly when he heard the agent's voice on the line. "Jerry Valdez here. The illegals set out in four groups of twenty or so each less than half an hour ago. They'll cross in one of several areas in the Boquillas Canyon, walk to some isolated spot in Texas, and be put on trucks to be taken to wherever it is they paid to go. But, Walt, Morales is not with them. My source says he set the four groups on their way and went back into the cantina and began drinking. Best bet is he'll hang there until morning and then drive back south to Monterrey."

The FBI agent was quiet for a moment. Then he said, "Okay, Jerry. We need to talk with Morales, and since he may be involved in a crime that occurred in your county, I want to talk with him here rather than there. So we'll bring him out. We'll have him in our office tomorrow. If you have questions, tell Archie he's welcome to come interview him tomorrow. But you rest. We'll handle it."

"How you going to get him out of Mexico, Walt? The extradition paperwork will take weeks."

"I'll arrest him in the U. S."

"But he's in Mexico. My source tells me he doesn't plan to come across."

"You ask a lot of questions for a sick man, Sheriff. Tell me, if you wanted to question him in Kendall County and he was in Mexico, how would you handle it?"

"Well, easy," Jerry responded. "I'd drag the sonofabitch across the Rio Grande and have Archie arrest him when he was on Texas soil."

"Well, hell, you ain't too dumb for a hick sheriff. Now get some rest, and we'll handle the extraction."

Jerry went back to sleep.

Chapter 41

His shoulder hurt like hell when he awoke on Sunday morning. He tried to reposition himself in the bed, but every movement caused the pain to increase.

His movement awoke Anna Maria, who had slept in a chair next to the bed, her head resting on a small pillow near her husband's right arm. She raised her head and smiled at her bewhiskered husband.

"You need a pain killer, Jerry?" she asked, stroking his wrinkled brow.

"Good morning, beautiful," he said. "Where are the kids?"

"Angie took them over to mom and dad's. Those young kids from Dallas, Geno and Mia, are spending the weekend with mom and dad, and Maria and Alex will enjoy playing with them. Angie'll bring them back here this afternoon for a visit. She didn't want to leave, but she knew the children were tired and needed some diversion. She's just a wonderful young lady, Jerry."

"Lord, yes," Jerry agreed. "Why some bright young man hasn't stolen her away, I don't know."

"Well, I know," Anna Maria answered. "Until she finds someone like you, she's not going to be interested. You're the model she measures everyone against."

Jerry looked puzzled. "You mean she's looking for a middle-aged, paunchy Mexican going to seed?"

Anna Maria smiled. "Well, not exactly. She more admires your mind. I don't think she's after your body."

"Damn," Jerry said.

"She may not be, but I am," she said seductively.

"That's even better," he said, trying to put a leer on his face. "I think I'll take a rain check, though."

"You need a pain killer?" Anna Maria asked again.

"No. Well, yes, I do. But I need to stay awake. I've got to talk with Archie, and that damned medicine puts me to sleep."

"That's what it's supposed to do, dear. Your body has been savaged, and it needs time to recover." She stood beside the bed and gently straightened the sheet and blanket.

"I do need to talk with Archie, sweetheart. Are any of the deputies still here?"

"Dorie is still sitting outside the door," Anna Maria said smiling. "Angie tried to get her to go home, but Dorie told her, 'With all due respect, no.' Angie thought it was adorable, so she just left her there. She let me take her place a few times when she had to go to the rest room, but mostly she just sits right outside the door."

Jerry was puzzled. This young woman who had been angry at the world in general and at him in particular had become his ardent protector. "Could you ask her to come in, please, babe. I need to talk with Archie."

"I'll find Archie for you, Jerry. I don't want to try to persuade Dorie to leave her post. Angie had to insist that she sleep a few hours last night. How do you feel this morning?"

"My shoulder hurts like hell. Did the doctor show up?"

"Yes, the surgeon stopped by very early this morning to check the wound and to have the nurse change the dressing. You slept through it all. He was of the opinion that he had done a wonderful job. He made me look at the stitches from three different angles. He insists that they are a work of art."

"He say when I can leave?"

"He wants to keep you here a few days, Jerry. You still have a bit of fever, and he wants to keep close tabs on you. That was a nasty wound. And he's afraid you had a concussion."

"I don't have a concussion. I just have a headache and a shoulder ache."

"We'll do what the doctor says, Jerry."

"How about when I can take these damned tubes out of my body?"

"He'll let you have liquids starting today—gelatin and broth and juice. If you do well on that, he'll remove the IV on Monday. And at the same time, he'll remove the catheter."

"It's a damned nuisance," he said. "But, okay. I still need to talk with Archie."

She did find Archie and put the phone on the pillow beside her husband's ear. Archie had executed a search warrant on bank president Monte Tritt, searching both his home and his office.

"We found a Honda motorcycle in his barn, Jer, but of course there is no way to tie it directly to your shooting. But we also found a scoped Winchester 30-06 locked away in his gun safe. It had just been cleaned and oiled. I've sent it over to ballistics, along with the bullet the doc pulled out of your arm. We'll have an answer tomorrow."

"You find a .22 pistol?"

"No, Jer, no pistol. I don't see how we can tie him to the INS agent."

Jerry was disappointed, but hoping he could find evidence was not the same as finding it. "Okay, Arch, good work. Thanks for getting all that done. You arrest Tritt?"

"Yep. He yelled like a stuck hog, called us hick cops, and threatened us with all sorts of reprisals. I told him we weren't hick cops; we are hick deputy sheriffs. But he wasn't amused. When we found the rifle, he stopped yelling and insisted on calling a lawyer. He finally got a guy from Houston on the phone, and I guess they'll meet tomorrow. 'Til then, Mr. Tritt will be our guest. You know, Jer, if we don't get a positive report on the ballistics, we won't be able to hold him."

"Yeah, I know. Um, Arch, do I remember right that we took some castings of tire tracks out by Harvey's ranch, on the shoulder of the county road?"

"Yeah, Smiley did that. I was there for some reason—to watch Smiley, most probably. But he got the castings. Smiley ran them by several tire dealers and identified them as, if I'm remembering right, Goodyear truck tires of some common type. I've got the notes here somewhere."

"Tritt drive a truck?"

"Tritt drives a Mercedes. But he has a truck, a Ford 150. We searched it, along with his car, looking for guns and blood and whatever else we might find relevant."

"What kind of tires does it have?"

"I'm ashamed to admit I don't know. I'll send someone to find out while I check the notes."

"Even if they match, it won't be conclusive. But, yeah, evidence can accumulate. One other thing, Arch. Will you call Walt McGarrett over in San Antone, please? He was going to try to arrest the honcho coyote for questioning. He's the only other one I can think of right now who might have killed the INS guy. I don't think he was around here when I was shot, but he could well have shot the agent. Talk with him, will you?"

"Sure, Jer. His number in your office?"

"Yeah, both his office phone and his cell. He's expecting you to call. I'm sorry as hell to put all this on you, Arch, but I wouldn't be much good to you if I were there. I keep falling off to sleep."

"Jer, you are right where you need to be. As long as we can talk about things from time to time, we have plenty of hands to get things done here. Keep your mind rested; that's what we need."

"Everybody seems to be interested in my mind recently. What's wrong with my bod?"

"Well, it's shot full of holes, for one thing."

"Shot full of ONE hole, Mr. Wiseass."

"What was that bandage around your head I noticed when they loaded you aboard the chopper?"

"Well, okay, two wounds. But otherwise it is the body of a god."

"If you say so, Jer. But if I were in the hospital with tubes running in and out of my body, I think I might be careful what I say about the gods. You will remember, Jerry, it was Catullus who said, 'It is not fit that men should be compared with gods.'"

"Well, hell, Arch, the point is, I'm not fit. If I was fit, would I be in the hospital?"

Chapter 42

Walter McGarrett greeted Archie Crane as the chief deputy was escorted into the regional FBI office in San Antonio. "Good to see you again, Deputy Crane."

"Thank you for the invitation to interview Morales," said Archie, shaking the hand of the special agent. "Please call me Archie."

"I'm Walt. Tell me how Jerry is."

"I stopped by the hospital on my way over here. The bullet, it was a 30-06 slug, did some damage to his shoulder; but the surgeon, I'm told, did a great job fitting all the pieces back. Jerry's anxious to get back to work on this case, but his body won't allow him to wiggle much right now. The mind is willing, but the body's weak."

"The sword outwears the sheath, I guess."

Archie smiled. "Sounds too phallic for Jerry, but something like that."

"I suppose you want to talk with Morales? We found him standing just on the Texas side of the Rio Grande in Boquillas Canyon and took him into custody."

"Just found him standing there, huh? That was wonderful thoughtful of him, wasn't it?"

"Damnedest thing I ever seen," the agent smiled.

"You've interviewed him, I presume?" Archie asked.

"I have. We had Special Agent Vilma Manteiga fly a bureau Cessna 182 over to pick him up at Alpine and fly him over here this morning. We arrested two *brincadores* and four scouts along with the illegals they were jumping across. Most of them the INS will just process and send back to Mexico."

"Um, Walt," Archie broke in, "excuse the interruption. Before I forget, do you know whether the INS has made a final decision on the earlier group of illegals Morales brought into the county? The ones we interviewed—when was it?—Thursday night?"

"Yeah, they didn't find any among them to worry about. Of course, they're still illegals, and we'll deport them if they attract any attention. But they are not high priority. If they stay quiet, they'll probably just be ignored. Not forgotten, but ignored."

"Okay, thanks. I've already had inquiries from family and employers in the county about them. Now about this latest bunch."

"Yeah, I was about to say, one of the scouts we arrested we believe was with Morales in Kendall County when the INS agent was killed. We flew him back here with Morales. Morales swore he was never in the U. S., that he was kidnapped out of his native land, that he knows nothing about smuggling illegals across the border, and he insists upon being sent back to Mexico. When I told him we had found all the illegals from his last run and that they could all place him in Texas earlier this month, he just shrugged and demanded to be deported. Which, of course, we ain't gonna do, under any circumstances. We're gonna prosecute him on a racketeering charge and put him in one of our jails for a nice long time as an example to other smugglers. That's at a minimum. But there's a kicker. He had a pistol on him when we arrested him standing just on the Texas side of the Rio Grande in Boquillas Canyon, a .22 caliber pistol."

Archie's eyes brightened. "It match?"

McGarrett shrugged. "Dunno. I called your district attorney, where Jerry said the two bullets taken from the skull of the INS agent had been sent. After Mr. District Attorney Peter Delgatto got through lecturing me about the dangers of laboring on the Lord's Day, he met one of our agents at his office and transferred the slugs to us. My lab guys here share Mr. Delgatto's aversions to laboring on the Lord's Day. I guess I'll know tomorrow whether or not we have a match. But from what we got from Morales, I don't doubt that they'll match."

"You question Morales about the murder?"

"Yep. He stopped being so cool then. He was obviously surprised that you guys had found and identified the corpse. He swears he had no idea that Madrazo was an INS agent, and he insists that he had nothing to do with killing him. His story is that he thought Madrazo was just a scout. Reason he, and all the other coyotes, got angry with him was that he let the illegals escape without paying what they owed. It amounted to something over thirty-thousand dollars. Morales says that the guy who put all this together—you and Jerry think it is this banker fellow…"

"Tritt, yeah."

"Morales says this Tritt went ballistic when he learned that Madrazo had released over thirty-thousand dollars of meat on the hoof. This guy's story is that Tritt grabbed Morales' pistol and shot our guy once in the back of the head and once again when he lay on the floor. All this, he says, happened at the safe house. Morales says he and the other coyote, one of the scouts, left that very night and went back to Mexico. Tritt told them he'd get rid of the body so that no one would ever find it."

"So, all this had nothing to do with their breaking the INS cover?"

"Not according to Morales and the scout. They say that Tritt was angry about the money."

"You believe Morales is telling the truth?"

"I do, Archie. We questioned the scout, who, after some encouragement, told essentially the same story. He identified Tritt as the shooter. I don't think we'll have any trouble getting him a life term. Killing a federal agent is frowned upon in federal court. Do you want to interview him?"

Archie thought for a moment. "I can't think of any reason I need to, Walt. Sounds like you have it pretty well nailed down. You sure you hadn't rather have us prosecute him for murder in state court? We can likely get the death penalty."

McGarrett shook his head. "No, Archie, he killed a federal agent, and we need to deal with him on our own turf. The INS guys feel very strongly about having a hands-on part of this, and they will with a federal prosecution."

Archie nodded. "Well, they won't really have any more control of a federal prosecution than they would in the state court. But if they THINK they do, then that means something. Jerry asked Peter Delgatto to cooperate with you guys to the fullest, so I'm sure you won't have any trouble. We're just glad to have the damned thing wrapped up. We don't like having unsolved murders in our county."

McGarrett stuck out his hand and warmly grasped Archie's offered hand. "Archie, I want to thank you and Jerry for the really super work you did on this case. If there is anything we can do to help you guys, let us know."

"Take away the grief of a wound?" Archie suggested.

"Would that I could, Archie. Take care of the old goose, will you?"

Chapter 43

Jerry was able to con the duty nurse into letting him have three eggs lightly poached and some English breakfast tea on Monday morning, but she absolutely refused to allow honey wheat berry toast. Jerry groused at her, but he was in fact delighted to have gotten the eggs and tea. Anna Maria had to feed him, since his left arm was incapacitated and his right still attached to IV tubes. Archie talked with his friend in between Jerry's bites of egg and Archie's of eggs, chorizo, and cheese wrapped in a flour tortilla. The Sunday morning issue of the *Boerne Bugle* lay on the bed, the headline "*Bugle* Guilty of Gross Libel' crying loudly in large print on the upper left of the front page. Both the retraction and the apology to the Sheriff of Kendall County appeared above the fold. Archie had read both front-page articles and Kenny Sellers' editorial explaining the newspaper's responsibilities concerning evidence printed on the editorial page. Jerry knew that the resolution of the lawsuit would do little to keep people generally from making unwarranted generalizations based upon inadequate or nonexistence evidence. Ignorance was always more expert about tough questions than knowledge was, and the ignorant were always with us, wandering in a cloud and spreading the shadow. Holding Albert Lane to the evidence in this one incident would do little to lift the general cloud of ignorance, Jerry knew. But some gentle wind of reason might remind one soul or two that the sun does shine. Jerry was satisfied.

Archie had brought the results of the ballistics test on the bullet taken from Jerry's shoulder. It had come from the gold-filigreed rifle found in Monte

Tritt's gun safe. They could get an easy conviction in the district court, but killing a federal agent trumped wounding a sheriff any day. The .22 caliber slugs taken from the INS agent's head were from the pistol taken from Morales. But the tire tracks found near where the body of Madrazo was found matched the tires on Tritt's truck. Of this, too, Jerry was satisfied.

"I see Dorie LaDeaux is still guarding your door, Jerry," Archie said. "I told her that your shooter was in jail. All she said was, 'Maybe.' Want me to make her go home, Jer?"

Jerry shook his head—easy, so as not to pull his shoulder. "No, I can't bring myself to be unkind to her. She's been at that door, except for a few hours sleep, ever since they brought me in. I want you to arrange for overtime for her, Archie."

"She'll take it as an insult if I ask her to apply for it."

"Don't ask her. Just do it."

Archie smiled at his friend. "Okay, Jer."

"Also, Arch, could you check with Walt McGarrett for us. I'd like for the department to be represented at Santiago Madrazo's funeral. Write a letter of condolence, will you please, to his family. I'd like his family to know we thought he was somebody, not Nobody."

Archie was taking notes. "Will do, Jer. I'll dress up in my class-A uniform and represent the department myself. I'll probably take Melina Rodrigo and Jesus Ortiz with me. They have family in the valley—maybe even know the Madrazo family."

"Good. Thanks, Arch. I want to write a note to those hunters who found Madrazo's body. I had the feeling that they were the kind of people we'd like to keep coming back to the county. Make a note to remind me to thank them for their help."

"Want me to write them?"

"No, just remind me to. I'd kinda like to do it. But talk to Walt, please, about giving some proper recognition to Sam Alton down in Coahuila. He's damned good people, and he helped us a lot. Get him a bronze plaque and a certificate making him an honorary deputy sheriff. And talk with Walt to see if the feds can't give him some suitable honor. He's a good man."

Archie nodded, his mouth full.

Jerry asked, "Everything copacetic back home, Arch?"

When he could speak, Archie said, "We'll get Tritt transferred to the feds sometime today. Peter and I have signed the transfer papers for the county, and Walt McGarrett will leave his signed copies with Stephen Abbot at the jail when his guys get Tritt. Nothing else much going on, for a change."

Anna Maria asked, "Will they get Mr. Ferguson to be president of the bank again, now that Tritt is arrested?" Jerry had finished his breakfast, but Anna Maria was waiting for him to ask for a second cup of tea before moving his tray table away from the bed.

Archie laughed out loud. "No, Ferguson was very clear. I ran into Walker Rains, who's on the bank's board of directors, this morning. He told me they'd asked Mr. Ferguson to resume the presidency '*ad-interim.*' Now, these are the same guys who bounced Mr. Ferguson in favor of that bastard Tritt. So, Walker told me that Mr. Ferguson was uncharacteristically blunt in telling them what they could do with their job. Walker said that Ferguson listed for him all the principles that Tritt had violated just to get more money for the bank and for himself, and then he looked Walker directly in the eye and said, 'You see how one gets rich.' Walker asked me what I thought Ferguson meant."

"Did you tell him?" Anna Maria asked.

"No," Archie answered. "I didn't figure he'd understand. And besides, I don't get paid to educate the muttering herd."

"And how are you doing, Archie?" Anna Maria asked. "Have you talked with Jo Anne?"

Archie's demeanor changed perceptibly. It was not a subject he either enjoyed or understood. "No, I don't really see much point in it. She's—well, I don't really know what to say she is. I thought she really liked me. But I think she also really finds me repulsive."

Anna Maria was quiet for a moment. "I know this is very hard for you. I'm really sorry that all of this other business has fallen on you, Archie—all this problem with Monte Tritt and all."

Archie waved his hand dismissively. "No, it's good that I have this to do. It keeps my mind off, well, other things, things I don't understand and can't control."

"Archie, I—um—I don't think Jo Anne's behavior has anything to do with you."

Archie looked at her in surprise. He knew Anna Maria to be bright and perceptive, but he did not understand her statement. "Well, it certainly appears to have everything to do with me, Anna Maria. At times she seems to detest me."

"She doesn't, though. She has a problem...."

"Yeah, me."

"No, Archie, I think she had this problem long before she met you. It is enormously complex, and it will take all our help for her to beat it."

Archie found the conversation unpleasant and awkward. "If she wants to beat it."

"Yes, if she wants to. But I believe she does. She just can't do it by herself. She's talked to me about it just a little, enough for me to realize how complex and deep-rooted it is."

Archie sighed. "I don't know, Anna Maria. Let's just let it be. I've got a bunch of stuff to do right now, things I understand and can do; and that's what I'll tend to. I've tried to be patient and understanding. But I really don't understand her. I'd do anything for Jo Anne, just as I'd do anything for you and Jerry. But with Jo Anne, I never know whether her response will be a smile or tears or disgust or what. With you, or Jerry, or even Tritt, I know what to expect."

They glanced at Jerry, expecting a comment. He was quiet, looking surprisingly small and tired. His left arm was bandaged tightly against his body, and his right arm was strapped to a board to protect the IV tubes taped to his hand. He had a slight smile on his face. He was sound asleep.

END

Printed in the United States
16841LVS00006B/142-147